MAD IN MISSISSIPPI

SHARON SALA

MAD IN MISSISSIPPI

AND

RAIN DOWN ON ME

MAD IN MISSISSIPPI
Copyright © 2024 by Sharon Sala

Paperback ISBN 978-0-7953-0114-8
eBook ISBN 978-0-7953-0113-1

RAIN DOWN ON ME
Copyright © 2024 by Sharon Sala

Paperback ISBN 978-0-7953-0114-8
eBook ISBN 978-0-7953-0113-1

Cover Art by Kim Killion, The Killion Group
Edited by Deborah Grace Staley, www.writebytheocean.com

DEDICATION

I'm dedicating this book to the girl who won't
back down from her truth.
To the woman who learned to say no.
To the mother who fights for her child.
To the woman who stands in the gap.
To all women alone.
Be your own champion.
Hold fast to your autonomy.
Let no one make your decisions.
Let no one put words in your mouth.

CHAPTER ONE

Thirty-four-year-old Bitsy Yarborough's world had never spread beyond the borders of Lone Bridge, Mississippi, where she was born and raised. It was where she first met Calvin Yarbrough, the boy she'd considered her destiny and had since she'd first laid eyes on him.

When his family first moved to Lone Bridge, he'd been sixteen years old, and full-grown in height. Three inches over six feet tall, chocolate-brown hair with a tendency to curl; he soon became the star quarterback of the football team. She wanted him, but when she found out every other girl wanted to date him, too, she pretended he didn't exist.

Cal Yarbrough had never been ignored by the opposite sex. Certainly not since he'd turned fourteen, and he didn't know what to make of Elizabeth Collins—Bitsy, to her friends. When he passed her in the hall and said *"Hello,"* she always responded, but she didn't bat an eye at his attempts to flirt. It became a point of pride to get a date.

Bitsy wasn't playing his game. She had no intention of being a notch in anyone's gun and never gave him the opportunity to ask. She just kept dodging and evading him, in the same way he evaded being sacked.

She went all the way through her junior year without much more than a daily hello, or good job when they won a game, but when school began her senior year, the first time she saw him in the hall, she flashed a pearly-white smile and gave him a soft, breathy 'Hi."

He'd stumbled.

She'd kept walking.

Within a week, they had their first date, and after that, there was no one else for either of them. Bitsy married him at the end of her first year of college, and today was their fifteenth wedding anniversary.

She'd woken up this morning convinced she was the luckiest woman in the world. For sure the luckiest in Lone Bridge, Mississippi. But that was before she started laundry. Now, she was feeling like there wasn't enough soap in the world to clean up Cal's act.

———————————

It all began as she was going through the pockets of Cal's clothes before putting them in the wash. She picked up a shirt to check the front pockets, and as she did, saw a lipstick smear on the collar, big as day.

Her first thought was disbelief.

There had to be an explanation.

Her heart was pounding as she reached into the cabinet for the stain remover, knowing she'd never worn a shade of lipstick that color in her life.

Even after she'd applied the stain remover and tossed the shirt into the washer, there was a knot in her gut. A soul warning that it was going to take more than Stain-Be-Gone to make this right.

The washer was already filling with water as she walked back into the kitchen and stopped in front of the three-layer cake she'd just made for their anniversary celebration. The irony of that strawberry-colored lipstick and this strawberry cake was not lost upon her.

Stain remover. I just used up the last of it, she thought, and turned around to look for her pad and a pen to start a new grocery list. That's when she saw them on the kitchen table where Cal had been sitting earlier.

She could see herself moving, but she couldn't feel her arms and legs. *Please let this be a bad dream.*

She reached for the pen to start her list and noticed it was a freebie pen from Rogers Motel. That was weird. Why would he even have a pen from that place? It was common knowledge that place served their guests by the hour. The knot in her belly tightened as she wrote *stain remover* on the list, then put the pen back on her list pad and took a deep breath.

The floaty feeling was fading, but now she wondered what else she might find if she went looking. She'd never used this particular instinct before—the one they called self-preservation--but at this moment, it was a big warning flare in her gut.

Cal had gone into town more than an hour ago to get the groceries for her to finish off their anniversary supper, because her car, barely two years old, had been sitting at the dealership garage going on six weeks now, awaiting a part. Or so she'd been told.

The dryer was still tumbling its load.

The washer was still filling with water.

She hated what she was thinking, and to prove herself wrong, she set out on a search, going through all the drawers in the house, looking for things that didn't belong.

She found grocery receipts, a recipe she'd been looking for, a broken tie pin, an earring missing part of the setting, dozens of gimme pens from nearly every business in town--from the insurance agency where Cal worked as an insurance adjuster, to the local funeral home, and the feed store. She'd even tossed some of them into those drawers herself.

But it was the pens from six other motels in the surrounding area that didn't make sense. And every time she found one, she kept trying to think of a reason why Cal would have it--maybe it was a pen he'd borrowed from someone else and forgot to give back. But six different motels? Locals didn't stay in local motels. But they did screw around in them. That she knew.

After she'd found the third pen, she began collecting them in a baggie, and every time she found another one, added it to the bag.

In the middle of her search, the clothes dryer stopped. She slipped the baggie into the pocket of her housedress, and went back to the laundry room to switch loads.

She put the dried clothes in a basket and took them straight to their bedroom to hang up before the wrinkles had time to set. It would have been a discredit to her if she sent her man out of their house looking anything but perfect.

Once the clothes were on hangers, she went back to the laundry room to sort out the whites for another load, and once again, began going through all the pockets of his shirts and her shorts, making sure there weren't any tissues in the pockets. They made such a mess.

Then it happened again. The same shock. The same acrid taste of bile that formed in her mouth before the urge to throw up.

It was the blue pop-off nail caught in the elastic waistband of his tighty-whities that didn't belong. She stared down at her plain, unadorned nails, and then back at the blue nail and moaned.

First the lipstick.

Then the motel pens.

And now this—the third 'nail' in Cal Yarbrough's coffin, and it had just set Bitsy on a path of destruction.

In her mind, she had two options.

Forget she ever saw it.

Or make him sorry.

Southern women did not lay down for anything but good sex. She would not ignore being cheated on and opted to make him sorry.

But first, she needed a court-worthy verification of her suspicions before she would act. If she was wrong, Cal would never know. But if she was right, she would string the guts of his deceit all over the county.

Bitsy had been raised to be a sweet, amenable southern lady, but like every southern woman, she also had "bless your heart" and a finely honed cut-your-throat smile at the ready when the need arose. And the longer she thought about it, the more comfortable she became about peeling away the lie.

Bitsy wasn't just hurt.

She didn't just feel betrayed in the absolute worst way.

Bitsy Yarbrough was hair-on-fire mad and going to war.

She dropped the blue nail into the baggie with the motel pens, then hid it beneath a stack of quilts in the hall linen closet.

For a few moments, she couldn't decide how to begin. She didn't want him to know that she was suspicious, but she needed wheels, and her less than two-year-old car had was still sitting the garage at the dealership waiting on a part.

Then it hit her! The reason why the car wasn't fixed. As long as she had no car, Cal didn't have to worry about what she might or might not see should she happen to be in town. Which also meant Bradley Beamer, who owned the dealership, had to be in on this ruse with Cal, or he would never have left work undone.

That made her even angrier, and that stunt was about to come to an end. She had the freedom to be mad at Bradley without raising Cal's suspicions, and she was going to raise hell at the dealership to make it happen.

She was still standing in the hall when she heard the front door open and close. Cal was home. Her hunk-a-burnin' love walked into the kitchen with a sack of groceries in each arm, and she found herself staring at him as if she'd never seen him before.

"I think I got everything," Cal said, as he put the sacks down on the island and then winked. "Maybe more. You know I like to shop around a little bit on my own, too."

"So, it appears," she said, as she watched him pulling out the items. "Thank you for running that errand, but I miss doing the shopping for us, and I'm sick of being stuck out here on my own. I've missed a book club meeting and haven't been able to do my charity work at the church Clothes Closet. Is there something you're not telling me as to why my car is still in the shop?"

He blinked. "You know I took it to the dealership. They said they're waiting on a part."

"I'm sorry, Cal. I have been patient, and I know Bradley is your friend, but I am also not a fool. I no longer believe that is true. Mechanics can order a part and get it in two days from almost anywhere in these United States. So, for my anniversary present, we are going to buy me a new car."

"Now, Bitsy . . . we just bought a new car less than two years ago," he said.

"And look where it is. I believe we have purchased a lemon. I don't want to drive a lemon. I need it to be dependable. I need safe."

Cal started to object, and then he saw the look in her eyes and shrugged.

"I'll go down to the dealer tomorrow and—"

"No. We'll go down today. And Bradley Beamer, himself, can explain to me why it's taken so long, and then he will give me the best trade-in deal he's ever given a customer or know the reason why."

Calvin stared at his wife as if he'd never seen her before.

"You're mad, aren't you?" he said.

"Why, honey . . . whyever would you think something like that?" Bitsy drawled.

"I don't know . . . it's just . . . you've never . . . oh, never mind."

"You put up the groceries. I'm going to change my clothes," she said, and walked out of the room.

The moment she was gone, Cal made a frantic phone call to Bradley Beamer. The call rang and rang, and he was afraid Bitsy would appear at any minute. Then finally he got an answer.

"Beamer Autos, Bradley speaking."

"Bradley, it's me, Cal. Don't talk, just listen. Bitsy finally had a meltdown over the car situation. We're coming in to buy a new car, and you need to give her the best trade-in deal ever. I'll make it up to you on the side if I have to, understand?"

"Yeah, buddy. No prob, but what prompted all this?"

"Hell, if I know," Cal said. "See you later."

By the time Bitsy came back, the groceries were put away and Cal was sitting at the kitchen table with his cell phone, sending a text.

"I'm ready," she said, eyeing the phone.

Cal immediately stopped what he was doing and got up. Bitsy gave him a sweet smile as she walked past him, then climbed into his truck and buckled up.

As they went up the graveled drive, they left a little cloud of dust behind them to mark their passing, and when they reached the main road, Cal didn't bother yielding. He just shot out onto the highway like he owned it.

Bitsy rode in silence with the sun reflecting off the hood of the truck and into her eyes, wishing she'd brought her sunglasses. Finally, she pulled down the visor to shade her eyes, and as she did, a waterfall of papers dropped in her lap.

Cal grimaced. "Oh, I'm sorry, sugar. That's my weekly filing cabinet. I'll drop them off at the office tomorrow."

"No problem," she said, and unbuckled her seatbelt before bending over to gather them back up. As she did, she saw what looked like a pair of black lace panties stuffed beneath the seat. Like the wrong shade of lipstick, she wasn't into black lace. Before she could react, Cal cursed and hit the brakes.

"Oh, hell," Cal said. "Art's bull is out again."

She righted herself and looked up. Sure enough, Art Warner's huge, white, Santa Gertrudis bull was standing in the middle of the blacktop.

Cal put the truck in Park and got out.

"Be careful!" she said.

He waved and was already pulling out his phone to call Art.

The minute he was out of the truck, Bitsy dug the black lacy bits from beneath the seat, and stuffed them into the bottom of her purse, then she shuffled all of the loose papers back into a stack and opened the glove box to put them inside and got another shock. The pretty pink hairbrush and a tube of lipstick beneath a pair of his work gloves did not belong to her.

She glanced up to see him still on the phone, and another car coming from the opposite direction was stopping as well, pinning the bull between their vehicles. Or, as Bitsy saw it, providing the bull with a choice of targets.

But since Cal was still distracted, she grabbed the lipstick to check the color. It didn't match the stain on his shirt!

What the hell? Was he cheating with more than one woman?

She shoved the lipstick and hairbrush into the bottom of her purse with the panties. It made her feel like a tech from a forensics lab, gathering evidence at a crime scene. Only the evidence was coming from so many directions it had begun to feel like a serial cheater and his accomplices were on the loose, and she was no longer the cop. She was the unwitting victim.

Finally, Art Warner arrived, pulling a stock trailer. Art, Cal, and the other driver managed to herd the bull inside. Bitsy watched the three men shake hands and wondered if those men knew Cal was cheating?

Moments later, Cal got back in the truck. He gave her a nervous glance, and then seemed to relax when she didn't say anything. He put the truck in gear and continued the drive into Lone Bridge, but the silence was getting to him, so he reached across the seat and gave her hand a quick squeeze.

"Hey, Bets . . . it's been fifteen years today! Can you believe it?"

She flinched. He only called her "Bets" when he was nervous. She nodded. "Time certainly has flown."

Pleased that he'd gotten a positive response, he kept talking. "That cake you made looks amazing. I can't wait to get me a big slice."

She nodded. "I know it's your favorite. I have your present, too, but I'm saving it for tonight."

"Uh . . . I was planning to pick yours up later," he said.

She rolled her eyes. "Don't lie. You didn't buy one. You never do. You just hand me a hundred-dollar bill and assume that covers anniversary sex. I'm picking out my own present this year."

Cal was speechless. Bitsy had always been forthright, but this was out of character. He shrugged and changed the subject. "Don't worry, darlin'. We'll find you a good deal. Something sturdy that can take our country roads."

"Silly boy. We live on a highway. I'm getting myself a girlie car," she said.

Cal frowned. He didn't know what had prompted all this, but he wasn't ready to cede his place as man of the house. "I don't know about all that. We don't need—"

Bitsy threw back her head and laughed. "Oh honey, there's no 'we' in this decision. I'm buying it. With my money."

His eyes widened. "But we put that money aside for our retirement."

"As the years have passed, it has occurred to me that my elder years are not all that secure. You wanted me at home, so I haven't been paying into Social Security. You're the one banking retirement. That's your money, and the only way I'd ever see that, is if you die. And we don't want that to happen. Daddy's money is my retirement . . . just in case," she said, and flashed him a big smile. "Besides, I might just find me a part-time job in Lone Bridge. I think it would be fun."

He blinked. "Yeah, right . . . I just—"

She interrupted with a laugh, pointing at the house they were passing.

"Jo-Jo Walker is half-dressed and mowing her yard in this Mississippi sun. Her double D boobs are bouncing like Jello shots, and her shorts are pretty close to near misses. She does love showing her ass."

Before Cal knew it, she'd reached across his arm to honk the horn, then thrust her arm out the open window and waved as Jo-Jo turned to look. "Hi girl!"

Jo-Jo looked startled, then waved as they drove past.

Cal's face was flushed, and now he'd become way too quiet.

She glanced at the side-view mirror, eyeing Jo-Jo's ass hanging off the sides of the mower seat and mentally added her name to a list of possible suspects.

The sun was still in her eyes, so she pulled the visor down again and turned it to block out the blistering rays.

"Cal, it sure is hot. Please, roll up the windows and turn on the air conditioner? I don't want to arrive at the car dealer looking like I've been in a wet t-shirt contest."

"Yeah, sure thing," Cal said, and turned on the cool air as the windows went up.

Bitsy sighed, raised her arms to lift the hair off the back of her neck, which thrust her boobs into full view of Cal's side-glance.

"Whew, that cool air feels amazing. I need to make some notes about what features I want on the car, so I don't forget." She pulled a grocery receipt out of her purse then kept digging for a pen. "Dang it. I don't have a pen," she muttered, and before Cal knew it, she'd opened the compartment in the console.

She dug through a conglomeration of candy wrappers, a partially smoked pack of cigarettes, a large assortment of pocket change, and finally, a few ballpoint pens. She grabbed one, tested it to see if it worked, and then closed the console and started making notes. She didn't let on that she'd seen a condom, still in its little wrapper, as well as two more pens from a motel she'd never heard of. She was writing down things like "backup camera," and "no leather seats," but her underlying thoughts were on replay.

What the hell has happened to the man I married?

As for Cal, he just kept driving. And praying. Praying was good. But he needed some luck to go with it. Something was up with Bitsy, but he couldn't put his finger on what was off. She was still smiling and teasing, and she'd baked his favorite cake. She'd been fine when he'd left to go to the store for her. She'd even given him a sweet kiss goodbye. Best he could figure, whatever had set her off had happened after he'd left and before he got home. But what the hell?

"I hope they've got a red one," Bitsy said.

Cal blinked. "Car? You want a red car?"

"I might," Bitsy said. "Unless I see something better. You know how it goes. You do the same thing day in and day out. Drive the same car. Wear the same clothes. Cook the same food. Have sex with the same person. I guess after a while, it all gets old." Then she giggled. "Oh, don't get me wrong. Sex with you is just fine, honey. Just fine."

A flush rose up the back of his neck. "Well, I'd hope to hell it's just fine. I wouldn't have a wife who fools around."

"I agree," Bitsy said. "Why . . . I don't know what I'd do if I found out you were cheatin' on me. I might be led to do something drastic."

His heart skipped. His eyes narrowed. "Like what? You don't mean you'd go and hurt yourself?"

"Oh, no way! But I'd sure as hell do some damage to you," she said, and then laughed.

Cal suddenly lost his desire for conversation and turned on the radio.

Bitsy loved to sing. Normally, she would have started singing along with whatever song was on the radio, but she was too close to mayhem today to start bursting into song.

A few minutes later, they crossed the bridge for which the town of Lone Bridge was named and drove straight to Beamers' Auto Sales.

Cal parked in the shade, but before he could get out, Bitsy was already walking to the showroom. That's when he noticed how short the skirt was on her yellow mini-dress and how high her heels were. Her shoulders were soldier-straight, and she wasn't walking, she was stomping toward the showroom.

He thought, *Yep, she is mad at Bradley Beamer*, and Cal ran to catch up.

***

Having been forewarned, Bradley came out of his office with a smile on his face, caught the panic on Cal's face as he was coming up behind his wife, and wondered what kind of trouble Calvin had gotten himself into now.

"Bitsy! How nice to—"

She rolled her eyes. "No, Bradley, it's not nice. Nothing is nice about this visit. I brought a nearly new car in to get fixed, and six weeks later, here it sits, and you think just because I'm a woman I won't know when I'm being played. Whatever your reasoning, this nonsense is over, and I am going to do you a favor. Rather than report you to the Better Business Bureau and then tell everyone in Lone Bridge that you are running some kind of scam, I will be buying myself a new car here today, and you will take the car you are unwilling to fix as a very nice trade-in."

Bradley was stunned. "Now, Bitsy, you misunderstand the difficulties of—"

She sniffed. "I don't have difficulties. Men have difficulties they bring upon themselves. I want a sports car. Not a used one. A new one. Like that red one on the other side of your showroom."

Calvin gasped. "Bitsy, that's a thirty-thousand-dollar Camaro!"

"Oh, but it's not going to cost *me* thirty thousand dollars. I have a lovely, already paid for, nearly new car sitting in Bradley's shop with less than nine thousand miles on it, worth about twenty-two thousand, allowing for depreciation. Don't I, Bradley?"

Bradley stifled a gasp and wouldn't look at Calvin.

Calvin was looking at a spot on the wall just over the top of Bitsy's head.

"Well, I guess that's right," Bradley said, and made himself smile.

"Then it's done," Bitsy said, and giggled. "Isn't this fun? A little anniversary present to myself. Go start the paperwork. I brought the title to the dead car sitting in your garage."

"Don't you want to try the Camaro out?" Bradley asked.

"I know how to drive. I'll 'try it out' on the way home. Do the paperwork, fill up the tank, and I want all the guarantees and that hundred-thousand-mile warranty, too, please."

"Some of those costs are extra," Bradley said.

"Just consider it what part of what you owe me for lying and leaving me stranded out in the country for the last six weeks."

Bradley had already lost control of the situation and knew the charade he'd been allowing Cal to pull was his fault, and it had come to a rather abrupt end.

"Then come into the office, and we'll get you fixed right up," Bradley said.

Bitsy started walking, heard Cal behind her, stopped, and turned.

"Cal, honey. You don't need to wait. Y'all go on home. I'll be along soon enough. I want to get the insurance switched before I leave town. Can't be driving around with no insurance, can I?"

"But I can tend to that insurance first thing tomorrow. After all, I work there."

"But there's a whole day between now and tomorrow, and I don't want to drive my new car without it. I'll stop by and let Paul switch it over for me, and that will be that."

Cal blinked, and made himself smile. "Right. Just don't forget we're having steaks and celebrating our anniversary," he said.

She heard the whine in his voice and wanted to slap him into the middle of the next week, but she just blinked her eyes and smiled at him instead.

"I am unlikely to forget what day this is. I just spent three hours in the kitchen making your favorite cake, like I always do, but when a woman has needs, they need be met, too."

Cal felt like he had in first grade, when the teacher put him in the corner, and he didn't know what for. As he watched her walking away, he realized it was still her mad walk, and he wasn't certain that the red sports car was going to make a lot of difference in whatever it was that had set her off.

CHAPTER TWO

Cal was on his third beer and glaring at the television. He'd been sitting here nearly two hours now, and she still wasn't home, or answering her phone. He was hungry and feeling sorry for himself when he finally heard a car coming up the drive and looked outside.

It was Bitsy in the little red sports car.

"About damn time," he muttered, downed the last of his beer, and got up, ready to read her the riot act.

"Where have you been?" he snapped.

She dumped the insurance papers and the new car papers on the sideboard, looked at the empty beer bottle in his hand, and rolled her eyes.

"Clearly, you have had one too many or you would remember that I was at the dealership and then the insurance company, hence the stacks of paperwork I just put down. I assumed you would have fired up the grill and started the steaks, but you didn't," and she sailed right past him.

"Don't walk off when I'm talking to you!" he shouted.

Bitsy froze. Stood a few seconds with her back to him, and then she slowly turned to face him.

"You did not just yell at me in my own house."

The look on her face sobered up Cal's three-beers' worth of stupidity.

"Look, Bitsy, I'm sorry, but you've been acting weird ever since I came home from town, and I want to know why."

"I'm sure I don't know what you mean. My problem was with your friend, and it has now been solved," she said. "And to answer the question you shouted, I am going to change clothes and cook supper. Then we're going to eat food and anniversary cake, and you can sleep off this hateful attitude. I would have expected you to see my side of this issue, but yet you seem to be more worried about what Bradley thinks. Maybe when you wake up, you will be my sweet man, again."

"Hateful? Well, I guess I don't want any dinner or anniversary cake. I'll just remove myself from the premises."

"Yes, hateful. Don't ever yell at me again!"

Cal knew he was wrong. But he didn't have the balls to say he was sorry.

Bitsy's heart was pounding. She wanted to cry. But she wasn't going to give him the satisfaction as she watched him grab his truck keys and stomp out of the house.

"Good," she muttered. "Since you're screwing another woman, being in your batting lineup is no longer an option."

She heard him spin out on the graveled drive and speed away and thought, *I wish I had a tracker on that truck to see where he goes next.* Instead, she picked up the anniversary cake, carried it outside, and set it in the grass by the chicken house, then she went to drown her sorrows with lilac scented bubbles in her Jacuzzi.

She stayed until all the bubbles had popped, and the water was cold before she got out. She put on a pair of shorts and a T-shirt then sat down at the kitchen table with an attitude, a Coke, and some cheese and crackers, and ate while watching the chickens pecking the hell out of that cake.

She was still sitting there when the sun went down, but instead of turning on the lights, she sat in the dark, waiting for his headlights to come down the driveway. The longer she sat, the angrier she became, thinking if her daddy was still alive, he would put a load of buckshot in that man's ass and dare him to ever set foot on this property again. However, Daddy was deceased, and it was up to Bitsy to make Calvin sorry.

It was six minutes past one a.m. when she saw headlights out on the blacktop, and the moment they turned toward the house, they went out. She snorted. That was Cal, trying to sneak in and lie about what time he got home.

She saw him park, kick a tire on her new car as he walked past, then heard him stumbling up the steps and fumbling with the keys before the door swung inward. For a brief moment, he was a looming silhouette in the doorway before he slipped inside and locked the door behind him.

He didn't see her when he stopped to pull off his boots, and he still hadn't seen her sitting in the shadows as he walked across her highly polished hardwood floors.

Then all of a sudden, she came out of that chair like she'd been launched and shouted out behind him.

"Where the hell have you been?"

Cal lurched like he'd been shot. His feet slid out from under him, and he fell backward with a thud. The boots he'd been carrying went up in the air. One came down on his crotch. The other one landed heel first on his forehead. It was a sucker punch he never saw coming.

"Oh, for the love of Pete," Bitsy muttered, and turned on the light.

He was laid out in her hallway like a body in a morgue. She checked his pulse. It was ticking just fine, which was more than she could say for him. There was a paper napkin sticking out of his shirt pocket which she quickly removed as evidence. It had a lipstick kiss and a phone number written on it, and she was contemplating all manner of revenge when sanity returned.

You are fortunate I do not want to go to hell, or to prison, she thought, and walked over his body, stashed the napkin in the baggie with her other evidence, and pushed it back under the winter quilts.

Then, to mark the end of their fifteenth wedding anniversary, she went to their bedroom, got his present, sat it out in the hall, then locked their bedroom door and went to bed.

The first thing Calvin saw when he came to, was the vamp of his boot in his face. When he shoved it off and saw ivy wallpaper, he thought, *I am in the hallway. Why am I sleeping in the hall?*

He remembered coming home and driving to the house with the lights off. He remembered pulling off his boots and then nothing. But it wasn't until he started to get up that he began feeling the pain.

His face hurt, and when he stood up, it felt like he'd been kicked in the balls.

What the hell? Did I have a fight in the bar?

He was walking a little bit bow-legged as he headed for their bedroom, and then saw the gaily wrapped present outside the door and groaned. At that point, he was afraid to go in, then realized it didn't matter, because Bitsy had locked him out.

He felt like ten kinds of a son-of-a-bitch as he carried the present into the kitchen, with the guilt of knowing he'd picked a fight with her for no reason and spent her hundred-dollar birthday bill on booze.

When he opened the box and saw the new hunting vest he'd been wanting, he left it where it lay, too ashamed to take it out of the box. He was beginning to feel sick and pretty sure it was from the lump on his head when he slipped and fell, and because the booze went sour in his belly.

He looked around for their anniversary cake, but didn't see it, and then felt the contents of his stomach coming up. He took off at a waddle for the back door, flipping on the porch light as he ran, and got outside just in time to puke off the side of the porch.

He was hanging onto the porch post to make sure it was over when he happened to glance out across the back yard. The light on that security pole was bright enough for him to see something laying out in the grass.

At first, all he could see was a lump of something white, and thought it was a dead chicken and that a critter had gotten into the coop. He went tearing off the porch and out into the grass in his socks and ran up on the cake.

In his half-drunk state, he saw the cake, clearly hen-pecked and crawling with June bugs, but he read it as a dead hen crawling with bugs and maggots, and once again, puked where he stood before staggering back to the porch. As he was walking up the steps, his foot slid. He grabbed onto a porch post to catch his balance, and that's when he noticed the white, greasy trail he was leaving behind him with every step.

He looked down at his socks, pulled one off, smelled the fresh chicken poop, and puked again, then he pulled off both socks and threw them in the yard, cursing loudly in garbled rage.

***

Bitsy woke when she heard him trying to get into the bedroom.

"At least he isn't dead," she mumbled, then laid there listening, knowing he'd gone outside. Curious, she got up and went to the window that looked out into the back yard.

She heard him being sick, and thought why do men make

so much noise when they fart or vomit? Women know how to do both delicately and blame it on someone else or bad food. Then she saw him walking toward the chicken house and pause beside the remnants of the cake and puke again.

She shrugged off his misery as well-deserved and went back to bed. A few moments later, she heard him launch into a cursing fit three octaves above his normal speaking voice, and she rolled over and pulled up the covers.

"Karma is a bitch," she muttered, and closed her eyes.

———

She was up making coffee and frying bacon when Cal appeared, already dressed for work. There was an imprint of a boot heel in the middle of his forehead. His eyes were squinty from the overhead lights and as red and bloodshot as the strawberries she'd put in their cake.

She poured a cup of coffee and set it on the counter.

He nodded his thanks as he picked it up, and even as he was taking his first sip, wondered if she'd poisoned it. But she was drinking from the same pot, and he decided his biggest issue today was having no excuse for last night.

"Do you want eggs, or would you prefer aspirin and dry toast?"

"Damnit it, Bitsy. Don't rub it in," he mumbled. "Something got into the hen house last night. I saw a dead chicken. The carcass was crawling with maggots. I was going to carry it off this morning, but it's gone."

She never glanced up. "You *were* drunk. That was our anniversary cake. I gave it to the chickens. It couldn't have been maggots. It hadn't been there long enough. Likely June bugs. And there were raccoon tracks around the chicken house this morning. Likely, they finished it off. Had you passed out in the yard last night instead of in the hall, I would have left you to the critters, too."

His stomach rolled. This reminded him of their entire junior year of high school, when she wouldn't even give him the time of day. He didn't know what to say or do, but had a feeling if something didn't get resolved, there wasn't going to be another strawberry cake or a sixteenth anniversary.

"Uh, Bitsy, about last night . . ."

"Go to work, Calvin. Go adjust someone's insurance claim or cry on Bradley Beamer's shoulders. I'm fine."

He walked out the front door, passing the red Camaro to get to his truck, and thought as he was driving away, that the worst decision he'd made in his life thus far was pulling that stunt with her car just to make his sex game and playtime a little easier. Unfortunately for Cal's well-being, the current discord wasn't enough to consider calling it all to a halt.

Embarrassment came when he got to the office with the obvious signs of a hangover and the brand on his forehead. He passed it off as having had "one hell of an anniversary," which wasn't a real lie.

It was their anniversary, and it had been the night from hell. They'd just happened to occur in two different places.

Bitsy, on the other hand, was full of righteous indignation, but she wasn't about to share it with the world. As soon as she finished her breakfast, she changed clothes and headed to Lone Bridge. This was her day to help at her church. The ladies of the First Baptist Church took in clothing donations, washed and mended them, then hung or folded them up like their own little clothing store for whomever was in need.

She liked being a part of it more than she liked the sermons. The preacher was always preaching about sin and retribution. The Clothes Closet was all about doing the right things out of the goodness of their hearts.

Arriving at the church parking lot in her new red sports car, she was met with the usual female glares or compliments, and the sweet smiles they didn't mean. It was her personal opinion that women were like feral cats. Just when you think you've tamed one to be your pet, it will scratch your eyes out just for practice. Just like she was going to shred Cal for cheating, and the woman participating in it, once she found out who it was.

She put up her things and went to get a work apron. Within minutes, she was sorting the new clothing donations, and JoJo Walker, who was also working today, was taking them back to the washing machines.

JoJo loaded up the three washers, then came back to where Bitsy was working.

"Nice car," she said.

Bitsy smiled sweetly. "Thank you so much. It's my anniversary present."

JoJo nodded. "Wow, Cal really came through for you, didn't he?"

Bitsy threw back her head and laughed. "Lord no. I bought this for myself."

JoJo blinked. "Well, I guess he still paid for it."

Bitsy paused. "Actually, he didn't. I have my own money. But why, exactly, is our business any of your concern? Do you know something I don't?"

JoJo went from flushed to pale so fast Bitsy thought she was going to pass out. "I don't know what you're talking about, but I do apologize for being nosy."

"Apology accepted. I won't hold it against you. Some people are blind to the boundaries of others." And then she pointed at the pile of clothing JoJo was leaning on. "I wouldn't lay all over those if I were you. That pile is the one with fleas and nits. It needs to go to the laundry. Did you ever have head lice? I haven't personally, but I hear it's nasty."

JoJo threw up her hands and shrieked, before heading for the ladies' room, while Bitsy took a moment to reflect upon the lie she'd just told in the house of the Lord.

"Sorry, not sorry, Lord, but I think she's been sleeping with my man. If I'm wrong, I'll apologize about it later."

***

It was nearing noon, and Bitsy felt good about what she'd done today to help people in need. She was at the back of the room with the sewing machine, repairing rips and replacing buttons, when she heard the long stride of a man wearing boots coming toward her.

She glanced up and saw Fisher Means heading toward men's coats and jackets, and she looked away before he saw her staring.

Fisher had been a year behind her in school. A quiet boy who'd joined the army out of high school and ended up smack in the middle of the war in Iraq. By the time he'd mustered out thirteen years later, there had been no one left to come home to.

His parents were deceased—killed in a car wreck just like hers had been. He lived alone in the family home he'd inherited, wore his long hair in a ponytail, and often had a couple of days' worth of black whiskers on his face. He could have passed for the bad guy or the good guy in any spy movie she'd ever seen, which kind of fit the job he had now. He ran a private investigation agency from his home and was known to disappear from time to time.

And now here he was in the clothes closet, looking at the men's jackets. She put her mending aside and went to see if he needed assistance.

"Hey, Fisher, are you looking for something in particular, or do you want me to go mind my own business?"

A slow smile spread across his face, changing the sharp angles to nearly handsome, which startled Bitsy that she'd even thought it. Right now, she was in no mood to admire anything about men.

Fisher still wore the half-smile as he met her gaze. "I would never be so rude as to tell a lady such a thing. I'm here because somewhere along the way, I seem to have lost my jacket. Maybe left it behind on a recent trip. I know it's a bit warm for jackets right now, but I like knowing I have one hanging in the closet should the need arise. I don't need charity. I would be happy to pay."

"That's fine. If you find what you want, we'll make a deal. I'll leave you to look."

"Thank you," he said, and kept sorting through the jackets as Bitsy went back to her mending.

But now she was watching him more than she was sewing and thinking about his job. Private investigators were supposed to be good at tracking and snooping. Last night, she had wished for a tracking device on Calvin's truck. Maybe Fisher could bug the truck and find out who he was cheating on her with, and where it was happening. The more she thought about it, the more it intrigued her.

She was still lost in thought when Fisher appeared before her holding a brown leather jacket as well as a denim one.

"What would be fair for these two?" Fisher asked.

"Maybe twenty-five dollars," she said.

"Deal," he said, and peeled off fifty dollars.

"Oh, Fisher, no! I meant for both of them," she said.

"They're worth it to me," he said, and put the money in her hands.

"The money will be put to good use," she said. "And thank you. Follow me up front, and I'll bag them up for you."

Fisher followed, trying not to admire another man's wife, but he couldn't help thinking what a fine sight she was coming or going. He laid the coats on the counter as Bitsy dug under the counter for a bag and then began folding them up to fit in it.

The whole time Bitsy worked, her thoughts were spinning, and before she talked herself out of it, just blurted it out.

"Are you still involved in private investigation?" she asked.

He looked up, and for a second, thought he saw tears shining in her eyes. "Yes, ma'am."

She handed him the bag with the two jackets and then whispered. "I don't know what you charge, or how all that works, but I want to hire you."

He glanced around to make sure they were alone then lowered his voice.

"It all depends. What, exactly, is the problem?"

Her voice was shaking. "I need to be sure you don't tell anyone what you're doing for me."

"Privacy is part of my job. I don't talk about anything I work on, or who I work for. If I did, I couldn't solve anything, could I?" he said.

"Right. I didn't think of that," Bitsy said. "So, my problem is that my husband is cheating on me with another woman."

Fisher was stunned and tried not to show it. "Bitsy . . . ma'am . . . are you certain?"

"I'm lipstick on a collar, condoms in the glove box, blue pop-off nail stuck in his underwear, black lace panties under the truck seat, pink hairbrush that's not mine, three different shades of lipstick, and ballpoint pens from at least six motels, certain."

"Holy shit . . . I mean . . . right. That's certainly enough."

"Do I pay you a retainer first, or how does this work?" she asked.

He definitely saw tears in her eyes now, and this was killing him. He couldn't stand to see a woman cry.

"Usually a retainer but—"

"I want pictures of him and the woman. I want proof. I am going to take him to court and her with him. Hanging is illegal now, but a public divorce with all the trimmings and suing the woman for Alienation of Affections will suffice. Would a thousand dollars be enough to start?"

Fisher was looking at the maddest woman he'd ever seen, and she had yet to raise her voice. This woman didn't just want a divorce. She wanted revenge.

He nodded. "Yes, it would be enough."

"I don't want to write a check he might see. I can get cash, or I can Venmo you or something."

"Venmo would be fine, Bitsy." He took one of his business cards out of his pocket, wrote his Venmo address on it, and handed it to her.

Bitsy wrote her phone number down on a piece of paper and handed it to him. "My phone number. I'm still living with the bastard. Text, don't call."

"Understood, and Bitsy, I will get the proof you want, and he'll never know it's happening."

"Thank you, Fisher."

"Just Fish. We've known each other too long to be formal. I won't send updates, and unless there's an emergency, I will not need to contact you until I have the full package. It would be helpful if you'd text me the motel names off the pens. Just go about your business as usual and trust that I've got your back." Then he picked up his bag and walked out.

Bitsy's heart was pounding. Either this would be the best thousand dollars she'd ever spent, or it would come to nothing, and Fisher Means wasn't all he was cracked up to be. Only time would tell, and right now, she was officially off the clock at the Baptist Church Clothes Closet.

She gathered up her things and went back to her car, then she sent the thousand dollars to his Venmo address. Next stop, Granger Feed and Seed to get chicken feed. Laying hens did not thrive on cake, alone.

Fisher said to keep to her routine, and this was part of it. She came home with chicken feed and a rotisserie chicken with the intention of making chicken and dumplings.

After unloading the chicken feed and gathering the eggs, she headed for the house. Normally, she would have cooked the chicken herself so she would have the juices from the stew pot to start the dumplings in. But Cal no longer qualified for the best of Bitsy. A box of store-bought chicken broth and a pre-cooked chicken would work just fine. All she had to do was get the meat off the bones, stir up some dumplings to drop in the boiling broth, and add the pieces of chicken in the bottom of the bowl before she served the dumplings. One wrong comment about the food, and he'd be wearing it.

Fisher Means went home long enough to hang up his new jackets, then he headed down the hall to his office. He was still reeling from the shock of Bitsy's request when her Venmo money arrived. He transferred it to his business account at the bank and felt sorry for her, for what was happening. Of all the people in Lone Bridge, he would have never seen this coming.

Then he shook off the thought and went back to the business at hand. What he needed first was a magnetic tracker to plant on Cal's truck, and once he decided which one to use, he opened the package, loaded the info into his laptop and synced it with his cell phone. Another practice of his was to put a new SIM card in his camera every time he began a new case. That way, every photo he took from then on would be photos pertaining to that case.

Once he had everything ready on his end, he headed out. It was going to take time to get a feel for Cal's daily routine, but the tracker would do that for him, and the camera was his gun. All he had to do was focus and click. A bloodless way to bring down the bad guys, and a far cry from spending thirteen years of his life in someone else's war.

Cal was at work, finishing up a report to send to the home office and wishing to God he could do rewind to six weeks ago, and let Bradley fix Bitsy's car. Never in a million years would he have expected what happened. She was always so agreeable and passive. But yesterday, she'd turned into a woman he didn't know. He should never have shouted at her, either. Three beers and he'd been ready to rumble until she turned around. One look at her face, and he turned tail and ran. Chicken Little had nothing on him. The sky was falling, and he was afraid to look up.

But Cal's focus on work was exactly what Fisher Means needed. He drove up the alley behind the Sullivan Insurance building, spotted Cal's truck, and stopped long enough to slap the magnetic tracker on the underside of the truck, and then drove away.

He parked a couple of blocks up long enough to verify the tracker's signal then went through the drive-through to get a Pepsi and some fries. Next stop was to find a place to park with a clear view of the alley by which Cal would be leaving, and wait.

Wherever Cal went, Fisher was sure to go.

Cal sent his report, checked the log to see if he had a clear calendar, and he did. Baring a fire, a wreck, or a natural disaster, his work week looked light, which meant his social calendar was looking up.

No sooner had he thought it, than his cell signaled a text.

#12. NOW

He grinned. Tansy Sullivan's bat signal left nothing to the imagination. He sent a reply.

ETA in ten

He logged off the computer and walked out the back door with his phone in one hand and his car keys in the other, heading for Rogers Motel on the outskirts of Lone Bridge without one ounce of guilt about having an affair with his boss's wife.

The tall pines lining the drive provided shade, and the parking lot behind the motel provided privacy. The perfect place for an illicit rendezvous.

He took the turn off the highway in a skid and gunned it down the pine-lined drive, then he slowed down as he entered the parking lot behind the building. Room Twelve was at the far end of the building, and that's where he parked. Just thinking about Tansy's hands and tongue made him hard. He got out of the truck on the run, knowing the door would be unlocked, and the room would be dark.

The moment he crossed the threshold, Tansy shut and locked the door behind him. She was a naked, shadowy wraith, waiting for a ride.

He kicked off his boots and began removing his clothes, but he wasn't fast enough. Tansy yanked. Buttons went flying, as they fell into a tangle of arms and legs and naked bodies, turning the bed into a horizontal trampoline.

When Fisher saw Cal exit off the highway into the motel driveway, he wiped the salt off of his hands, started his truck, and began following the blip on his phone. It didn't take long to figure out where Cal was going.

A few minutes later, Fisher turned off the highway and followed the drive all the way back to the parking lot, pulled into a spot two rows behind Cal's truck, and killed the engine.

He took his camera out of the case, fitted it with the telescopic lens, and took a couple of pictures of Cal's truck and the car parked beside it. Fisher wondered who she was and settled down to wait.

Twenty minutes after liftoff, Cal was flat on his back in the bed, still reeling from the blood rush, while Tansy had already pranced herself into the bathroom. She'd gotten what she'd come for and had places to be, and Cal was on the same schedule. He'd used up this week's freedom to dither.

Tansy emerged from the bathroom and grabbed her clothes to put on as Cal rolled off the bed. "You're the best," he said, and gave her butt a quick pat.

She was applying her makeup when he came out of the bathroom and began getting dressed. As soon as they were ready, they left the room key on the bed along with a tip and walked out together, unaware of the man in the back of the lot taking picture after picture of them, including their goodbye kiss, and then shots of them driving out of the lot, one behind the other.

After they were gone, Fisher drove around to the front of the motel and went into the office. The clerk looked up and smiled.

"Fish! Long time—no see," he said.

"Evening, Dooley. How's it going?" Fisher asked.

"Could be better. My kid broke his collarbone a couple of days ago. I'm working two shifts to make up the money for the doctor bills," Dooley said.

"That's rough. Sorry to hear that," Fisher said, then leaned on the counter and lowered his voice. "I need a little information, and it's worth the hundred-dollar bill in my pocket."

Dooley frowned. "What kind of information?"

"About the people who just rented room twelve." Fisher said.

"I ain't supposed to give out that information," Dooley said.

Fisher laid the money on the counter between them.

Dooley looked around to make sure they were alone and then slipped the money in his pocket.

"Calvin Yarbrough and Tansy Sullivan. They take turns paying, but that's their go-to room."

Fisher nodded. "Out of curiosity, how long has this been going on? I mean . . . them meeting here?"

Dooley's brow furrowed. "I'd say . . . once a week for at least four, maybe five years."

"Do you have any way to print out that history for me?" Fisher asked.

"It'll take a minute," Dooley said.

"I'll wait," Fisher said, and a few minutes later, he had the proof.

"Thank you, Dooley. I hope your son heals up okay," Fisher said, and walked out.

He got back in his car to check the blip that was Cal's truck, noticed he'd already gone through Lone Bridge and was driving toward the home he shared with Bitsy. Fisher wondered if she would suspect anything when Calvin walked in the door?

He watched until the blip ceased movement, checked the location, and saw Cal was home, which meant it was time for him to go home, as well.

Bitsy had her mama's tureen full of chicken and dumplings and a bowl of sliced cucumbers and raw onion slices marinating in a salt and pepper vinegar dressing. They'd been her daddy's favorite version of a salad, and she had the need to hold the memories of her family close, today more so than ever.

She didn't have Cal anymore.

She wasn't even certain he'd come home.

All she had for sure was her rage—and Fisher Means.

A few minutes later, one question was answered when she saw Cal's truck coming up the drive. It remained to be seen if he intended to stay.

CHAPTER THREE

Cal was felt good about his rendezvous with Tansy until he was almost home. Before Bitsy's blow-up about the car, he'd never thought about having sex elsewhere then going home to her. It wasn't about loving any other woman. It was all the sex.

But after he'd walked out on their anniversary, he'd screwed himself sideways with her, and the uncertainty of which incarnation she'd be inhabiting when he got home was just the tiniest bit worrisome. He parked beside her car then sat a moment, staring at the front door and started psyching himself up.

"I'm the man of that house. I put food on the table, and I pay the bills. She doesn't get to call the shots! She owes me!"

He got out of his truck and headed to the house with purpose in every step. He slammed the door behind him as he walked in.

Within seconds, she appeared in the doorway with a knife in her hand and a look of disbelief on her face, and Cal crumbled like a dry biscuit.

"Sorry. I guess the wind caught it."

"There hasn't been a breeze all day. Supper's ready."

"Uh . . . right . . . I'll just get out of these work clothes first."

She laughed, but somehow it didn't feel friendly. "I swan, Calvin. You sit at a desk. Your clothes are fine. Just wash up and come eat while it's hot."

He bolted for the bedroom then wondered if she'd locked him out. But the knob turned, and then he was inside. He sniffed his clothes and rolled his eyes. They smelled like Tansy's perfume.

All he could do was fight fire with fire, spritzed himself with his manly cologne, then washed up. When he went back to the table, his face was washed, his hair combed, and he was ready to take back his house.

The moment Cal took a seat, the scent of his Ralph Lauren Polo Blue became an assault on the aroma of the food Bitsy had cooked.

She said nothing, but suspected a lot, and when she passed behind his chair with the tureen of chicken and dumplings and saw the bite mark on the back of his neck, the urge to pour it in his lap was so strong, it made her shake.

But she could hear her mama's voice. *Waste not, want not,* and carried it to the table instead. She smiled sweetly as she sat.

"Help yourself," she said.

He frowned. "You don't want to bless the food?"

"I'm taking a break from piety, right now," she said, and served herself from the bowl of peas and carrots, while Cal dipped into the tureen.

Their plates were filled, and they'd had their first bites. Cal was reaching for the salt when Bitsy sniffed the air like a hunting dog trying to lock onto a scent.

"Hon, I think your cologne has gone bad. It smells a little like a fifty-dollar tart waiting for her next fuck."

Cal gasped. "Bitsy Yarbrough! I have never heard that word come out of your mouth before."

She shrugged. "I've said it plenty of times. Just not while you were around. We all have our little secrets. I'll bet you do things I don't know about, too, but it hasn't killed us yet. Anyway, the point being . . . your cologne is off. I can take it back to the department store next time I go to Jackson and get you a new bottle."

"I'll deal with it myself next time I go that way," he said.

She picked up the bowl of veggies. "Peas and carrots?"

"What? Oh . . . yes, sure," he said, and served himself a helping.

It was the longest, most uncomfortable meal he'd ever eaten with her. Clearly, she wasn't over his late-night bar stunt. It would probably be helpful if that mark was no longer in the middle of his forehead as a reminder.

"Do we have dessert?" Cal asked.

"No. I spent half the day at the clothes closet at the church, sorting donations and mending clothes, then I had to pick up chicken feed and groceries. I was too tired and hot to think about baking. What did you do today? Did any disasters come your way?"

He shook his head. "It was all desk work today, making final reports for the home office."

"Then while I'm cleaning up here, I would appreciate it if you would make sure the laying hens are put up for the night and have water."

He got up from the table and went out the back door, while she began putting up the leftovers and loading the dishwasher.

By the time Calvin came back, she had the kitchen cleaned and was sweeping the floor.

"I'm going to take a shower," he said.

She just nodded and kept sweeping, knowing he'd never see that bite mark on the back of his neck unless somebody told him, and that would likely happen tomorrow, when he went back to work.

She was embarrassed to call him husband with that brand in the middle of his forehead and a hickey bite on the back of his neck. As far as Bitsy was concerned, he'd just dulled all the shine she'd ever seen in him, and there weren't enough apologies this side of heaven to make it better.

The shower was steamy by the time Cal stepped in. He started with shampoo and then scrubbed himself from head to toe, removing all of the fifty-dollar tart, before getting out.

He was drying off in front of the mirror, as always, admiring his fine physique and sizeable manhood, when he saw a huge hickey just above his belly button. His heart started to pound, and there was a knot in his belly going to war with the dumplings.

If Bitsy saw this, he was done for. Now he wished he was still locked out of their bedroom. He always slept in the nude. She'd know something was up if he didn't. How the hell was he going to get out of this?

He put on a pair of shorts and a T-shirt, stepped into a pair of flip-flops, then snagged a beer and went out onto the back porch for a little privacy.

Bitsy had carried a bowl of vegetable peelings out to the chickens and was on her way back when she saw Cal come out on the back porch with his phone and a beer. His phone began ringing as he sat, and he was laughing by the time she came up the steps. She passed him without a word and went inside. She was halfway to the kitchen when she made a U-turn and went back to the window behind him. Never in her life had she eavesdropped on her husband, but circumstances changed, and this was about the fight of her life.

She leaned in, listening to his side of the conversation.

"Not for a couple of days." Then there was a pause before he spoke again. "Not at your place." A pause. "She said what?" Pause. "Blind to the boundaries of others? What does that even mean?" Pause. "Probably nothing."

Still clutching the empty bowl, Bitsy backed away and carried it to the kitchen, put it in the dishwasher, and started it up. Her ears were ringing. She felt faint. Finding inanimate clues was one thing. Hearing that conversation was a physical pain. She knew who he was talking to—JoJo Walker!

She needed not to be looking at him when he came back inside. She wasn't sure she could control what she felt. Fisher told her to act as if everything was normal, but that would never include having sex with her husband again. She wasn't sure how this was going to play out, but she needed a reason that didn't make him suspicious.

And then fate intervened in the form of a blast so loud it rattled the windows.

Bitsy thought it was thunder, but when Cal came flying back into the house with a wild-eyed look on his face, she guessed she was wrong.

"What was that?" she cried.

"Explosion. Somewhere between here and Lone Bridge."

"Lord. That will set the laying hens back a week. I may be buying eggs in town for a bit," she said.

But Cal was already playing into the escape plan that had just landed in his lap. "It looks like it's somewhere between here and town. There's already smoke rising. I have to change clothes and get to the site. It may involve one of our insured. Stay inside. If it's something toxic in the air, I'll let you know in case there's an evacuation notice." "For pity's sake, Calvin. You should wait until someone calls you. You're already wearing a brand between your eyes from a simple trip to the bar. Lord knows what you'll get into out there. Whatever's happening, they won't be needing their insurance adjustor right now."

Cal knew she was right, but this gave him the reason he needed to be AWOL at bedtime.

"I'll be fine. Don't wait up, but I have my phone. Call if you get worried."

She bit her tongue to keep from saying what she was thinking, but being worried about him was the last thing on her mind. He was flirting with danger on his dime. She shrugged and went to the living room to turn on the television as he ran to change clothes.

A few minutes later, he came hurrying back through the house. "I'm leaving now," he said.

She looked up. "Yes, I can see that. And if you set yourself on fire, don't blame me. I already told you what I think about this decision."

"Yes, well . . . take care," he said.

"Unless I fall off the sofa, I should be fine," she drawled, and upped the volume on the TV.

It wasn't her usual sendoff, but then Bitsy wasn't her usual self, so he didn't think much about it. He bolted out the door, leaving her to get up and lock it after him. And as soon as she saw him on the blacktop, she went to their bedroom and began going through the clothes he'd just removed, looking for clues.

Besides the reek of perfume mixed with cologne, she noticed two missing buttons on the front of his shirt.

"Tore that right off him, didn't you, bitch?"

There was no way in hell she was sleeping with that smell and took everything he'd just put in the laundry basket straight to the washing machine. Some laundry soap would take care of the smell, and the hot water cycle should shrink up that shirt just fine.

She started it to washing, then went to get her sewing box. She was going to need two small buttons to replace the ones missing. Preferably something pink and pearly.

Cal drove like a madman, using the rising smoke ahead as a beacon, and the closer he got, the more certain he became that it was closer to the river than the blacktop. As he sailed past JoJo's house, he saw her in the yard, eyeing the rising smoke, and he honked at her.

She flashed a big smile and waved.

The closer he got to the smoke, the more he noticed the increase in traffic. Probably lots of curious looky-loos, he thought, and never considered that he was one of them. It wasn't until he got to a section line road directly north of the smoke, that he realized who lived down there.

It was the old Turner place. It had been empty for years, but gossip was that it had become a meth house. And if that was true, then it was quite likely some meth heads had just blown up their own lab. At that point, he made a knee-jerk decision to keep driving and glean gossip in Lone Bridge, instead.

As he drove down the main drag, he noticed lights on inside his office, and so, he drove around to the back and went inside.

His boss, Paul Sullivan, was at his desk with a headset on, talking on the phone at the same time he was pulling up info on his computer.

When Cal walked into his line of vision, he gave him a thumbs up and waved him over, still talking to someone on the other line.

"Yes, ma'am, we're just learning of this. Yes, ma'am, your policy is still valid. No, ma'am, it is not our responsibility to oversee squatters. That is all in the homeowner's realm. You'll have to speak to the county sheriff about that. No ma'am, it would not be advisable to come to the site. It's near nightfall. They will be trying to put out fires and remove bodies. You need to get clearance from the sheriff, like I said. When we're cleared to photograph the scene, we will do so. But that's not happening until we also get clearance. Yes, ma'am, you're welcome. We'll be in touch."

Paul disconnected, then pulled his headset off and leaned back in his chair. "I'm a little surprised to see you, but kudos for thinking you might be needed. That was Eliza Turner, the great-granddaughter and present owner of old man Turner's property. Somebody already called her and told her what happened."

"I guessed that's where the explosion happened. Do you know details?" Cal asked.

"Not really, but I suspect a meth lab just blew up what was left of that old plantation house. In its day, it was grand low-country style architecture. Right now, they're trying to put out the fire. Then they'll have to dig through the debris for bodies, and you know they'll find them. Empty houses with no functioning utilities do not blow up without some fool lighting a fuse, accident or not."

"So, let me know when it's cleared, and I'll get some photos. Do we even have anything for comparison?" Cal asked.

"That's what I was looking for," Paul said. "The most recent photos were taken three years ago when the policy was renewed as a vacant home policy. It didn't look so great then, but it has an insured value, so we'll have to go by that. Don't worry about it tonight. Go home. We'll talk again tomorrow."

"Yes, sir," Cal said, and left the way he'd come.

It was too soon to go home, but he wasn't going to the bar. The last time he'd done that, he'd made it home but hadn't got past the hall and had slept on the floor all night.

What he needed this go-round was to get close enough to the scene to get all smoky, then go home and claim to be emotionally wrought about what he'd seen, and sleep on the couch.

Fisher was already in for the night when he heard the explosion. It wasn't long after that when his tracker signaled Calvin

Yarbrough was on the move. He knew the man was an insurance adjustor, but Fisher's job was to keep track of Cal, so he sat a few moments to see which way Cal went and realized he was headed into town. Fisher sat in his driveway, watching the blip until he realized Cal had had gone to the office.

Fisher started the car, then he drove to the same place he'd waited before and got there in time to see Cal driving away. He followed, only to end up in the traffic coming and going from the scene of the explosion.

When he saw Cal stop on the side of the highway and get out, Fisher wondered what the hell the man was doing. He glanced in the rearview mirror as he drove past and saw Cal getting into the back of his truck bed to watch the orange glow on the horizon.

Fisher parked farther down on the side of the highway to keep an eye on Cal's next move, and after about fifteen minutes, he saw Cal get back in his truck, drive right past where Fisher had parked, and then he drove home.

Satisfied that Cal had not planned to double-dip, Fisher turned around and went home. As he walked into his house, he noticed how smokey his clothes smelled, stripped, and showered.

Later, as he was going to bed, he thought about how smokey Cal's clothes must have been sitting out in the open like he had for so long, and guessed Bitsy would not be appreciating the scent of smoked jackass.

———————

But Cal's arrival didn't go as planned. The lie he'd cooked up and his elaborate plan to back it had all been for nothing. The house was dark, but for a light Bitsy had left on in the hall, and she was in her nightgown, curled up asleep on the sofa. He quietly locked up and went to the laundry, stripped off his smoky clothes, left them on the floor, and went to take another shower.

Just before he came out, he turned off the bathroom light in case she'd moved herself to the bed, but it was still empty. In all the fifteen years they'd been married, except for a couple of out-of-town work trips—and sleeping passed out in the floor the other night—he'd never gone to bed without her.

As he crawled between the covers and turned over onto his side, the sight of her empty pillow tugged at his heart. He wanted their old life back. The one where he cheated on her in the day and slept with her through the night.

Bitsy had pretended to be sleeping, and it had worked. She'd smelled the smoke on his clothing when he came in the house and guessed he had actually done what he'd said. But it wasn't a get-out-of-jail-free card; it just saved her from a night together in their bed.

And when morning came, she woke up to smokey clothes in the laundry room floor. She calmly dropped them in the laundry basket and reminded herself that the day was coming when she would never have to pick up after him again. She went back to the kitchen to start the coffee and then to the bedroom to get dressed.

As she opened the bedroom door, she could hear Cal in the bathroom and guessed he was shaving. It was enough time for her to change and get out before he emerged. She dressed in their walk-in closet faster than she'd ever dressed before and was back in the kitchen, standing at the kitchen counter eating a bowl of cold cereal, and watching TV when he strolled in.

"Meth lab, wasn't it?" she said.

He blinked. "How did you know?"

She pointed at the TV airing the local news. "Coffee's made. Help yourself to cereal."

He frowned. She was furnishing food, but she wasn't handing to him ready to eat like she used to. He poured himself a cup of coffee then sat down and fixed his cereal. Just a little bit of milk. He didn't like the cereal to float. As he ate, he watched the broadcast with her.

When the show went to commercial, he spoke up. "We have that property insured. Once they've cleared the site, I'll have to go take pictures."

She glanced up. "Of what? Surely, there's nothing left but a big hole and burned spot."

He frowned. "Well, I still have to do it."

"Wear old clothes when you do. If you come home smelling like a meth lab, I'll be setting fire to those clothes."

"Jesus, Bitsy! What's got into you?"

She blinked, then looked up and smiled. "Bless your heart, Calvin. I'm just conversating. Oh . . . my book club is this afternoon. I'll be gone for a couple of hours."

He looked up. She'd said, "Bless your heart," and now she was giving notice she'd be absent from the house.

"Who's hosting this time?" he asked.

"I'll have to check our calendar, but I think it's JoJo's turn."

"The JoJo Walker who lives two miles up the road?"

Bitsy laughed. "Yes, that JoJo Walker. Surely to God there aren't two of them?"

"Well, no, that's not what I meant, I just didn't know she was part of your book club," he said.

She shrugged. "I've been going to book club for five years. You never asked about it before."

"I guess I didn't think what it meant," he said.

"It means me and seven other women read the same book and get together and talk about it. Then the next month, we pick a different one to read and do it all over again."

"So, what do y'all talk about at those meetings?" he asked.

Bitsy gave him a strange look. "Are you even listening to me? I just told you. We talk about the book. This meeting, we'll be talking about a book called *The Broke-Ass Women's Club*. The genre is women's fiction, and the author's name is Sharon Sala. She's a writer from Oklahoma. We've read other books by her as well in the past few years. This story is about four women who find out after they are notified of their husband's death, that they were all married to the same man—a bigamist who had been stealing their money and lying to all four of them. The story tells how they come together to save themselves after he destroyed their lives. There are some really great scenes in that book. One very memorable one is when all four of the women meet up for the first time at the funeral home. They're so mad at him by this time that no one wants to claim his body, so the legal wife just tells the funeral director to nuke him and throw the ashes away."

Calvin's eyes went wide from shock. His mouth fell slightly agape. A Rice Krispy was hanging in the corner of it, and Bitsy wondered if it was going to fall in his lap, or if he'd finally eat it.

"Good Lord! What the hell kind of a book is that?" he mumbled.

She laughed. "It's very pertinent to the way life is these days. You never know who you can trust, you know? In the book, the four women become great friends and recover together from what he stole from them. It's the perfect climax, after being screwed three ways to Sunday by a conman."

"Well...I guess...if that's what turns you on," he muttered.

Bitsy leaned forward. "I like to read, Calvin. It's a pleasure to get lost in a story. And it's a gift to find writers who can give that to you. When you're out and about, other than getting drunk at the bar, what turns you on?"

His face flushed. He stood abruptly and glanced at the clock.

"I'm going to be late. Have fun at your meeting," he said.

"Thank you ever so much. I surely will," she said, and watched him walk out of the house with that Rice Krispy sticking ever tighter to the corner of his mouth.

Then she waited until he was driving away before she called him.

"Hello?" he said.

"You left so abruptly I didn't have a chance to tell you . . . you have a Rice Krispy stuck in the corner of your mouth, so check yourself. It's my job to make you presentable to the world."

She hung up and grinned.

Cal ran his hand over his mouth, felt the cereal hanging from his mouth, and brushed it off. He was immediately pissed off that she'd sat there talking to him, saw it, and said nothing.

She'd turned all weird. He didn't know what was going on, but he didn't know how to take her anymore.

Fisher had already showered and shaved, but he was still bare-foot and sitting in the kitchen in a pair of jeans, having toast and coffee, with an eye on the TV, as well as the tracker app on his phone. He glanced down at his chest, frowning at the toast crumbs on his six-pack abs, then brushed off the crumbs before reaching for his t-shirt and pulling it over his head.

He knew Cal would be leaving for work, and when the blip on the screen began to move, he watched Cal leave his property, drive into Lone Bridge, and then park behind his office.

Satisfied with Cal's status, he put Kielbasa with sliced onions and Bell peppers into a slow cooker on low, and he then began researching the locations of the other motels on the list of ink pens Bitsy had recovered. Next, he ran a background check on Calvin and found out he had a sealed juvie record from before he'd moved to Lone Bridge.

So, the star quarterback from high school wasn't as squeaky clean as one might have expected. However, he had a clear record as an adult, which may or may not have proved that he had learned at least one lesson. He'd just shifted from stealing things to cheating on women.

"Class act, dude," Fisher muttered, and kept on working.

JoJo Walker had spent most of yesterday cleaning for the book club meeting this afternoon and was on her way into town this morning to pick up some goodies at the supermarket deli. Unlike most southern ladies, JoJo did not bake and was only a passable cook. She'd always considered it her own private joke that she and Bitsy shared the same man, the same charity work at the Baptist Clothes Closet, and membership in the same book club. It was the curse of living in a small town, and no small miracle that she and Cal had not been found out.

What JoJo didn't know was that she wasn't the only one. She didn't know about Cal and Tansy, and Tansy didn't know about Cal and JoJo, and Sue Ritter, the local librarian, didn't know about either of them.

As JoJo drove into Lone Bridge, she eyed the door into the insurance agency and sighed knowing Cal was so close, and yet for her, so far away. That man was her sin to live down, but she wasn't doing much to stop it. He was too good at sex, and it was too hard to say no to heaven on a mattress.

She parked at the supermarket and hurried inside. The day was getting hotter, and she needed to get home where it was cool before her hair fell flat. She needed height in her hair to draw attention from the unfortunate shape of her face. On a good hair day, her chin didn't look so square. On a bad hair day, her whole face looked a little squished, like the last burger bun in the bag.

She went straight to the bakery, picked out tartlets and cookies as well as a small tray of fresh fruits, then she checked out and hurried home. She had a new summer outfit she'd been dying to wear. Bitsy Yarbrough always looked so cute and put together without even trying, but just once, JoJo wanted to outshine her. Today might just be the day.

Bitsy had an early lunch before the book club. JoJo always served sweets, and Bitsy wanted a bit of something substantial first and had chosen leftover pasta salad, with a piece of fried ham from their supper a couple of nights ago.

As she forked a piece of ham, it dawned on her that when she'd cooked and served this, she'd been the happiest little wife ever. Clearly, her leftovers were better than her marriage.

She kept reminding herself it wasn't the end of the world. It wasn't even the end of her. She had a wrong to make right, and there was justice to be had. She'd cry when it was over.

After she ate, she went to the bedroom, took off her housedress, and stood in their closet eyeing her wardrobe, trying to decide what to wear, and thinking, *How does one dress to outshine a whore?*

Flashier? Classier?

Wearing the family pearls?

Or letting the diamonds on her left hand speak for themselves?

Hair up? Hair loose and sexy?

Décolletage prim or trashy?

Then she spied the perfect outfit and reached for her pink denim shorts, the ones in a bib overall style, and chose a white camisole to wear under them. She dressed where she stood, then reached for her white sneakers and carried them into the bedroom, got a pair of white anklets with a lacy edge from the chest of drawers, and turned to face the full-length mirror.

Almost there.

She went to the bathroom, brushed her hair to a shine, and then put it up in a ponytail on the top of her head, dabbed on a tiny bit of mascara to her already thick lashes and a lipstick called Pretty in Pink, then went back to the mirror and saw herself as she'd looked ten years ago—still fit and tan, boobs still standing at attention, and not a wiggle of flab on her arms or legs.

She traded her usual purse for a little white shoulder bag and called it done.

Now she was ready to go to the book club meeting. She picked up her copy of *The Broke-Ass Women's Club* as she passed through the living room and locked the door behind her as she left, but it wasn't until she thought about where she was going that her heart skipped a beat. She was heading for enemy territory unarmed, with nothing but her tongue and wit. She had to make this count for something without giving herself away.

Then a calm washed over her, and for a heartbeat, she felt as if her mama was riding shotgun beside her.

"Yes, Mama, I know. Never let them see you cry."

JoJo was playing hostess to the hilt, keeping the snacks and conversation lively, while waiting for their last member to arrive. She'd spent a lot of time on the preparation, and had chosen to wear her new floral turquoise and yellow silk lounging pajamas to make a statement. Even her sprayed-to-helmet-worthy hair was cooperating.

"I swear, I don't know what's keeping Bitsy," she said, and then Connie Parmeter looked out the window and pointed.

"Oh, there she comes now, and I just love her new car, don't you?" she said.

"Yes. I saw it the other day when we were doing Clothes Closet stuff at church," JoJo said, and went to the door. She opened it just as Bitsy was coming up the steps with the book clutched to her chest and her little white purse swinging at her hip.

"Oh gosh! Looks like I'm the last hen in the pen," Bitsy said. "Thank you, JoJo. It's like a sauna outside today. Feels good to be inside where it's cool."

And just like that, JoJo felt like the guest at the party who hadn't gotten the notice about casual dress. *Damn Bitsy Yarbrough forever for still looking like she's twenty-five!* And then JoJo flashed her best smile and waved her arm toward the buffet.

"You know the drill, Bitsy. Help yourself and find a seat," JoJo said, while every other woman in the room began exclaiming over what the little bitch was wearing.

Bitsy had not missed seeing the same kind and color of blue pop-off nails on JoJo's fingers that she'd plucked off Calvin's tighty-whities, and was, at the moment, resisting the urge to bitch-slap her into the next county. Instead, Bitsy smiled her sweetest. "Is this chair taken?"

"All yours," JoJo said.

Bitsy dropped her purse and book beside the chair and then headed for the buffet with her ponytail swinging, chatting with the others as she chose fruit and a cookie. Instead of the punch in the elaborate punch bowl, she chose bottled water and went back to her seat, while JoJo watched from across the room.

She wanted to hate Bitsy, but there was no basis for it other than she wanted Bitsy's man—all of him. Not just the hit and miss sex they had in secret. She needed a reason to justify what she was doing, but there wasn't one. Her mama always told her she wouldn't amount to a hill of beans. So, she sighed, grabbed a cookie and napkin to add to her little plate of fruit, and found herself a place to sit.

Rita Dubois, their book club leader, clapped her hands to get everyone's attention. "Ladies, this meeting of the Lone Bridge Book Club is called to order. Has everyone read our book of the month?"

"Yes," they echoed.

"Wonderful," Rita said. "The floor is open for comments. Did you like it, and if so, what did you like about it? Were there scenes in the story you identified with? What was your takeaway? Anyone?"

The first comment came from JoJo, and it was about the bigamist.

"I will say, it's the first time I've read a book where one of the lead characters was killed in the first few pages and yet stayed a main protagonist throughout the story," JoJo said. "I couldn't decide if he was a horrible conman, or a lonely man who created the family for himself he never had."

"He wasn't too lonely to lie to them and steal their money," Bitsy said. "I had a lot of favorite scenes in that book, but the four widows meeting at the funeral home almost felt real. I forgot it was just a story, and I was already worrying about their situation when they met. The surprise was how Janie opened her heart and her home to them. When she told the funeral director to nuke his body and throw away the ashes, I thought, that's my kind of woman!"

"I loved that scene on the Fourth of July, when they were all on the back porch singing along with the music, and how the author kept giving us moments with each woman, showing how they struggled with the hate they felt for someone they'd loved. It was real, y'all," Sandy Loveless said.

"I'd never forgive that," Bitsy said. "I wouldn't waste my tears. I'd be out for revenge. In the book, their revenge was surviving in spite of what he'd done, and with Janie giving them a place to live, they found their footing and thrived."

"What about when they discovered all those boxes in the attic? One for each woman he'd scammed. I never saw that coming," Lilah Marshall said. "And what Gretchen found out when she went through hers! Now that was revenge on a whole other level with her first husband . . . the one who basically sold her to the bigamist to get out of paying alimony."

They all had opinions and weren't shy about sharing them, but JoJo had seen a side of Bitsy she wouldn't have known existed. Bitsy's world was black and white. A kind of "betray me and you pay" mindset, which was a revelation for JoJo.

Every time she and Cal had their little rendezvous, they were playing Russian Roulette with their own welfare. Bitsy Yarbrough wasn't all sweet smiles and fluff. One might even consider messing with that woman could be dangerous.

CHAPTER FOUR

The book club was in full swing when Paul Sullivan got the all-clear from the parish sheriff about Turner property and went to give Calvin the news.

"Hey, Cal. We just got the okay to get photos at the Turner place. I need you over there now before the looters show up looking for scrap to sell. Better take a disposable mask, too." He started to walk away, and as he did, glanced at the back of Cal's neck and grinned. "Dang, Cal. That's an epic hickey you're supporting. Did she suck your brains out with it?"

Cal froze. "What the hell are you talking about?"

Paul poked the back of Cal's neck. "That hickey right there. That's what I'm talking about. I haven't seen one that perfect since high school." Then he laughed and walked away.

Cal's heart was pounding as he reached for the back of his neck. He couldn't feel it, but he remembered how it had happened. Tansy was like a damn spider monkey in bed. Climbing all over him, grabbing and licking and biting. *Dang it, Tansy.*

Bitsy surely hadn't seen it yet, or she would have beheaded him where he stood, but he was going to have to conceal it or come up with a different, but plausible, explanation for what had caused it until it faded. But first things first.

He went to get the camera from the supply room, checked to make sure the SIM card was in it and the battery charged, then he grabbed a mask from a box on the shelf and headed out the door.

———————◆———————

On the other side of town, Fisher Means had been going down the list of motels Bitsy had given him, calling them all and identifying himself as Calvin Yarbrough. He fed them all the same story about losing a watch and wondering if they'd found it.

He was on the phone with the desk clerk at the Sleep-Inn Motel when he saw the tracker on Cal's truck begin to move. He kept an eye on it as he continued his conversation.

"I don't often wear a watch, which is why I didn't realize it was missing," Fisher said. "It might help me narrow down the window if you could remind me of the last date I was there."

"Sure thing, Mr. Yarbrough," the clerk said. "I'm just pulling up your name on the registry. Let me see. Oh, here you are. Every other Thursday, for the past year, and regular as clockwork. The last date was a week ago Thursday. I remember after you left, your friend, Miss Ritter, came back to get the key, because her phone was missing. I walked her to the room, and she found it on the floor near the desk. Maybe she found your watch then, too, and forgot to mention it. You could check with her."

"Oh, I didn't know!" Fisher said. "I'll have to check it out with her."

The clerk laughed. "That's a good one, check it out with your librarian, like checking out a book."

Fisher grinned. "Yeah, like that. Thanks for your help," he said, and hung up.

That was the last motel on the list, and he'd just discovered the name of a second woman. Sue Ritter. The librarian in Lone Bridge.

He got up on the run, grabbed his camera and his gear, and headed for his car. While he tracked Cal, he couldn't stop thinking about having to break the news to Bitsy. Not only was there more than one woman, but the affairs had been ongoing for years, and he suspected they purposefully used different motels from time to time for a reason—thus the existence of the number of pens Bitsy had found. Now he needed pictures of Cal and Sue Ritter to add to Bitsy's evidence.

Cal went straight to the Turner property, parked a short distance away from the site, masked up, then began getting shots from all angles. Once he'd finished with those, he sent up the drone to get aerial shots of the blast site, then stowed it and the camera in the truck, before walking a couple of yards away to take a pee in the bushes. He was on his way back to the truck when he tripped on a piece of wire hidden in the grass and went belly down in barb wire.

It was like being shot pointblank by a double-barrel load of buckshot. Pain followed the shock, but when he moved, the wire began coiling and catching on every article of clothing he was wearing, and the shriek that came out of his mouth sent a flock of herons in the nearby water into the air. Not only was he caught in the wire, but the dust all over the ground and the grass were actually meth ash from the explosion.

He cursed the wire. Cursed his luck. Cursed the meth heads who'd been cooking it and wished them all to hell as he kept trying to get up. When he finally managed to stand and move toward the truck, the barbs dug in, and the loose wire began coiling around his neck and back, and then down the back of his left leg like mutant ivy.

He cursed a blue streak as he shuffled to his truck, dug through the toolbox to get the wire cutters, and with many curse words and tears, began cutting himself out of the mess, one small section of wire at a time.

By the time he got free, he looked like he'd gone ten rounds with a bobcat and was wearing enough meth ash to be dangerous. He dusted himself off as best he could, then crawled into the truck and headed home. If he was lucky, Bitsy would still be at her book club meeting. He could clean up, bag his clothes for disposal, and then take himself to the ER.

He'd need a tetanus booster for sure, and God only knew what else regarding the cuts and scratches. He'd worried about his visible hickeys, which had now been defaced by the other injuries. He couldn't decide if God was helping him or punishing him. Either way, he was going to be miserable as hell, and no more sex with anyone until he healed.

It never occurred to him to wonder how Bitsy would view his temporary disfigurement when it came to sex. She was his wife. It was her duty, and she had always succumbed.

Until the car thing.

Clearly, her recent displeasure with him had been because she'd figured out that he'd been in on it. It was her silence about it that was eerie. Like waiting for a hurricane. You know it's coming. But you don't know the power of the blast or if you'll survive it, until it's come and gone.

He rolled all the windows down as he drove home, hoping even more of the dust would blow off before his arrival, and when he went past JoJo's house and saw the little red sports car in the driveway, he breathed a sigh of relief and just kept going.

———

The book club meeting had ended. The new book for next month had been chosen, and Bitsy was getting ready to leave when she happened to glance out the front window of JoJo's house and saw

Cal driving past. She frowned. It was way too early for quitting time, so something was up. She turned to thank her hostess.

"Everything was lovely, JoJo. I hate to be the first one to leave, but I have a dozen things yet to do this afternoon. See y'all around town."

JoJo walked her to the door. "I'm so glad you could come. We missed you at the last meeting."

"Because my car was in the shop, but that problem was solved, and won't happen again," she said.

Moments later, she was out the door and walking to her car. She started it up, then drove out of the driveway and headed home.

Cal's truck was parked in its usual place as she pulled in beside it, then got out on the run. The last thing she expected was Cal walking in the back door buck naked, with bloody scratches all over him. He looked like a bait dog.

She gasped.

Cal looked up. "Fell in barbed wire out at the Turner property."

She started toward him, but he took a step back and held up his hand.

"Don't touch me. I'm covered in meth dust. My clothes are in a garbage bag in the middle of the yard. I need to shower."

"Oh. My. God. I'm so sorry. Get yourself cleaned up, and I'll take you to the ER. At the least, you'll need a tetanus shot."

He nodded, and then pointed at the camera and box on the floor.

"That's my work camera and the drone. They were already in the truck before I fell, so they didn't really get contaminated. Would you put them in your car, please? I need to drop them off at the office before we go to ER."

She nodded, got the keys from her purse, and went one way as Cal went the other. She felt sorry for his misery, but his pain was physical and an accident. He'd heal. What he'd done to her was selfish, intentional, and mean.

"Shit happens," she muttered, and headed for her car with his things.

———————

Bitsy had thrown an old quilt over the passenger seat so he wouldn't bleed on her new upholstery, and when he got in her car, she had to scoot his seat back for leg room. He was used to his truck, but right now it was a biohazard.

Betsy adjusted the air conditioning vents to keep him cool and then headed into town, with Cal trying to make small talk.

"Did you have a good book club meeting?" he asked.

"It was fine."

"Did you have good stuff to eat?" he asked.

"It was okay. JoJo doesn't bake. It was all bought stuff from the deli. I don't know how she supports herself, or what she does with her time. She isn't married. She doesn't have a job. Maybe she has a sugar daddy somewhere. But on the other hand, I don't suppose it's any of my business."

And suddenly, Cal's need for conversation ceased as he shifted in his seat, trying to find a comfortable position to sit.

Bitsy guessed he was uncomfortable and sped up. Once they got to Lone Bridge, their first stop was the office.

"Just stay in the car where it's cool," Bitsy said, got the camera and the box, and carried them inside to his boss.

Paul saw her entering and stood up from his desk. "What's wrong? Where's Cal?" he asked.

"In the car. He said to tell you he got the shots you need as well as aerial footage. But when he turned around to go back to the truck, he tripped on some loose barbed wire and fell in it. The clothes he was wearing are in a bag in the yard, covered in meth ash. He had to cut himself out of the wire. We're on our way to the ER. He's scratched and cut all over. Looks like he tried to pill a cat. He may or may not be at work tomorrow. He'll call and let you know."

"Oh dear! I'm so sorry," Paul said. "What a horrible thing to have happen! Remind him this will fall under workers' comp. I'll take care of the paperwork."

"Yes, I'll let him know. As for the horrible stuff . . . there's a lot of that going around," Bitsy said, and strode out with purpose in every step.

When she got back in the car, Cal was looking at himself in the visor mirror.

"Good thing it didn't get my face," he said.

She rolled her eyes. "Yes, good thing," she said, and carefully backed away from the curb.

By the time they entered the ER, his sweatpants and t-shirt were dotted with bloody spots that had seeped through the fabric.

"Sit," she said, pointing to one of the faux leather chairs. "Paul is doing the paperwork for a workman's comp claim for you."

He nodded, watching as she went to the desk to check him in, thinking as he did, how cute she looked in those pink overall shorts, and how tanned and toned her legs were. For a brief moment, he wondered what the hell was wrong with him to be chasing tail all over Lone Bridge when this cute little thing was waiting for him at home. Then he shrugged off the thought. He liked variety, and nothing was new and exciting between them anymore. But the sex game he'd invented kept everything buzzing.

They'd just had their fifteenth wedding anniversary. Not that they'd celebrated it, but it had been a memorable day, nonetheless. Just not in a good way. A few minutes later, Bitsy sat down beside him, and there they were, silently waiting for his name to be called.

Fisher Means had followed Cal as far as the turnoff to the Turner place, but since there was nothing and no one at the end of that road, he turned around, went home, and followed Cal's trips from his laptop.

He didn't know Bitsy was sitting in the ER with Cal, and it wouldn't have been any of his business if he had, but word was spreading around town anyway.

Paul Sullivan told his receptionist, who told her friend, that Cal was injured on the job.

And that friend was in the library when she got the text, and mentioned to Sue, the librarian, that Cal Yarbrough was in ER, and he'd fallen into barbed wire and been ripped to shreds.

Sue fainted in her chair.

Rita Dubois got a text about it before she'd left JoJo's house, and told JoJo about Cal's terrible accident, and it was all JoJo could do to hide her horror.

Tansy Sullivan was in the supermarket when she heard someone talking about Cal being taken to ER covered in blood. She left her shopping in the cart and ran out crying.

And there they were—three women who had no right to go check on him. To console him. To even be in the same presence as him and his wife.

Wondering if their handsome lover was ever going to be the same.

Wondering if they'd still want him if he wasn't good-looking anymore.

While Bitsy sat beside her husband, waiting for his name to be called.

Finally, a nurse came out. "Calvin Yarbrough."

He stood up, then realized Bitsy was still sitting. "Aren't you coming with me?"

"You're a big boy, Calvin. They're pokes and scratches. They'll clean them up with disinfectant. You're getting a shot. I'll be right here when you get back," she said.

And that's when Calvin acknowledged the wall between them. He'd put it there. But he didn't know how to take it down.

"Right," he said, and followed the nurse through the open doors.

Bitsy watched those doors swing shut and saw them as the symbol of what their marriage had become. All the secrets. All the lies. All the betrayal behind closed doors.

Fisher Means had become her secret. Her spy. She just needed him to come through for her soon, before she lost her shit on the whole damn mess. And while Cal was with the doctor, she sent Fisher a text.

JoJo Walker is the owner of the blue pop-off nail I found on Cal's underwear. I am in ER with Cal. He got tangled up in barbed wire taking pictures at the Turner place today. He's fine, just pokes and scratches. Brought him to get a tetanus shot. He may or may not be at work tomorrow, but if he's roaming around town, he'll be up to no good.

Fisher read the text with interest. If Bitsy was right, then that was woman number three for Cal, not counting his wife. He already knew the workplaces and home addresses of Sue Ritter and Tansy Phillips, and now he had one more address to add to his list.

This is where trailing Cal would take more than watching a blip on a screen. He needed photos of the other two with Cal, and that meant physically following him everywhere he went. But that wasn't going to present a problem, because Fisher was the original invisible man.

A quiet kid who turned into a quiet man who'd gone to war, come home in one piece, and slid back into the daily life of Lone Bridge without anyone paying attention. Being invisible in his business was a valuable trait. And since Cal was otherwise occupied for at least the rest of this day, Fisher loaded up and headed out to two different motels to get hard copy proof of Cal Yarbrough's repeated visits.

One thing Fisher discovered was that Cal had a special motel for each woman. He already had what he needed from Rogers' Motel, but there was still the Sleep-Inn and Mimosa Manor, and no guarantee he hadn't visited the women at their homes, as well.

Fisher hadn't ever given the man much thought until he'd taken this case, but he'd quickly found out Cal Yarbrough was a lying, cheating ass, whose hunting days were about to come to a swift and painful end.

Cal came back into the ER lobby a chastened man. He'd never been naked in front of so many women and at such a disadvantage. He'd shriveled up like a wrung-out dishrag when they'd begun swiping disinfectant on all of the pokes and scratches. He hadn't been able to get dressed fast enough.

When they'd walked him back to the lobby, and he'd seen Bitsy still sitting in the chair, absently staring at the muted TV monitor on the wall, he could see her thoughts were elsewhere. He just didn't have the guts to ask where she'd gone, but when she looked up and saw him approaching, she quickly stood.

"They called in a prescription for infection," Cal said.

"Then we'll get it before we go home. If you're too sore to walk, lean on me," she said.

"Thank you, baby, but I'm good," Cal said.

"Just wait here by the door where it's cool, and I'll bring the car around," she said, and then walked off.

No hug. No kisses. No sweet tones of concern in her voice. Cal was scared. He wasn't sure, but it felt like a really important part of Bitsy was gone. However, the longer he stood, the more his attitude shifted. He was the injured party here, and she was acting like a cold-hearted bitch. When she pulled up to the entryway in that little red sports car, he was mad all over again.

Damn car.

Damn woman.

That's fine, too.

If she wasn't putting out, he knew women who would.

CHAPTER FIVE

Bitsy went into the pharmacy to get Cal's prescription while he waited in the car. She could see the street through the pharmacy window and her car parked directly in front. Cal was on the phone. Oh, for the days when she would have seen that and thought nothing of it. How utterly blind and stupid had she been?

The pharmacist, Josie Lavelle, was bagging up the bottle of pills when Bitsy pointed to the little candy display by the register. "I'll take one of those Snickers bars, too. Cal loves his sweets."

"Sure thing, honey. You take good care of your man. Prayers for healing from all of us," Josie added.

Bitsy smiled her sweetest smile. "Thank you so much. He's going to need them."

She exited the pharmacy and saw Cal end his call. She just kept walking, and when she got in, handed him the bag.

"Your meds and instructions are in the bag. I bought you a Snickers bar, too."

Cal's surprise was evident.

Good. I want him off guard, she thought, and backed away from the curb, then she drove straight to the Fish Shack drive-through and got both of them cold drinks to-go.

"I know you must be hurting. Maybe something cold and sweet will make the ride home a little easier," she said, and took a sip of her Coke before putting it in the cupholder in her console and headed home.

"That was so thoughtful," he said, as he dug the candy bar out of the sack and took a bite.

She gave him a quick sidelong glance and added a tinge of surprise to the tone of her voice.

"I have always been thoughtful of you," she said.

He thought he heard an emphasis on the word *I*, which could be construed as her saying *he* wasn't. But then he shrugged it off and enjoyed the treat.

Even with the windows up and the air conditioning on, the thick sweet scents of wisteria, crape myrtle, and lilac coming in through the air vents were redolent of happier times. Bitsy blinked back a single tear and kept driving, but every time she felt like stopping the car and kicking him out on the highway, she just took another drink of her Coke. By the time she got home, there was nothing left in her cup but swiftly melting ice. So much for her need to have a hissy fit. They were home, and she hadn't given herself away.

"Can you get yourself out, okay?" she asked, as she parked and killed the engine.

He nodded. "I'm just sore as hell, not crippled. I'll be fine by tomorrow."

"Okey dokey," she said, then gathered up their refuse, got out, and headed for the house.

Cal followed her inside to the kitchen and watched her dump their cups in the trash.

"What now?" he asked.

"I'm going to change clothes and go to the garden. Green beans need picking. I should have done it this morning while it was still cool, but I didn't. I'll put one of the old quilts on top of the bedspread. You can stretch out on that and rest. Don't forget to take your first dose of the antibiotic. You don't want all those pokes and scratches getting infected. Your normal workday has been put on pause, but mine hasn't," she said, and flashed a quick smile.

He opened the bag, read the dosage instructions, then took the first pill before going to the bedroom.

Bitsy had already changed into a loose mini-length cotton house dress that hid her shapely body but showed a goodly portion of her legs.

"That dress is short. When you bend over, your ass will show."

She pivoted so fast his first instinct was to duck.

"I have been wearing this dress for six straight summers, and you never paid attention to what I was wearing before. It's one of my everyday work dresses. My garden is behind the house. What's getting short around here is my patience. What the hell is wrong with you, Calvin? You have never once come into this house and asked me what I did during the day or commented upon what I wear. Daddy always told me when a man started criticizing his wife, it was all because of his own guilty conscience. So, either lie down and shut up, or come on outside with me in this godawful heat and hold the tail of my dress down while I pick my green beans."

"Uh . . ."

She rolled her eyes. "That's what I thought," she said, and walked out.

Cal didn't move until he heard the back door slam, and then he walked to the window overlooking the back yard and saw her stomping toward the garden. When she got to the first row to start picking, he realized the rows ran horizontally, which meant only the chickens in the hen house were going to see a damn thing.

He turned away from the window and flopped down on the bed. But his phone was already buzzing with texts. He let them all go to voicemail and closed his eyes.

———————————————

That evening, supper consisted of scalloped potatoes, the green beans Bitsy had picked, and a fried ham steak. She cooked it, served it, and ate it sitting at the same table with Calvin, waiting for him to start the conversation with an apology.

Other than, "Please pass the salt," the dinner conversation did not happen, because Calvin had not apologized, and Bitsy wasn't giving him a break.

When they'd finished eating, Calvin stood, patted his pocket to make sure his phone was there, and pointed toward the back porch.

"Thankyouforsupper. Itwasgood. I'mgoingtositoutonthe—" Bitsy gave him her back, turned on the water, and began rinsing dishes and banging pans.

He sighed. "Bitsy . . . I'm sorry—what I said about your dress."

The butcher knife she held was dripping water on the floor when she turned around. "And I'm sorry those words ever came out of your mouth, because I cannot unhear them," she said.

He bolted for the back door, moving faster than was comfortable, anxious to put some distance between them. Not once in his life had he ever been afraid of a woman, but as of today, he was officially afraid of his wife.

Bitsy knew he was uneasy, which was fine with her. She didn't have to spurn his advances. He was dodging her. And tonight, she had an even better excuse for not having to sleep beside him. He was going to have the whole bed to himself, so she wouldn't accidentally bump his wounds.

She knew he was outside so he could text all his girlfriends. All she could hope for right now was that he got mosquito bites. That way he could itch and hurt at the same time.

Sue Ritter had a floor burn on her backside from sliding out of her seat when she fainted. It was embarrassing and a bit too revealing to have done it upon hearing about Cal's condition, but she managed to cover it up by claiming a reaction to low blood sugar. Later, she'd sent him a frantic text.

My poor darling. I just heard about your injuries. Please let me know if you are okay.

Then she waited anxiously until he finally responded.

I just got tangled up in some old, barbed wire. Got some cuts and scratches and a tetanus shot. You are a darling for asking. I'll come by sometime tomorrow and you can see for yourself. I'll be in the alley behind the library.

Relieved by the news, Sue could hardly sleep for the thought of seeing him tomorrow.

Tansy Sullivan had been horrified when her husband told her about Cal, and her reaction to the news was real.

"Oh my God! Paul! How terrible!" Tansy said. "Poor Calvin."

"Indeed," Paul said. "Bitsy took him to ER. I doubt he'll be at work tomorrow, so I'll likely be here early and staying late."

"Of course," Tansy said, but her thoughts were swirling, trying to figure out how she could check on Cal for herself without raising attention. But the woman standing beside her in the grocery store had overheard enough of her conversation with Paul to be curious.

"Tansy, what happened? Is your husband okay?" she asked.

"Oh yes, he's fine. He was just telling me what happened to Cal Yarbrough, our insurance adjustor. He was taking pictures of that explosion site at the old Turner place and tripped and fell in a bunch of barbed wire. He got all cut up, and Bitsy just brought him to the ER."

After that, the news began to spread, and so did Tansy's plans. Once she learned Cal had not been hospitalized, she sent him a text.

Damn it hotshot. I'm so, so sorry. I would give anything to just hold you and make all the bad stuff go away.

Cal smiled when he read Tansy's text and sent her a reply.

Missing my best girl. I could do with a hug, if it's not too tight. I might be able to slip by sometime tomorrow. I'll let you know if I make it to town.

That was all Tansy needed to know. She wasn't budging from her house until she saw him, no matter how long it took.

The last text came from JoJo.

I am so sorry you've been injured. I suppose Bitsy is taking good care of you, but I wish it was me. When you can, let me know you're okay.

Cal frowned when he got her message.

It was an unwritten rule between him and his "girls" that no one mentioned his wife. It turned up the guilt factor, which ruined the mind games he played.

It had started years ago, when he'd cheated the first time and told himself the women meant nothing more to him than a real-life version of a computer game. Instead of a war game where he shot enemies hiding behind buildings and evaded traps and bombs online, he was the playboy, counting off how quick he could make them climax, and bonuses for how many times in one session he could make that happen. In return, he had good sex.

A good psychiatrist would have had a field day with him. It would have been hard to determine how much of it was narcissistic behavior, and how much was due to a total absence of empathy and decency. Unfortunately for Bitsy, she'd been fooled by his good looks and charm.

———

Cal was back in the house watching TV when Bitsy went out to put the chickens up for the night. After she came back in the house, she locked the doors behind her, and got the last load of laundry from the dryer, and she carried the basket through the house to hang up the clothes in their closet. The last thing she did before she quit for the evening was to sweep the kitchen floor.

As she went into the living room, she was tired, but even more, soul weary. She and Cal used to watch TV together in the evenings, and now all she could think about was staying as far away from him as possible. She also used to think he was the handsomest man in Mississippi, but now all she saw was depravity, and everything she heard that came out of his mouth, blatant lies.

He looked up as she walked in, but before he could open his mouth, she spoke.

"Calvin, out of consideration for your poor body, I am going to sleep in the guestroom to give you all the room you need in the bed. I would feel horrible if I accidentally bumped into you and caused you pain. Everything is cleaned up and locked up. Retire at your leisure, and don't forget to take your meds."

She made herself smile and left the room. She wanted to soak in the Jacuzzi, but she didn't want him in there eyeing the goods, so she opted for a bubble bath in the guestroom. After she started the water and added the bubble bath, she went to get her robe and nightgown, then took them back across the hall, locking the door behind her.

Even as she turned the lock, she saw the irony. A locked door was a symbol of the deterioration of their marriage. He'd broken her heart and all the vows he'd made to her at their wedding. It was only fitting that she dismantled his playhouse and his playmates with it.

Her hands shook as she stripped, then she clipped her hair up on the top of her head and crawled into the tub. Lies were stressful, and she was living one. She slid down into the heat as the bubbles began popping against her skin and sighed with relief.

This left Calvin alone with the TV and the remote, but Bitsy had caused him to lose interest in the show he had been watching. He couldn't get a read on her. On one hand, her words were as sharp as that knife she'd been holding earlier, and on the other hand, she was all sweet words and smiles. It was like living with two different women.

Later, when he got up to go to the bathroom, he tried the doorknob to the guestroom. It was locked and very quiet.

So much for the smile.

A short while later, he took his pain and antibiotic meds, then went to bed. It took forever to get comfortable, and as he was tossing and turning, he realized how considerate it had been of Bitsy to take the spare bed. All of this would have been easier to bear if she'd just have a hissy fit.

What Calvin didn't know was that Bitsy was holding all the aces.

With the evidence she'd found on her own, and the stuff Fisher Means was gathering on her behalf, he was a walking time bomb, and she held the detonator.

Cal didn't sleep well, and got up early to get dressed, thinking she would still be asleep. But when he went into the kitchen and smelled fresh coffee, he sighed.

Moments later, he heard her coming in the back door and watched her come in with a bowl of fresh eggs. Her and her chickens.

"Did you get any rest?" she asked, as she set the bowl on the counter.

"Not much."

"Did you take your morning meds?"

He blinked. "No, I forgot."

She stood there, just looking at him until it hit him. She was waiting for him to go take them. Aggravated with himself for having to be reminded, he stomped out of the room.

When he came back, she was taking sausage patties out of the skillet and breaking eggs to fry in the leftover grease. He got a cup and poured himself some coffee then sat down at the table. When she slid his plate in front of him, he looked up and smiled.

"Thank you. It looks amazing," he said.

"You're welcome, but it's just breakfast like always," she said, and set a little plate of toast in front of him.

She went back to get her egg. She hated soft eggs. If the yolk wasn't done all the way, it wouldn't be going in her mouth.

As soon as it was done on both sides, she slipped it on her plate with a sausage patty and a piece of toast and sat down at the table with Cal.

"So, what are you doing today?" he said.

"Watering the flower beds and picking tomatoes before it gets too hot. If there are a lot of tomatoes, I'll probably put some of them up, but it's too hot to can. I'll just chop and freeze them," she said.

He nodded, and kept eating as he sorted out the best way to let her know he was going into town, and then she gave him the perfect out.

"I know you aren't up to going back to the office, but if you decide to go into town for anything, I could use a gallon of whole milk. I want to make bread pudding."

"Sure thing," he said. "I can do that. Do you need it before noon?" he asked

"No, but it will be tonight's dessert, so if you can get it to me anytime around noon or after, that would give the mixture plenty of time to set up before I bake it off," Bitsy said, and primly plopped a dollop of blackberry jelly on the corner of her toast.

"Consider it done," he said, and took another bite of his food while trying to hide the glee he felt from getting the break he needed.

He was so wound up in his own drama that he missed the flash in Bitsy's eyes. She'd just set him up for Fisher. She wanted this over with, and she needed him out of her house. And, after her request, he didn't waste any time leaving.

She was still cleaning up breakfast dishes when he went outside to work on getting the meth ash off and out of his truck. After he'd finished, he came inside, showered and changed.

She was on her way outside to gather tomatoes when he called out. "Hey Bitsy, I'm leaving now. I'll be back later. Call if you need anything else before I leave town."

He went out the front door as she went out the back, but Bitsy didn't go straight to the garden. Instead, she stood on the porch listening, waiting for the sound of his truck to leave their property, and when it did, she got her phone out of her pocket and sent Fisher Means a text.

He just left the house.

Fisher was scooping Frosted Flakes into his mouth with razor-sharp precision. No milk drops between the bowl and his mouth. Just the crunch of each bite, chewing and swallowing, and repeating it over again, when his phone signaled the text. He already had the app pulled up and was watching his laptop for movement when he got the text at the same time he saw Calvin on the move.

He sent a quick response.

Already on it. I've got your back.

He calmly finished his cereal, downed the last of his coffee, and was cursing himself for breaking his personal rule not to get involved with his clients' cases. With Bitsy, he'd done it anyway. The only thing left now was to make good on his promises. He put the bowl and coffee cup in the sink, then went to get his things. He was going to dog every step Cal took and do what he did best. Become invisible.

Once Bitsy got Fisher's text, she took a deep breath and headed for the garden. Everything within her wanted to scream. But not now. All she had to do was stay busy. Just stay busy.

When she got to the rows of tomatoes, she paused, set her bucket down in front of her and began picking the ripe ones. Sometimes when she was in the garden, she would pick a couple of big green tomatoes to fry up, but not today. She just kept picking the deep red ones, and slowly, the simple act of gathering food began to soothe the turmoil within her. When she reached the end of the first row and started back up the last one, she paused and straightened up to rest her back then looked toward the house.

It was the same green-roofed, white single-story home with a wrap-around porch where she used to play when it was raining, and the porch that had turned into a racetrack she'd used to run with her daddy. He'd go one way, she'd go the other, and whoever got back to the starting point first was the winner. She could almost hear her mama yelling out the back door, telling them they sounded like stampeding goats and to stop making so much noise, because she was trying to watch "her shows."

Bitsy sighed. Those days of Mama watching the soap operas and shelling crowder peas, and Daddy carrying Bitsy to bed at night when she fell asleep on the couch, were long gone. Some days she was sad she'd lost both her parents so young, but knowing they'd passed away together made it a little easier to accept. Even if one had survived the car wreck, they would have grieved the loss of the other one forever.

She used to wonder why she and Cal never had a baby. It wasn't for lack of trying, but it just hadn't happened, and now, after all of this mess, she was glad.

Thank you, Daddy, for deeding this home and property to me, and enough money in the estate to keep insurance and taxes paid. No matter what happens when this is over, I'll be fine.

She sighed, wiped the sweat off her forehead, and started back up the last row, working her way to the house.

***

Cal wasn't taking chances of getting caught out, but he did have to pacify the other women in his life. And after finding out Bitsy and JoJo belonged to the same book club, it added another edge to his game.

Tansy and Bitsy did not attend the same events, or the same churches, so she was his secret weapon, and having sex with the boss's wife was good for bonus points in his game.

Sue was the dark horse. The prim librarian who wore big black glasses, wore her long blonde hair wadded up in a messy bun, and hid her rock-solid body beneath loose-fitting clothes. No one would ever suspect her of being a wild woman in bed.

So, as soon as he arrived in Lone Bridge, he went straight to the local café to lay rest to the stories of his near demise. Within moments of him taking a seat at a table, Bradley Beamer joined him to commiserate.

It soon became obvious to everyone that yesterday's gossip about him being ripped to shreds had been a slight exaggeration. But it was also obvious he was in pain. He was moving slower, and when he sat down, he did so with caution.

"Sorry about you getting hurt," Bradley said.

"Perks of the job," Cal said. "Insurance adjustors get flak from people who aren't satisfied with their assessments, and being onsite at fire and explosion sites isn't necessarily a walk in the park. That barbed wire was not on the property when old man Turner died, so I guess the dudes who blew themselves up added it as a deterrent from people sneaking onto the property. Then when the whole place exploded, the wire went up with it. I just happened to stumble into it in the grass. It's a damn mess out there."

Bradley shuddered. "I'll stick to selling cars." Then he glanced up at Cal. "How's Bitsy liking her new car?"

"She likes it just fine. I, on the other hand, am in the doghouse," Cal said.

Bradley shrugged. "I told you it wasn't a good idea."

Cal grinned. "And you were right. But she'll get over it."

"Why did you do it?" Bradley asked.

Cal shrugged. "Just a whim that bit me in the ass."

Bradley didn't say anything more about the car, but knowing Cal, he suspected it had to do with another woman and felt guilty for even participating in something that might hurt Bitsy. She was a good woman, and he'd helped Cal play a dirty game.

"Well, it's good to see you upright and in one piece, buddy. I need to get to the dealership. Have a good day, and take it easy," Bradley said, then laid down money for his coffee and waved at the waitress as he walked out.

She came by to pick up the money. "Refill, Mr. Yarbrough?" she asked.

"Yeah, sure," Cal said, and settled in with an eye on the clock.

After he'd killed another hour visiting, he left the café, checked to make sure his boss's car was parked at the office, and went straight to see Tansy.

The Sullivan house was on a dead-end street. The house across from it was for sale and empty, and the tall green Arborvitaes on both sides of Tansy's home walled it in via carefully landscaped elegance.

Cal and Bitsy had been here a couple of times in the past for a Christmas gathering, but it had also included every insured local, as well as office staff. A perfectly innocent reason to visit—unlike today.

Arriving like this was him leveling up in his cheating game, so he drove down the street like he owned it and turned up the driveway like he lived there. He went up the steps, rang the doorbell, and when Tansy opened it wide, she threw her arms around his neck.

He immediately winced.

"Oh, Cal, I forgot about your wounds," she said, and grabbed his butt with both hands instead.

"That hurts too," he said, laughing, and kicked the door shut.

———

By eyeing the blip tracing the streets Cal was traveling on now, Fisher took a wild guess as to where he was going next and took a couple of back streets to get there sooner. He parked in the alley behind the house that was for sale and was lying in wait within some overgrown shrubbery when Cal pulled up in the Sullivans' driveway. He had his camera aimed and snapped pictures as Cal strode up the steps and rang the bell. He got pictures of Tansy greeting him with open arms and her hands on his butt as the door closed between them. And then he settled down to wait.

When Cal exited less than five minutes later, he caught their goodbyes, as well, then took off running through the back yard of the empty house, jumped in his car, and checked the tracker.

As soon as he saw Cal was heading for the library, Fisher took the back streets and beat him to the parking lot. He had just pulled into a parking place when he saw Cal's truck appear.

"Creatures of habit. Always the easiest ones to trap," Fisher muttered, and adjusted the telescopic lens on his camara, but when Cal got out and sat down on a bench facing the parking lot, Fisher scooted down in his seat.

Cal sent Sue a text to let her know where he was then sent another one to JoJo to let her know he was heading her way soon. He made a mental note not to forget to take home Bitsy's milk. Satisfied that he was on schedule, he settled in to wait for Sue.

Within minutes, the back door to the library opened. A tall blonde in navy-colored pants and a blue and white tunic-length top came flying down the steps.

Cal stood up and moved toward her as she threw herself into his arms.

Fisher saw it all through the lens of his camera, snapping picture after picture of the embrace and then the passionate kisses. Their meeting was brief because it had to be, but there was no mistaking it for what it was. He got one last picture of them saying goodbye, and then one of Sue darting back inside the library, and the smile on Cal's face as he got back in his truck.

"You are one sorry son-of-a-bitch," Fisher muttered, and slid back down in the seat as Cal backed up and left.

Fisher sat, eyeing the blip on his laptop to see where Cal was off to next, and when he saw him stop at the supermarket parking lot, that meant he was likely headed home. But then he remembered JoJo Walker. She lived just off the highway between Lone Bridge and the Yarbrough property.

It would be on his way, and if Bitsy was right about JoJo being the one who'd left the pop-off nail in the elastic on Cal's underwear, now was the time to check out that theory.

Fisher drove past the supermarket, saw Cal's truck still in the parking lot, and headed out of town to find a place near JoJo's house to set up his stakeout. Thanks to kudzu and rural Mississippi side roads, it wasn't hard to find a spot in an overgrown lane between the two properties across the highway from JoJo's place. He backed far enough in to hide his car, then got out and secreted himself within the hedgerow of kudzu.

What he hadn't expected was to see JoJo come around the side of her house on her riding lawn mower and start mowing her front yard.

Fisher eyed her lack of clothing and guessed JoJo wasn't one of those people who burned easy. The weather was sauna-worthy, but that was a lot of flesh left bare to sun and skeeters.

He glanced down at the screen on his phone and brushed a mosquito off his arm. The blip that was Calvin's truck was on the move again, this time on the highway heading back to his house. And then he wondered if JoJo was in the front yard just to let Cal know she was home. The other two women had certainly been prepared for his arrival. Clearly, JoJo Walker was displaying her presence and her wares.

According to the blip, Calvin would be passing at any moment, and Fisher began watching the highway, waiting for that truck to pull up in JoJo's driveway—and to see how this meeting played out.

Cal glanced at the time. JoJo knew he was coming. He'd make this last stop to reassure her he was still in one piece and see where it went. When he saw her in the front yard on her riding lawn mower, he turned off the highway and pulled up into her drive, then he stopped and got out. He leaned against the cab of his truck with his arms crossed and a big smile on his face as she drove her way across the yard to where he waited.

Fisher snapped shots in rapid succession as she parked the mower, swung her leg over the steering wheel, and then fell into his arms. Cal's hands were on her breasts and then her butt when he went in for the kiss, unaware their actions were being photographed.

Fisher waited until Cal was gone, and JoJo had ridden her lawn-mower back around the house before he headed back to town. He had everything he needed. Now it was time to collate the compelling evidence he'd collected, and give Bitsy the ammunition she'd paid for.

But as he pulled up into his driveway and gathered his things, he felt a little bit like a pilot with a load of bombs on the way to destroy someone's pretty little world. Even though Bitsy had asked for it, it was going to be a shock finding out there were three of them, and that it had been ongoing for years.

After Bitsy came in from the garden, she went straight to their bedroom to shower off the sweat and get into clean clothes, taking care to lock the door behind her. She didn't expect Cal to come rushing home, but the pressure of what was happening had started to get to her. She was going to need a job, but she had zero work experience at anything but homemaking.

The humiliation of being cheated on was inevitable. There would be people taking sides. Some would surely point the finger of blame at her for not being enough to keep her man happy. And others would vilify Cal for being a cheater. But none of that was within her control, and she'd have to weather its passing. As she took off her dirty clothes, she found a ladybug on the hem of her dress.

"Sister! You are so in the wrong place," she said, and carefully picked up the dress, then went through the house and out the back in her undies to let the little bug fly free. Then to make sure there weren't more hitchhikers, she shook off her dress before going back inside.

Getting in the shower and scrubbing herself clean felt good, but she wished it would be this easy to wash off the taint of what Cal had done. The knot in her stomach grew bigger and tighter by the day.

As she got dressed, she caught a scent she hadn't smelled in years. Old Spice. Her daddy's go-to aftershave. Her eyes welled, and her throat tightened, but she wouldn't let herself cry.

"Daddy . . . I know you're here. You never did like Calvin, did you? Now I understand why." She sighed. "'Live and learn' you used to say, and I guess I'm learning the hard way."

But even after she'd left the bedroom, she couldn't bring herself to start a new task. Instead, she made herself an iced tea and took it to the living room.

She sat down and started to turn on the TV, then let the remote lie, and closed her eyes instead. The house was so quiet. The cool air after the hot sun in the garden felt wonderful. The sip of sweet tea was refreshing as it slid down her throat. And that's when it hit her.

This was how it was going to feel after Cal was gone. It was different, but it wasn't awful. And in time, it might become a blessing, or it might become the impetus she needed to fly away from this tiny, insulated piece of the world.

She closed her eyes and saw Fisher Means' face as he'd stood before her that day at the Clothes Closet. He'd been looking for a jacket, and she'd been looking for answers. It was at that moment fate had stepped in. A single tear rolled from the corner of her eye and down her cheek. She'd asked for answers. This was no time to be afraid of them.

CHAPTER SIX

Bitsy had the bread pudding ready and was waiting for Cal to get home with the milk. She was at the kitchen island, chopping up tomatoes for salsa, and blinking back tears from the onion, jalapeno, and cilantro already chopped up in the bowl when she heard Cal's truck pull up to the house. She glanced up as he came into the kitchen in long, hurried strides.

"What's wrong? Why are you crying?" he asked.

She rolled her eyes. "I'm making salsa. It's just the Jalapeno and the onion. The force is strong with these veggies," she said.

He grinned. "Oh. Right. The force is strong. That's a good one, Bets. Here's your milk. I'll put it in the fridge, okay?"

"Yes, please," she said, and then scrapped the chopped tomatoes into the bowl as he headed down the hall. She added the rest of the ingredients, then covered it up and put it in the refrigerator then took out the milk. It didn't take long to mix up the egg, milk, cinnamon, and vanilla mixture then pour it over the bread and raisins and put it in the refrigerator to set up before baking.

She was cleaning up the counter and putting things in the sink to rinse when Cal came back into the kitchen carrying a hangar with one of his shirts on it—the one with the two pink pearly buttons she'd used to replace the missing ones.

"I was going to wear this shirt to work tomorrow but not now! What the hell is the meaning of this?"

She turned around, blinked, then looked him straight in the eye. "Meaning of what?"

He was trying not to shout, because the last time he'd done that, it hadn't gone well, but he couldn't keep the disdain out of his voice.

"Pink. Fucking. Buttons?"

"Since I didn't ask you how you managed to tear two of them off at the same wearing, I don't see as how you have a right to complain about what I sewed on. It could have been because it's all I had on hand, but it still doesn't matter unless you're planning to flash someone tomorrow. Keep your shirt tail tucked into your pants, and no one will ever know. Calm down," then she turned her back on him.

A cold chill washed through him. There he still stood, holding the shirt like a white flag of surrender. He walked out of the kitchen, hung the shirt back in the closet, and kept staring at it as if it was going to tell him something he didn't want to hear.

He was still mulling over what sounded like a hidden message in what she'd said, when all of a sudden Bitsy was right behind him, and he hadn't heard her come into the room.

"It's time to take your meds," she said.

He jumped. "Damn, Bitsy. I nearly had a heart attack, what's with you sneaking up on me like that?"

She pointed down at her feet. "I wasn't sneaking. I'm just not wearing shoes. Take your meds," she said, and started to walk off, but then she paused and turned around. "Do you ever look at me anymore? I mean . . . really see me? I've always liked being barefoot in the house. Once upon a time, you knew that."

And then she was gone.

He walked into the bathroom, shook the pills out into his hand, and swallowed them without water. When he glanced into the mirror, all he saw was that damn heel-shaped bruise in the middle of his forehead.

Weary of the game he'd been playing, he went back into the bedroom and stretched out on the bed. All his running around this morning had been exhausting, and he was suffering the consequences. He had a headache, and all his wounds stung and burned. Too much hugging. Too much fussing. He closed his eyes and fell asleep.

He didn't know Bitsy came back into the room and stood at the foot of their bed. If he had opened his eyes at that moment and seen the look on her face, he would have known it was over. But he didn't, and she walked out as quietly as she'd walked in and put her bread pudding in the oven to bake.

The moment Fisher walked into his house, the scent of the Kielbasa, peppers, and onions he'd put in the slow cooker this morning met him at the door. His belly growled just thinking about it, but he'd eat later. The urge to print off the pictures he'd taken was uppermost. He needed to know that they were clear and showed everything needed to stand up in court as evidence.

So he went straight to his PC, uploaded the photos from his camera, and then printed them all off in color on 5x7 photo-quality paper, in duplicate. One set for his files in case of an emergency. One set for his client. He was lining them up and sorting them in the order in which they'd been taken and thinking it was a shame that tarring and feathering was no longer an accepted method of punishment, because this man was a total disgrace.

Once he had the photos collated, he went to shower and change clothes. He'd spent half the day in overgrown bushes and kudzu, and he felt the need to clean up before he sat down to eat.

He stripped, left his dusty, buggy clothes on the floor of the utility room, and then went back through the house naked, started the water running in the shower to get hot, then stepped beneath the showerhead and squirted shampoo in his hand.

He washed his hair first, then his body. Once he was out and dried off, he put on an old pair of sweatpants, slid his feet into some slippers, and pulled a T-shirt over his head on his way back to the kitchen.

It was chow time!

He made a sandwich with the sausage and pepper mix using a hoagie roll he'd heated in the microwave, got himself a bottle of ale, and took it to the living room to watch TV as he ate. He finished off his meal with a handful of cookies from the supermarket deli, but as he ate them, he remembered how good his mom's chocolate chip cookies had been, still warm from the oven, and the laughter that had once been in this house.

He was grateful it had been here to come home to, but it didn't feel like home anymore. Nobody lived life here. He owned the place, but it wasn't anything more than a home base—the place he stayed while waiting for the next job to appear. He'd long since given up looking for love. He wasn't disliked, but it was hard to make an impression and still be his quiet, invisible self.

After he'd satisfied his hunger and cleaned up the kitchen, he went to work, compiling the facts and data he'd been collecting on Calvin Yarbrough and his women. He made copies of the records he'd collected from the random motels, complete with dates, times, and which woman he'd been with at each one.

He knew from the background checks he'd run on all of them that JoJo Walker had been widowed twice and was living off life insurance money and inheritances from both husbands.

He knew Sue Ritter was from Las Vegas, and before coming to Mississippi, she had been an exotic dancer.

Tansy Sullivan had a squeaky-clean clean record, which was more than he could say for her soul, and he included all that information in the file he would turn over to Bitsy.

Once he had the info recorded in detail, he began printing it off, along with a cover letter to Bitsy stating the retainer she'd paid covered expenses and the fee, and there was a zero-balance owed. It wasn't even close to what he would charge a regular client, but Bitsy was different. She was special—a friend from home—and he wasn't going to lie to himself. She would be so easy to love.

He glanced at the time as he shut down the computer. He'd wait until tomorrow to contact her and set up a meeting, then he'd retrieve the tracker he'd put on Calvin's truck, and the file would be closed. After that, as difficult as it may be, he was going to have to debrief himself from Bitsy Yarbrough's life.

Unaware that the next shoe was about to drop, Bitsy spent the night in the guestroom again, while Cal sprawled out in the middle of the bed, trying to find a comfortable position in which to sleep.

The next morning, Cal dressed for work wearing the white short-sleeved shirt, with the two pink pearly buttons he'd objected to, neatly tucked into his pants. He'd chosen a pair of gray linen slacks, a fabric that was kinder to his body than the denim pants he'd worn yesterday.

Bitsy had his breakfast ready when he entered the kitchen. But as good as it looked, smelled, and tasted, every bite stuck in his throat. He wasn't sure if it was from guilt or fear, but he let out a sigh of relief when the meal ended.

"What's on your agenda today?" Cal asked.

"I guess whatever I am moved to do," she said. "I may even go to Jackson and buy myself something new to wear, since you spent my anniversary present in the bar. I also need to go to the bookstore and pick up a copy of our next book for the book club. I'll leave a note, if I do."

He was too embarrassed to admit he'd never given her anything for their anniversary and inserted his own preference for being notified if she left.

"You could just text me," he said.

"Yes, I could do that, too," she said. "Did you take your meds?"

He rolled his eyes and went back to the bedroom to take them, but when he came back to tell her goodbye, she was gone. He saw her walking across the back yard toward the chicken house and sighed. He left the house, locking the door behind him.

———

Bitsy relaxed after she heard him drive away, then gathered the eggs and fed and watered the chickens. She was on her way back to the house when her phone signaled a text, but she waited until she was back in the house to look. When she saw it was from Fisher, she quickly opened it, and the moment she saw the words, her heart skipped.

I have what you need. Where is a good place for us to meet?

She thought a moment, remembered it was summer and school was out, and sent back a reply.

One hour. Behind the high school field house.

Fisher smiled when he read her reply. That was a damn good place to meet up. Bitsy was on her game.

She went to change out of her work clothes, brushed out her hair, and put on a white sundress with yellow sunflowers woven into the fabric. When it was time, she headed for town with her chin held high and her sunglasses on.

She drove past the city limit sign and immediately took back streets, heading straight for the school grounds. She drove down a back alley and then out across a street that took her straight to the field house. Upon arrival, she backed up to the building beside an empty dumpster, and seconds later, Fisher pulled up beside her.

"Get in," she said.

So, she does want to talk. He grabbed the file, got into the passenger seat, and handed her the manila envelope.

She took off her sunglasses and put the envelope in her lap instead of opening it straightaway. Her voice was trembling. "Tell me first before I look. I know he cheats, but I hate surprises."

"There are three women. He's been seeing one of them for almost five years. One for over a year, and one for at least two, maybe three years. The motel pens were a dead giveaway. You were smart to have caught onto those. I have copies of the history of his motel visits with each woman. Motel clerks don't get paid enough money to keep secrets. I think they have moved their meeting places to different locations over the years, which is why you had so many pens. I ran background checks on him and all three women. The information is in the file I gave you. The pictures included are all the proof you'll need to prove his infidelity and their participation."

He paused, eyeing her expression, but the only giveaway of her stress was a little muscle jerking at the corner of her eye.

"I'm not supposed to have personal feelings about the cases I take, but I grew up with you. I have always admired you, and I just want to say to your face that I am incensed on your behalf, and that I have imagined beating his sorry ass to a pulp so many times I can't even say his name aloud without cursing. You did not deserve this, and I am sorry."

Bitsy hadn't expected a champion, and it took everything within her not to fall apart where she sat.

"Thank you, Fisher. For the help, and for the speed with which you have gathered what I need. And for the friendship. It will not be forgotten."

"Look at the pictures, Bitsy. It's always wise to know who not to turn your back on," he said.

She reached into the envelope and pulled out three packets of photos. He heard her soft intake of breath, and then her eyes flashed in sudden anger.

"Well, it's not the butcher, the baker, or the candlestick maker," she said, quoting from an old childhood nursery rhyme. "Here we have the boss's wife, the prim librarian, and my neighbor down the road. How trite," she said, then looked him straight in the eye. "I'm okay. I suspected, and now I know. Don't worry about me. I will get revenge before I give myself permission for regrets. When I began to suspect all this, my first thought was that I was glad we hadn't been able to have children. I wanted them, but it never happened, and now I'm glad there are none to be caught up in a custody battle."

"What are you going to do now?" he asked.

"I'm going home to call the family lawyer for a favor. Then I'm making a trip to Jackson to find the sharkiest divorce lawyer in the city, get papers drawn up, and sue three women for Alienation of Affection which contributed to the downfall of my marriage. Who knew I would ever have need of that law, but it seems ordained that Mississippi is one of six states that still has it in the books. I am going to drag Calvin and his women ass-backward through the mud of public opinion and social media."

Fisher's lips twitched. He wanted to laugh at her fierceness. She was the maddest woman he'd ever seen, but she was a freaking warrior to boot.

"Then more power to you, Bitsy Yarbrough. But remember what I said about being careful. Once the cat's out of the bag, they may start to pressure you. Don't turn your back on any of them. Don't talk to them. Don't take calls from them. If you have to, get restraining orders against all of them. Change the locks on your house and pull all the strings you can to get this case in court as fast as you can. When the truth comes out and everyone knows is when you'll know you're safe. And if you need backup, you have my number." He gave her one last look, then got out of her car and drove away without looking back.

Bitsy returned all the pictures to the envelope and headed home. She drove the five miles in a daze, and when she pulled up to the house, for a second, it didn't look like her home, and she thought she'd accidentally come to the wrong place. Then she blinked, and the mirage was gone.

She ran inside and hid the file Fisher had given her in her mama's old roasting pan, then shoved it all the way to the back of the shelf beneath the island. Cal couldn't even find a fork for himself. He'd never be digging in her pots and pans for anything.

Then she sat down and made a call to Earl Justice, Esquire, the family lawyer who'd managed her father's estate. It rang four times, and then his secretary answered.

"Justice Law Office, this is Carrie."

"Carrie, it's me, Bitsy Yarbrough. I have an emergency and need advice. Is Mr. Earl in?"

"Yes, just a moment," Carrie said, and buzzed her boss's office.

"Yes, what is it, Carrie?" Earl said.

"Bitsy Yarbrough is on the line. She said she has an emergency and needs advice."

"Put her on," Earl said, waited for Carrie to connect them, and then spoke. "Bitsy! What's going on?"

Bile rose in the back of Bitsy's throat. Just saying the words was going to make her sick.

"Cal's been cheating on me. I hired a private detective to confirm my suspicions, and I have photographic proof of him with three different women, for God's sake! Coming out of motels with them! Embracing them! Kissing them! I haven't confronted him, and after some consideration, I decided not to kill him. I thought it best to just divorce his ass and drag him and all three women into the limelight, instead."

Earl was shocked. "Bitsy! I am so very sorry. Do you two have joint property that could be contested?"

"No. As you know, the house and land are mine. I have never worked outside of the home because he didn't want me to. Now, it's obvious why. He liked me out on the farm and out from under his nose. He owns his truck. I own my own car. I could throw his clothes out in the yard and that would be all his belongings. Everything else that's here came from Mama and Daddy . . . even the bed we sleep in, and the furniture we sit on. He has no claim on anything except me, and that's about to change. But I intend to sue the three women, whom I know personally, for Alienation of Affection. They aren't sliding under the fence on this. These affairs have been ongoing for years, and I can't imagine how many times I've been laughed at behind my back."

Earl blinked. "Well, that's an old law, but I know it's still in the books. Listen . . . this sounds like you're going to need some specialized representation. I have a friend who's a sharp divorce lawyer, and he owes me a favor. Sit tight. I'm going to make some calls, and I'll get right back to you, okay?"

"Yes, okay, but make sure he knows I don't just want a divorce. I want revenge."

Earl chuckled. "Yes, ma'am. I heard you loud and clear. I'll call you back in a few." He disconnected, then pulled out his cell phone, scrolled through his contact list, and then called Charlie Cowan.

Charlie Cowan was a forty-something divorce lawyer with a receding hairline and a shark-bite reputation. He didn't believe in nibbles of recompense when a marriage failed, and the clients he accepted were always the spouses who had been wronged. It had to do with an event in his personal life when he'd been just a kid.

His father had walked out on him and his mother when he was nine years old, and they never saw him again. No alimony. No child support. But Charlie's mother didn't raise him to hate the man. She'd just instilled the belief in Charlie to get even.

She'd worked two jobs to keep them afloat, and Charlie had worked two jobs to put himself through college and law school with one goal in mind. Not to get rich. To get even. The fact that he'd become well-to-do in the process was the collateral benefits gathered from sticking it to the cheating spouses.

Yesterday he'd brought a very contentious divorce to a successful ending for his client, and he was still riding that satisfaction high when his cell phone rang. When he saw who was calling, he smiled.

"Earl! What's up, my man!"

"It's about that favor you owe me," Earl said.

Charlie kicked back in his chair. "What do you want?"

"I have a thirty-four-year-old client, named Bitsy Yarbrough, who just found out her husband of fifteen years has been cheating on her for at least five years with three different women. She had suspected something fishy was going on and hired a P.I. who came back with enough proof to choke a horse. The man has three women on the hook, and she has physical proof, photographs, and paperwork proving the timelines, places, and pictures of him with all three women in different locations."

"Damn," Charlie said. "What's her husband do for a living?"

"He's an insurance adjustor, but here's the deal. Bitsy isn't after big money. She owns her family home, and her father left her a small estate. She wants revenge. She made the comment that she decided to divorce him instead of killing him, so that's how mad she is. Her dad and I were friends for years. He's deceased, and I think the world of her. I'm just sick about what has happened. She's full of anger, but I know Bitsy. Her heart is broken, but she's southern to the core. She'll deal with this shit first and cry later."

Charlie was already hooked. He just hadn't said so. "So, what's she hoping to gain?"

"You would have to ask for details, but I know for sure, she wants a very public divorce for adultery and intends on filing Alienation of Affections on all three women, calling them out for contributing to the failure of her marriage. I know this sounds like some Lifetime movie, but it's real, and it's happening to a friend. She's not rich. But she's at the point of willing to go bankrupt to make them pay."

"I don't see the need for that to happen," Charlie said. "It's been a while since I did a case *pro bono*, but this sounds like one that needs tending. Give me her information. I'll call her right now."

"I'll text it to you after I call to let her know who you are, because right now, her trust in men is at an all-time low. And be prepared to fast-track this, because if this drags out, I don't know what she might do."

"Understood," Charlie said. "As soon as I get her info, I'll reach out to her... and Earl?" "Yeah?"

"Thank you. This might be the one that finally evens the score for me and my mom," Charlie said.

Earl ended the call and breathed a sigh of relief as he called Bitsy back. She answered on the first ring.

"Hello?"

"I got you, girl," Earl said. "I'm sending your info to a Jackson lawyer named Charlie Cowan. I told him your story. All I'm going to say to you is trust him. He's got a thing against cheating spouses. Just do everything he says, exactly as he says."

"Thank you, Earl. Thank you," she said.

He heard the tears in her voice as she disconnected and shook his head. Some days life just sucked eggs.

As promised, he immediately forwarded the necessary information, knowing Bitsy's future was now in Charlie Cowan's hands.

Bitsy hadn't moved from her chair since Earl had told her to wait. She'd already jumped off the cliff by calling a lawyer. Now she was waiting to see if she landed on her head or her feet.

This was a most horrible feeling, but it was also a most horrible thing that had happened. There was no other way to be. Now that Fisher had finished his job, she felt like she'd lost an anchor.

What she didn't know was that Fisher had not untethered himself from her. Right now, he was between jobs, and he had a gut feeling Calvin was not going to take kindly to being kicked out of the house. He was not the kind of man who could accept embarrassment or defeat without causing chaos, and for that reason, Fisher had left the tracking device on Calvin's truck. Just in case.

Bitsy was so lost in thought that when her phone rang, she jumped and then scrambled to get it answered.

"Hello, this is Bitsy."

"Nice to meet you, ma'am. My name is Charlie Cowan. Earl told me all about your problem. Are you ready to do this?"

"Yes, sir. As soon as possible."

"You're from Lone Bridge?" he said.

"About five miles outside of it," Bitsy said.

"Do you have transportation to get yourself to Jackson?" he asked.

"Yes."

"I'll need you to come to my office. Bring everything you have with you. Your proof, your evidence, and I mean everything."

"When? Today? I can be there in about an hour. Tomorrow? Anytime. I can't stay under the same roof with this man much longer and pretend I don't know what he's doing."

Charlie blinked. The fire in the tone of her voice was scary real. He glanced at his calendar, then made a knee-jerk decision. "Can you be here today by three-thirty?"

"Yes, and thank you. All I need is your address," she said.

"I'll text it to you," Charlie said. "Just do me one favor. Take a breath and drive carefully. I've got your back."

"Yes, sir. Thank you, sir," Bitsy said, and hung up. Moments later, she received the address. She entered it into her GPS app, then got a flat box she'd saved from an Amazon delivery and began gathering up the evidence she'd hidden in the linen closet, retrieved Fisher's file from her mother's roaster, and packed it in with everything else, then left a note on the counter for Cal.

I'm going to Jackson. Back late. Please feed yourself and the chickens and gather the eggs.

B—

She locked up on her way out and within moments, she was in her car and driving just under the speed of sound, heading into the unknown. It dawned on her as she drove that this reminded her of how she'd felt right before the first time she'd had sex. She knew it was going to hurt, but she was willing to endure the pain for the end result.

She also remembered that the first time she'd had sex hadn't felt good at all. Not even after it was over. It had taken time to learn how to be the woman and not the girl. But the woman she'd become did not suffer fools gladly. She'd made a believer out of Bradley Beamer and was getting ready to shake the foundation of Calvin Yarbrough's world. She would be back tonight, but he would never see the hell she was bringing with her until it was too late.

Charlie had already alerted Wanda, his secretary, to the change in his schedule. While he was waiting for Bitsy Yarbrough's arrival, he began researching the details of the alienation of affection laws, as well as the *stare decisis*—the legal precedents—for prior judgements in such cases. He didn't know for sure what her ultimate goal was in doing this, but he was about to find out.

Two cups of coffee and a package of peanut butter crackers later, Charlie was still reading and making notes when his secretary buzzed him.

"Mr. Cowan, Mrs. Yarbrough is here," she said.

"Send her in," he said, marked the place where he was reading, and checked his shirt for cracker crumbs as he stood.

He'd had all manner of people of varying ages and with varying emotions enter his office. But he'd never had one come in wearing a white sundress with yellow sunflowers—a "don't fuck with me" look on her face, carrying the requested paperwork like she was bringing in a casserole to the church dinner. He was somewhat enchanted and wanted to smile, but it wasn't the appropriate response to her arrival.

"Mrs. Yarbrough. I'm Charlie Cowan. Please, have a seat."

"Please call me, Bitsy, and forgive me, but I need to get this all said before you ask me questions." She paused for a breath and continued. "I am married to a lying, cheating man named Calvin Yarbrough. Our fifteenth wedding anniversary was about a week ago. I had just made our anniversary cake and was doing laundry when I saw lipstick on the collar of Cal's shirt and knew I had never worn a shade that red in my life. You know the feeling when all of a sudden everything you thought you knew about your life no longer makes sense?"

Charlie nodded.

"Yes, well, that's what happened to me. All of a sudden, there was a reason why my nearly new car was still sitting at the dealership awaiting a part to repair it for the past six weeks— because it left me stranded on the farm while he played loose without fear of getting caught. So, I started looking through my house and found ballpoint pens for a lot of local area motels and tried to tell myself there were a dozen different reasons why he would have them. He's an insurance adjustor. He does have times when he has to travel, but never overnight. And then I found a blue pop-off nail caught in the elastic of his underwear. Later that day, when he came home, I made him take me straight back to town to visit my unrepaired car, at which time, me and the owner of the car dealership had a 'come to Jesus' meeting about the delay of the repairs. On the way to town, we stopped on the road because Art Turner's big bull was out. And while Cal was out helping Art catch his bull, I found black lace underwear under the car seat, another tube of lipstick, then a pink hairbrush, and yet a different color of lipstick in the glove box. After that, there were signs everywhere. Long story short, I came home that same day with a brand-new red Camaro that cost me eight thousand dollars because I knew the dealer, Bradley Beamer, had to be in on the ruse, and I made him take the nearly new car back for a big trade-in. After that, everything went downhill at home, and I hired a private investigator who got me more than I bargained for."

Charlie listened and nodding, while making notes and hearing the hurt beneath her words.

At that point, Bitsy removed everything in her Amazon Box, placed it on his desk, and then pointed at the various clear plastic storage bags in which she'd gathered her evidence. "The ballpoint pens from all the different motels are in that bag. This bag has that single blue plastic pop-off nail. The black lace underwear I found under the passenger seat of his truck is in that bag. The pink hairbrush and lipstick I found in his glovebox are in that bag. I don't wear pop-off nails. I do not own black underwear. I do not use those colors of lipstick. I have not owned a pink hairbrush since I was twelve. Those are the files from my private investigator. There are three women. I want them sued for Alienation of Affection. I want them outed right along with my sorry-ass husband. There is nothing to contest in this divorce. He committed adultery. I am the victim. I own the house and the land it sits on because I inherited it from my father, and I own my new car. I paid for it with my own money from my dad's estate. Calvin has it job, owns his truck, and his personal belongings. Please tell me he does not have the right to demand part of my inheritance, and how fast can you serve papers on all of them?"

"Give me a couple of minutes to glance through the paperwork from your P.I. so I'll know what we're working with," he said. "Can I get you something to drink? I have cold drinks and coffee."

"Anything cola would be appreciated," Bitsy said.

Charlie buzzed his secretary. "Wanda, would you be so kind as to bring us a couple of Cokes?"

"Right away, sir," she said, and moments later, Wanda came in carrying two cold bottles of Coca-Cola. She handed one to Bitsy, set one on her boss's desk, and slipped out of the room.

Bitsy had the lid off hers before Charlie knew it, and had taken a long, slow drink.

"I needed whiskey, but I have to drive home," she muttered.

Charlie grinned. "Yes, ma'am. Point taken," he said, and began to sift through the photos and the paperwork. A few minutes later, he looked up from the private investigation files. "You hired a good investigator. This is very detailed information backing up any accusations we choose to make. Am I to understand you are not suing for any financial recompense?"

"I want fifteen thousand dollars from Cal for the fifteen wedding anniversaries he ignored. I want the women outed for what they did, but I wouldn't touch a dollar they put in my hand," she snapped.

"And you and your husband have no jointly owned property, is that correct?"

"That is correct," Bitsy said, and took another drink. Now that she'd spoken her mind, she felt lighter, like she had after she'd hired Fisher. He'd uncovered the truth about Calvin and the three women, and now this man was going to destroy them with it.

Charlie was still making notes and confirming details. "So, you've been married fifteen years. Have you ever worked outside of the home?" he asked.

"No, because Calvin had a good job, and since we didn't have the burden of paying rent or a mortgage, he wanted me to stay home. Stupidly, I agreed. I raised chickens, grew a huge garden, and preserved the food from those crops just like my mama did. He liked knowing I was home. I thought that was him being good to me. Instead, it was him making sure it gave him a clear playing field. Even though it probably doesn't sound like it to you, I need you to know my heart is broken, but my mama taught me three things: be good to people; be honest; and never let your enemies see you cry. I will cry when this is over. I don't know what this is going to cost, but it has to be done."

And that's when Charlie knew he was going to war for this woman for free.

"I'm taking your case. And I'm doing it *pro bono*. Your only job is to stand firm and do everything I tell you."

Bitsy gasped. Her chin quivered and her eyes welled, but the tears never rolled.

"Oh, my God," she whispered. "Thank you. I will stand firm, and I will do everything you say."

"Good. We'll get this done as fast as humanly possible. Courts are slow, but since you're not demanding any huge settlement, and he has no recourse to ask anything of you, this will be what is called an uncontested divorce. While it's a little unorthodox, I will be adding the names of the women who committed adultery with him into the divorce papers, and the three women will also be served paperwork informing them of the impending lawsuits against them, with timelines to appear in court on the same day as you and your husband's divorce hearing."

"Can you do that?" she asked.

"Yes, ma'am, I can, and I will. I know people," Charlie said.

Bitsy was still trembling. "Sorry. A piece of me just died. I'm trying to pull together what's left."

"Go home, my dear. Say nothing. I will let you know the day the process server delivers the papers to each guilty party."

"How long?" she asked.

"Within the next seven days. Don't lose faith. The hard part is over. All that's left are repercussions." He handed her his card. "If shit hits the fan, just call me. Restraining orders can be issued ASAP. After that, the threat of going to jail for ignoring them is a good deterrent."

She slipped the card into her purse.

"Are these your only copies?" Charlie asked, referring to the file.

Bitsy nodded.

"Then they are going in my safe. And they will be coming to court with me on your day of deliverance," he said.

"Is this all?" she asked.

"Yes, ma'am. That's all for now."

Bitsy stood.

Charlie was walking her to the door when he thought to ask. "What's your next move?"

"I'm going to the bookstore to buy a copy of the next book for my book club and buy myself a large chocolate malt to drink on the way home."

Charlie smiled. "I salute your fortitude. Before you know it, this will all just be a memory."

"And a lesson in what never to do again," Bitsy added, and left without looking back.

CHAPTER SEVEN

Cal was tired and sore. Sitting most of the day had been uncomfortable, but there were new claims being filed, and they were busy all day. He was actually looking forward to going home and wondering what they would have for their supper when he drove out of Lone Bridge.

He passed JoJo's house with little more than a glance, thinking of how good it was going to feel to get out of these clothes and stretch out. Another couple of miles and he'd be home. But as he topped the rise and saw that the little red car was gone, he frowned. She hadn't sent him a text. Then he remembered she hadn't said she would. Bitsy had just agreed with him that she could.

Now he was in a mood and walking into the house without the smell of good things cooking only added to his snit. Then he read the note and cursed out loud.

"To hell with the chickens," he muttered, and went to change. Stomping in chicken shit in these clothes wasn't happening.

The whole time he was putting up the chickens for the night and gathering eggs, he wondered what she was doing in Jackson. He didn't like not knowing where she was, but he never equated what he'd done to what he expected of her.

When he came back inside and washed up, he opened the refrigerator and realized there were all kinds of good leftovers.

All he had to do was pick what he wanted and zap it in the microwave. So, she hadn't ignored his needs. She'd provided good food. She just wasn't here to eat it with him.

He made a plate and a drink and took them into the living room to eat so he could watch TV. After a few bites, he decided this wasn't so bad after all. He wasn't getting any go-to-hell looks, and the comfort of being home was not lost on him.

He was all the way through his meal and kicked back in his recliner when he saw her red car turn off the highway and come up the drive. He watched from where he reclined to see how many bags she was carrying, but when she got out with only her purse, one small sack, and drink cup, he frowned and sat up.

The door opened.

Bitsy sailed into the room in her little white sundress with the yellow flowers and her flat-heeled sandals slapping the hardwood floors.

"Oh good, you ate. I'm going to get out of these clothes. It's been miserably hot today. I'm sweaty all over."

"You didn't shop for anything. What did you do?" he asked.

She paused and frowned at him. "I beg your pardon. I didn't even leave the house until after 2:00 p.m. I came home with the book I said I needed. I decided I didn't need to pretend I was buying myself an anniversary present, since that day has come and gone, but I did treat myself to a chocolate malt to drink on the way home. Now, get over yourself, because I'm not in the mood to be cross-examined," she finished, and flipped out of the room.

Cal frowned. She was never going to get over the mess of their anniversary, or the car debacle, and he'd waited too long to apologize, so here they were. She'd been insulted, and he'd let it slide.

He got up and carried his dirty dishes into the kitchen, rinsed them, and put them in the dishwasher. Then he stood listening to her banging doors and slamming drawers. Frowning, he went back to the TV and turned up the volume. Two people could play that game.

He just didn't expect her to sit on the sidelines because his stunt fell flat. When he got up to get a cold drink, he found her sitting at the table eating a sandwich and chips with her new book open, totally engrossed in the story.

"What's the name of that book? Another hate story about men?" he asked.

"You're just trying to pick a fight. If that man hadn't been a criminal and a bigamist and a liar, he wouldn't have been hated. The title of this book is Demon Copperhead. The author is Barbara Kingsolver. It's a Pulitzer-prize winning novel about a hard-up kid," she mumbled, and poked another chip in her mouth.

"For your book club," he added.

She sighed, paused, and looked up. "I hear doubt in your question. You know JoJo. She's in my book club. Why don't you verify my truth with our neighbor? And while we're clarifying things, you and Bradley Beamer started this shit when you lied to me. I have never lied to you. But I am also done talking to you tonight. Go away."

"Damn it, Bitsy. I . . ."

She just stared at him, and for the life of him, he had no explanation that wouldn't give away his game. He finally shook his head and shrugged.

"That's what I thought," she said, went back to her book, and shoved another chip in her mouth.

There was no longer a question of where they would sleep.

By nightfall, Bitsy had moved all her toiletries into the spare bathroom, as well as her nightgowns and some changes of clothes, leaving Cal with the king-size bed and the ensuite to himself.

On the one hand, he was still in enough of a healing phase to relish the extra space in the bed. But on the other hand, he hadn't cuddled up to Bitsy in bed since the night before their anniversary. It was like walking with a limp. Both feet and legs were still there, but the crutch she'd been in his life was missing. He was off kilter, without a way to recalibrate.

As for Bitsy, she was just biding time, waiting for Charlie Cowan to tell her the process server was coming to Lone Bridge. In the meantime, tomorrow was her day to work at the church Clothes Closet. There was every likelihood she'd see JoJo again. She'd say prayers tonight before she went to sleep, asking God to help her keep her words sweet. After the process server hit town, the nails would come out, and Bitsy's weren't the kind to come unglued.

And the longer she thought about it, the more certain she became that after everything was over, she wasn't going to want to live here anymore. All these years, and not one person had ever cared enough about her to let her know what was going on. Bradley Beamer had known. And if he'd known, then there were others.

She'd lost faith and trust in the people she'd grown up with. This divorce wasn't just about cleaning out her house. It wasn't even about starting over. It was about finding out who she was as a woman, alone.

———————

When Bitsy went to bed that night behind a locked door, it was the official beginning of the end, leaving Calvin under the misapprehension that he was sleeping alone because of his injuries, and that the locked door was Bitsy sulking.

The next morning, he woke up to the scent of fresh coffee and bacon frying, and he bailed out of bed, showered, shaved, and was dressed for work when he came into the kitchen. He expected to see his wife in one of her work dresses, but she'd obviously dressed to go out.

"Scrambled or fried," she asked, as he stopped at the end of the island.

"Scrambled is fine," he said. "Going somewhere?"

"As always for the past eight years, it's my day to work at the Clothes Closet." Then she looked up at him and gave him the once-over. "Where are you going today?"

"Well . . . to work, of course."

"I meant . . . as an adjustor? I ask, because the only time you wear that jacket, and those shoes is when you're going to be out of the office."

He frowned. "How do you know this stuff?"

She began cracking eggs into a bowl and then beating them with a fork without looking up.

"Because, as your wife, it has always been my job to send you out of the house looking all put-together." At that point, she did look up. "I know just about everything there is to know about you, Calvin Yarbrough, yet it has become blatantly clear that you know nothing about me. Not my charity work at church. Not the book club I've been going to for years. Not the fact that I am usually barefoot in the house until cold weather sets in. You don't seem to care that you've hurt my feelings every year on our anniversary, and continue to do so, because never once in those fifteen years have you brought me flowers or a present on that day. You just sail in expecting *your* favorite cake. And I put up with it. But no more. You are clearly oblivious to everything about me except when I feed you and fuck you, and you've lost privileges there. Be glad I'm still cooking your food. Pour yourself some coffee, your eggs will be done in less than a minute. Clearly, I am invisible in your world, so don't bother with conversation. I don't want to hear your voice."

He was so shocked he didn't know how to respond, but truth hurt. He just poured his coffee and sat down, watching the stiffness in her shoulders as she scrambled the eggs then divided them on two plates. As always two-thirds for him, and the leftovers for her. She added bacon and carried the plates to the table, went back to get her coffee and the little plate of toast for the table, then sat down and began buttering her toast, and peppering her eggs.

She was just about to take her first bite when her cell phone rang. She glanced at it and then answered, while all Cal got was her side of the conversation.

"Good morning, Pastor Samuels. Yes, I'm coming as soon as I finish breakfast. Yes, I will do that," she said. "See you soon."

"What . . ."

She glanced up. "He wants me to pick up some soap. Laundry soap, and what part of 'no conversation' do you not understand?"

He glared back, cleaned his plate in gulps, and stomped out of the house.

"Good riddance," she muttered, and spread peach preserves on her toast to finish eating.

Calvin was mad, and he was about to call a damn halt to her attitude, whether she liked it or not. *She isn't the boss of our house. It even says in the bible that the husband is the head of the wife. He's the leader. She's meant to follow.* But he still chose to ignore quite a few other verses and commandments, like the one about not committing adultery. By the time he got to town and walked into the office, he was full of indignation.

"Good morning, Cal. Glad you're here. There was a three-car pile-up north of town on Highway 49. Two of the three vehicles are insured by our agency. I've already gotten the phone calls from the drivers. I don't think anyone was seriously injured, but that will likely evolve, too. I'll need you to get out there and take photos ASAP. Hopefully, before the police arrive and start moving vehicles. I don't know who's at fault, but everybody's going to be filing lawsuits. We'll get accident reports later."

"Right," Cal said, and went to get the camera out of the storeroom, checked the battery, then grabbed a second battery just in case, got his briefcase and notebook, and took off out the back door.

It didn't dawn on him until he was driving out of town that he was wearing the kind of clothes he normally chose when going out on a job—like he'd known this was going to happen, but then he shrugged it off. There was no such thing as precognition. Unfortunately, for Cal, it would have been a handy skill to have, because then he might have foreseen the coming chaos.

———

As soon as Bitsy got to Lone Bridge, she went straight to their little Neighborhood Walmart and picked up six large jugs of laundry detergent to take to the church, per Pastor Samuel's request. The laundry area at the Clothes Closet had just received a donation of clothing, and they were out of detergent to wash them, which had to happen before they got worked into the donation side of the store. So as soon as she'd checked out and loaded everything up in her car, she headed to the church and met a couple of other women arriving as she pulled in.

She popped the trunk of her car and then called out to them. "Hey, y'all! Will you help me here?"

JoJo and Retha from the book club had come to work together and quickly came to help. They each got two, Bitsy got the other two and followed them into the church back to the Clothes Closet.

Pastor Samuels met them at the door to the laundry area. "Thank you, ladies! And Bitsy, thank you for running the errand. Go see Fern about being reimbursed."

"Just consider it an extra tithe," Bitsy said, and stored her purse.

"JoJo and I will sort," Retha offered. Neither of us can sew worth a flip, so we'll leave that to Bitsy."

JoJo sighed. "Okay, but I hate sorting through fleas and head lice."

The pastor frowned at her. "It's nothing a little cleanliness won't cure. We aren't all blessed the same."

JoJo flushed. She'd just been chastised, although quite nicely by the pastor, and she followed Retha to the pile of clothes that had been dumped in a corner.

"There are quite a few rips, tears, and missing buttons at the sewing area," the pastor added.

"Right up my alley," Bitsy said, and left them to it.

Once she got to the sewing room, she thought of Fisher. Had it only been last week when he'd walked in to find a jacket? It seemed like a lifetime ago but revisiting old wounds did not hasten their healing, so she dismissed the mood and got to work.

There was satisfaction in repairing something to be used again, and as she did, Bitsy thought of who might wear each item next, and what needs or disasters had driven them to seek clothes to wear. Such a simple need, but without money to buy them, not an easy one to fill.

As she worked, she thought of what kind of a job she might get when she was divorced and tried to remember what she'd wanted to do, what she'd wanted to be besides Calvin Yarbrough's wife, when she'd graduated high school.

Her one year of college had been almost over when her parents were killed. She'd come home to an empty house with a broken heart, and Calvin Yarbrough had been on her doorstep with sympathy and open arms. She'd taken it, and him, and had given up everything else.

Looking back, part of her wondered if he'd ever really loved her, or if she'd just been a good catch. She'd come with a beautiful home and a hundred acres of Mississippi fields and woods, and they were good together in bed. Bitsy had been so grief-stricken that his attention had helped her get past being a nineteen-year-old orphan.

She was so deep in thought that she wasn't paying attention to what she was doing and accidentally pricked her finger as she was sewing on a button.

She gasped and flinched, and then got up to douse it in alcohol and get a Band-Aid. There were tears in her eyes when she walked past the laundry room where Retha and JoJo still worked.

Retha saw the tears and stopped her. "Bitsy honey! What's wrong?"

Bitsy held up her bloody finger. "War wound," she said. "Going to get a Band-Aid so I don't bleed all over everything else. It's not a big deal. Comes with the job."

"Do you need any help?" JoJo asked.

Bitsy paused, then flashed her a sweet smile. "No, but that's so sweet of you to care."

JoJo started to smile when she caught the flash of fire in Bitsy's eyes and didn't know how to read that. A little shiver ran up her spine, which she quickly shrugged off.

A couple of minutes later, Bitsy came back by, flashed her bandaged finger at them, and kept walking. Retha didn't see it, but JoJo did. She gave her a thumbs up as she was putting a new load of clothes into the washer. But it wasn't until she'd poured in the soap and turned it on that she realized which finger had been bandaged, and now she wasn't sure if Bitsy had been just showing her the bandage or flipping her off.

———————

Cal was just finishing up at the wreck-site when tow trucks began arriving. The highway patrol had traffic blocked off both ways, and Cal had a few words with one of the officers, thanking him for his assistance in getting the needed photos. Then he was headed back down the road to retrieve his truck, patting himself on the back for having the foresight on his arrival to turn around and park on the shoulder of the southbound lane, so he wouldn't get blocked in by the traffic being stopped.

Before he got back in his truck, he took care to clean the broken glass from the soles of his shoes. As soon as he was seated, he called the office.

To his surprise, Tansy answered. "Sullivan Insurance, this is Tansy."

"Um, Tansy, this is Cal. Would you let Paul know I have the pictures from the wreck, and I'm headed back to the office?"

"Yes, of course. He's with a client. I'll let him know," she said, and then whispered in his ear. "Miss you, wild man," and disconnected.

He liked being called that. It was all part of their game. And since Bitsy had put him out to pasture at home, he was going to have to count on the girls to step up.

He was still smiling when he started the truck and headed back to town, unaware that Fisher Means was tracking him everywhere he went.

Bitsy spent four long hours at the Clothes Closet, either at the sewing machine or in her mending chair, wishing that it rocked and thinking about her career choices.

There was one thing she could immediately cross off, and that was raising chickens ever again. That had been her mama's joy, and she'd just carried it on out of love. But since her world had crashed down around her, she saw no reason to grow old and die in the same place she'd been born. Things happen. Dreams come to abrupt ends. Such is life.

She was still in her little out-of-the-way corner when she caught movement from the corner of her eye. She glanced up and saw Fisher. It was the first time she'd seen him with his hair down, and once again, was startled that she'd never noticed the sharp, but handsome angles of his face. She smiled and waved him over.

"Looking for another jacket?" she asked.

"No, ma'am. Just checking on a friend."

"I have a lawyer. The wheels are turning. Process server is supposed to be here within a couple of days."

His voice lowered to just above a whisper. "Are you afraid?"

She shrugged. "Of the unknown? Maybe a little."

"Let me know when he's been served, and you have put him out of the house. I left the tracker on his truck. If he bothers you at home, I will know it."

"Oh Fish . . . you don't have to do this," she whispered back.

"Yes, I do," he said, and walked away.

Bitsy blinked back tears as she sewed up a ripped seam on the underarm of a shirt, then tossed it in the finished pile, and got up. It was well after the noon hour, and her shift was over as she carried the clean, repaired clothing to another table where the garments would be sorted and either hung on hangers or folded up on tables according to size. She didn't let anyone know she was leaving. She just walked out.

The sky had clouded up. It looked like rain. She needed to get home and put up the chickens, so she drove out of town in haste, arriving just ahead of the storm.

She grabbed her purse and ran, let herself in, and locked the door behind her, then she slung her purse on the kitchen island as she headed out the back door, still running.

The hens had already taken shelter inside the coop, but she counted heads anyway, just to make sure they were all in, then she closed the gate and ran back to the house.

She heard the crack of lightning somewhere nearby, then the roll of thunder overhead as she went in the back door, but she'd made it just in time. She kicked off her sneakers in the laundry room to clean the soles later and went barefoot through the rooms to change into one of her housedresses. Then she washed up and headed to the kitchen to make herself some lunch.

The first drops of rain were already falling as she diced a tomato, a small cucumber, and a little bit of raw onion. She put it all in a bowl with salt and pepper and a splash of Italian dressing, and set it aside to marinate. After that, she got leftover fried chicken out of the refrigerator, put two of her favorite pieces on her plate along with the salad she'd just made, poured herself a glass of iced tea, and sat down at the kitchen table to eat.

Between the rain and the food and Fisher Mean's promise, her nerves settled, and so did her determination.

Fisher was traveling new ground.

Bitsy Yarbrough had shown him a whole new side to the word, "Woman," and he was in awe, both of her strength of character, and the cold precision with which she was facing the fall of life as she'd known it.

He had no place in her life, but he wished he did, and was aghast at what Cal had thrown away. The only thing Fisher *could* do for her was make sure she stayed safe through it and be grateful knowing she trusted him enough to do it.

He'd long ago accepted that some things were meant to be, and others were just pretty wishes without foundation. He'd been a damn good soldier, and he was good at what he did now. His skill set wasn't for everyone, but it served a purpose for those in need—like a police officer, but without the same rules. He answered to no one. He was his own boss. And he could pick and choose the cases he wanted to work.

And he chose Bitsy's.

CHAPTER EIGHT

Cal left work late. The rain had passed by mid-afternoon, but they were still dealing with the wreck victims and getting copies of both medical and police reports, and they already were aware that lawsuits that would be pending.

He was tired as he began the drive home, and he wished life was back the way it had been before he'd pulled that stunt with Bitsy's car. Even as he approached the house, his stomach began to knot, wondering what mood she would be in. But then he walked into the scents of supper cooking, and if he wasn't mistaken, they were having meatloaf.

"I'm home," he called out.

"So am I," she answered.

He walked into the kitchen and sighed. She was barefoot, and in her house dress. Maybe if he kept his damn mouth shut about her business, their world would get back on track sooner.

"Something smells good," he said.

"Meatloaf, baked potatoes, squash casserole, and left-over bread pudding," she said, and checked the timer to see how many minutes were left on her baked potatoes.

"Sounds wonderful. I'm going to change clothes," he said, and when she didn't have anything else to add, he left the room.

"Lord, give me strength," Bitsy muttered, and took a sip of her iced tea.

A few minutes later the timer went off and she took the meatloaf and the baked potatoes out at the same time, removed the casserole from the warming oven, and put everything on the table, then she went down the hall to tell Cal the meal was on the table.

The bedroom door was wide open, and he was sitting on the edge of the bed, facing the mirrored dresser with his back to the door and talking on the phone in a gruff whisper.

"I know, I know. I miss you, too, but I need to heal up a little more. I feel the same way. Yeah, can't happen too soon for me. Gotta go. Talk to you later."

He disconnected and looked up, saw himself in the mirror and then the woman standing in the doorway behind him, and came off that bed like he'd been ejected.

"Uh . . . Bitsy, I . . ."

"I came to tell you supper is ready," she said, and then turned around and walked away.

And just like that, his appetite was gone. He followed her, shoulders slumped, feet dragging, expecting the third degree. But it didn't happen. The meal passed as they'd been passing for the last week. Eating to assuage their hunger, and in the coldest, quietest, imaginable silence on earth. She wouldn't even look at him. And then he remembered he'd been going to set her straight about who was the boss around here and cleared his throat.

"Bitsy, I'm damn tired of this cold shoulder business. You seem to forget who's putting the food on this table and paying the bills. You are not the head of this house, and I'm not going to—"

She slapped her hands on the table so hard the ice rattled in his glass, then she rose from her seat like the Kraken coming out of the sea, and in that moment, Calvin realized that Bitsy was the hidden trap in his sex game that he'd never seen coming.

"You don't talk to me like that! You are head of nothing. This house, and all the one hundred acres with it, is mine, not yours. The food you buy and the utilities you pay are what it costs you to live here rent free. I cook for you because I choose to, not because I owe it to you. The last time you set foot in church was on the day we got married, so don't throw bible verses at me. All these years, I thought I was the luckiest woman alive until you began showing me who you really are, and I don't like it, and I don't much like you, either. I don't know you anymore. Maybe I never did."

Then she started taking food off the table.

"I'm not done eating!" he shouted.

"Actually, yes you are. You *are* done. In fact . . . you are *so very* done!" she said, and turned her back on him, picked up a spoon and started scooping the squash casserole into a refrigerator container.

"Look . . . I don't know what you think you heard, but it wasn't—"

Bitsy threw her spoon across the room, splattering squash and cream sauce all over the wall, and then let out a scream that was somewhere between utter despair and pure rage.

Cal froze on the spot, too shocked to speak or move until she stopped as suddenly as she'd begun. She straightened up, then turned around, and the look on her face sent him running. He grabbed his car keys and his wallet and shot out the front door without looking back. He spun out of the driveway when he left.

Although there'd been no weapon in her hand, he felt like he'd been shot at and missed. He didn't know where he was going, but it wasn't back home. Not tonight. And then he thought of the Royal Motel and accelerated. He'd never been there on his own, but there was always a first time for everything.

He'd go back tomorrow in the bright light of day to get some clothes. Maybe a temporary separation would be the way to heal the rift between them.

———————————

For Bitsy, the moment Cal ran, it broke the last of their bond. She heard him leave, but she didn't bother to look. She just locked the door behind him, cleaned up the kitchen, and threw the last of the bread pudding out into the yard by the chicken house.

First cake. Now bread pudding. She didn't know if sugar was bad for chickens, but it hadn't hurt them yet, and it was the last dessert she'd ever cook for that man. But instead of going back in the house, she sat down on the porch swing, gazing out across the heavily wooded land behind the house and remembered the little creeks she'd played in, and the fishing hole where her daddy taught her how to catch crawdads.

She sat until the sky darkened and the stars came out. The ache in her heart wasn't going away anytime soon, and when she was gone from this place, memories would be all she had left. But for the time she was here, she was reclaiming her space.

She went back inside and began carrying everything that belonged to Calvin to the spare room. She dumped his clothes on the bed and his toiletries in the smaller ensuite. Everything in the dresser that was his went onto the floor beside the shoes.

Back and forth, back and forth, until everything related to him was gone, and then she moved her things back into the primary bedroom and stripped the sheets off the bed. He'd slept with other women and then come to this bed for the last time, and if the sheets hadn't been Egyptian cotton, she would have burned them. So, she settled for extra detergent in the washer and started it up.

When she went back up the hall to the linen closet to get a fresh set of sheets and pillowcases, she remembered that this had been her first hiding place of the clues she had gathered. When she'd finished making the bed, she locked her bedroom door and started filling up the Jacuzzi, tossing in a liberal amount of lavender scented bath salts. Lavender was supposed to be a calming scent, and she needed to not feel like murder was still an option.

———————

Fisher was kicked back on his sofa in the middle of watching Hacksaw Ridge for the umpteenth time, when his laptop signaled movement from the tracker on Cal's truck. He frowned, glanced at the clock, and then went to get his boots on. He grabbed his laptop and headed for his car, then sat watching the blip heading toward Lone Bridge and wondered which woman would get lucky tonight.

When Cal went through town without stopping anywhere, Fisher took to the highway and made sure to stay back within the traffic so he wouldn't get made. When he realized Cal had just taken a turn into the driveway of the Royal Motel, he sped up, curious to see who Cal was meeting with, but to his surprise, Cal stopped out front and went into the office.

When he did, Fisher immediately went to the back lot and parked to wait and see how this played out.

A few minutes later, Cal drove into the parking lot, parked in front of the third door down instead of his usual at the far end of the building. He got out alone, walking like he was going to his own hanging, and went inside.

Fisher frowned. He knew what the three women drove, and none of their cars were here. In fact, from the looks of the parking area, it appeared to be a slow night all around.

And then he had a thought. What if Cal had been kicked out of the house already? Whatever was going on, Bitsy might be the reason he was looking for someplace else to sleep. He sat there for almost two hours until all the lights went out in the room, then he started up his car and drove home.

Cal couldn't sleep. After Bitsy's last meltdown, he couldn't shake the feeling of impending doom and wasn't sure how much she'd heard of his phone conversation with Tansy. If it hadn't been so late, he would have gone to the bar, but it was 4:00 a.m. and nothing was open in Lone Bridge at this time of the morning except the police station and the hospital.

He glanced at the clock again, reminding himself that he could go home. She was his wife, and he had just as much right to be there as she did, or at least he'd always felt that way until she'd thrown the ownership of the property in his face.

To be honest, he'd never given that a thought. Not even once. Even when he'd been cheating on her, he had never worried he'd be found out. His main concerns had been making sure the three women didn't know about each other.

And then, to add insult to his situation, he heard a woman laugh in the room next to his, then a man's gravelly voice, and a few seconds later, the beginnings of a steady thump, thump, thump against the wall behind Calvin's bed. He sat up on the side of the bed and scrubbed his face with his hands, wondering if this is how his rendezvous sounded and rolled his eyes in disgust.

Seconds later, the woman began moaning and groaning, and yelling "Harder, baby, harder," and Cal was on his feet. He couldn't take it anymore and stomped into his shoes, pocketed his wallet, threw the room key on the bed, and bolted out the door. Seconds later, he was in his truck and driving out of the parking lot as fast as he could go.

———

Bitsy's sleep was fitful. She kept waking at every little sound, fearful of his return and desperately hoping he wouldn't. She'd finally drifted off to sleep sometime after midnight, then woke again just before 4:00 a.m. and laid in her bed, motionless, but listening. Self-preservation had fine-tuned her senses to the slightest of sounds, and even though she was in a room on the backside of the home, she heard the rumble of his truck as it turned off the highway and moved toward the house.

The crunch of gravel beneath the wheels set her heart to pounding, and she flew out of bed and ran to the door to doublecheck that it was locked, then she got his old baseball bat out of the closet. She stood in the middle of the room with the bat, heart pounding in the shadows, in case he was mad enough, or drunk enough, to try and kick down the door.

She heard him come inside, but he wasn't stomping. He was slinking, and when his footsteps paused in the hall outside the door, she held her breath, but nothing happened. Then she heard him go into the spare room across the hall and close the door. *Thank you, Lord.*

After she heard the shower come on in the other bathroom, she put the ball bat back in the kitchen and got dressed, then sat down in the easy chair by the window. Whatever happened next, she didn't intend to be vulnerable or naked.

A short while later, she heard the water go off, then a few mumbled curses and guessed he was trying to sort out clean clothes from what she'd piled on the bed and dumped on the floor.

After bumping and thumping, she heard his footsteps in the hall again, moving toward the front of the house, and later, when she smelled coffee brewing, she decided to make an appearance. But instead of going into the kitchen, she went through it and out the back door without acknowledging his existence.

Cal heard her moving about and stilled, waiting to see what she was bringing to the war this morning, then she walked right past him, as if he wasn't there. He didn't know whether to be sad or relieved and decided to pour his coffee to go, and eat breakfast in town. He left the house while Bitsy was still messing with the chickens.

She heard him leave and didn't care.

Two whole days had passed, with Cal and Bitsy playing dodgeball. The less they saw of each other, the better his day went.

It was mid-morning when Bitsy's phone dinged a text. Her heart skipped when she saw it was from her lawyer, Charlie Cowan.

Batten down your hatches. Process server is on the way. I will notify you when all the papers have been served.

She sent him a thumbs up emoji then went to get suitcases and garbage bags and began packing everything Calvin owned and dragging it all to her car, then she headed into town. The closer she got, the faster she drove, readying herself to deliver a message of her own.

It was the fastest trip she'd ever made, and she had but one destination—the parking lot behind Sullivan Insurance. It was fenced in behind it and bordered with tall trees. She'd be in and out before anyone ever saw her.

Cal's truck was parked nearest the back exit. She pulled up behind it, dumped every suitcase and every garbage bag filled with his things into the truck bed, and drove off, feeling a thousand pounds lighter than when she'd arrived.

She would never spend another night under the same roof with him. Never cook him another meal. Never wash any more of his clothing. She was going to have to make peace with what had happened, but it would take time.

She stopped at a drive-thru to get a cold drink, hoping it settled the panic she felt. Part of it was being uneasy about what might happen next, and part of it was just shock that it had come to this. As she drove home, she made a call to Earl Justice, the family lawyer.

"Morning Bitsy," Earl said. "How goes your day?"

"Bordering on chaos, as usual," she said. "I have a question. Cal and I never made a will. What might happen to my property if I died before we were divorced?"

"It would go to him, because there is no other proviso mentioned in your father's will."

"Okay . . . but just FYI . . . I've been told that the process server is going to deliver divorce papers and lawsuit papers to all parties involved in Cal's adultery today. So, if anything happens to me, it's likely murder."

"Oh hell, Bitsy. That's not okay. Do you really have that fear?"

Her voice was shaking. "It's in the back of my mind."

"Then I think the more people who know about this as soon as possible, the safer you'll be. I'll draw up a public notice for you to put in the local papers, stating that you are responsible for your debts only, and no one else's, which is an immediate flag, letting people know there has been a separation or a divorce. And then get all the utilities transferred into your name alone. Start separating him from you."

"The utilities have always been in my name. He just paid them. I'm going to sell the home when this is over. I can't live there anymore. I don't know who's left in town that I could trust," she said.

Earl sighed. "I'm sorry, honey, but that might turn out to be the best thing you ever do for yourself. I'll email you the public notice today. You can get it in the local paper ASAP."

"Thank you, Earl. For everything."

"That's what I'm here for," he said. "Chin up, lady. Chin up."

Randy Arthur had been a process server for almost fifteen years. He'd been chased by dogs. Shot at. Punched in the face and cursed roundly. Over the years, he'd learned a few tricks to getting it done without bodily harm, and today, he was traveling to Lone Bridge with paperwork to be served, and three small bouquets of on-sale flowers in the seat beside him. At this point, all he was hoping for was that the petals stayed on the stems long enough for him to make an exit. As for the man he was serving, this was going to be an easy one. He'd catch him at work.

He had orders to serve the man first, then the two women who lived in the city limits of Lone Bridge, and then the last one, who lived three miles outside of town.

Randy had the address to the Sullivan Insurance office at the far end of Main Street and was fortunate enough to get a parking spot directly in front of the building. Without hesitation, he picked up the envelope with Calvin Lee Yarbrough's name on it and got out.

Brenda, the secretary at the front door, looked up.

"Good morning, sir. How can I help you?"

Randy smiled. "I need to speak to Calvin Yarbrough, please."

Brenda turned in her chair. "Cal, someone to see you."

Cal had just taken a bite of a doughnut when he heard his name, looked up, and waved him back to his desk.

Randy reached the desk, still smiling. "Calvin Lee Yarbrough?"

"Yes," Cal said, nodding and still trying to swallow his bite.

"This is for you, sir," he said, and held out the envelope. The moment Cal reached for it; Randy laid it in his palm. "You have been served," he said loudly, then made a U-turn at the desk and walked out, leaving Cal in momentary shock.

Forgetting the bite he still needed to chew and swallow, he ripped open the envelope, saw the words "Petition for Divorce," and then saw the word "ADULTERY" in bold font, and the names of three women, and "ALIENATION OF AFFECTION." He gasped, sucked the chunk of doughnut down his throat like a sock going through a vacuum hose, and then it went no further.

The divorce papers went flying as Cal grabbed at his chest, choking and gagging. His face went from ashen to flushed, and he was slowly turning blue when Paul leaped to his feet and ran toward him.

Brenda grabbed the fallen papers as Paul began the Heimlich maneuver, applying it over and over, until finally dislodging the clog.

"Cal, buddy, are you okay?" Paul asked, as he helped him back to his chair.

Cal nodded, breathing deeply as the panic began to subside, and then he took the bottle of water Paul gave him to drink.

Unfortunately for Cal, Brenda had taken it upon herself to read the papers she'd picked up and was already incensed on Paul's behalf. She walked up behind her boss, tapped him on the shoulder, and handed him the papers.

Paul frowned, glanced down at what she'd handed him, realized what it was, and then read the rest of it in disbelief. It wasn't until he saw his wife named as one of the cheating women that he spun the chair Cal was sitting in to face him, drew back, and punched him in the jaw.

Cal never saw it coming. One minute he was sitting upright, and when he came to again, he was still in the chair, but on his back, looking up at the ceiling, and Paul was pouring water in his face.

"You are a sorry, son-of-a-bitch, and you are fired," Paul said. "Get your shit out of the desk and get your truck off my property."

Cal groaned, rolled out of the chair, spit the blood in his mouth into the wastebasket, and looked up. Brenda stood at his desk glaring at him. She held a box with his things in it, the divorce papers on top. He didn't say anything because there was nothing he could say. It's not like he'd just wrecked Paul's car and could pay to have it fixed. He'd wrecked his boss's marriage, and Bitsy had ended theirs.

His head pounded. His throat was raw. It hurt to draw breath, but he made it to his truck. Then he saw the suitcases and bags in the back and realized he not only had no job, but he also had nowhere to go.

What a mess. What a gawd-awful mess. And all the while, he wondered how Bitsy had ever found out. He needed a lawyer, but not until he took himself to the emergency room—again.

Cal's steps were slow and unsteady as he walked into the ER. He couldn't stand up straight for the pain in his ribs, his lower lip was puffy and bloody, and his jaw was already swelling.

"I need a doctor. Now. I can't breathe right," he mumbled.

Within moments, a nurse emerged with a wheelchair, rolled him into the examining area, and got him settled on a bed. They were taking his blood pressure and pulse when a doctor rushed in and started asking questions about chest and arm pain.

"Not heart attack," Cal mumbled. "I nearly choked to death, and my boss did the Heimlich thing. Now it hurts to breathe."

"Ah . . . you might have a cracked rib. It can happen. I'll get you into x-ray. In the meantime, what happened to your face?" the doctor asked.

Cal started to answer, then danced around the truth. "I think it happened after I fell . . . maybe . . . I'm not sure."

The doctor began examining Cal's jaw, with Cal wincing and groaning at every touch. "We'll get some shots of your jaw, as well, just to make sure you didn't crack a bone. Hang tough, Calvin. Someone will come get you and take you to x-ray, and then we'll talk."

By the time Cal was released two hours later, news of his personal life had become a gossip epidemic. His diagnosis was a bruised rib, a bruised jaw, and a shredded reputation.

"I recommend over the counter pain meds and ice packs," the doctor said. "You need rest to heal."

"Yes, sir," Cal said, and sat up on the side of the bed as an orderly came in with a wheelchair and gave him a ride to the exit.

Cal got in his truck and drove out of the parking lot, then out of Lone Bridge and never looked back. He didn't notice he'd already passed JoJo's house. He was watching for the sight of their home, and when he passed the driveway, he took a good, long look, knowing it would also be his last.

Tansy Sullivan sat on her front porch with a glass of iced tea, wearing one of her favorite floral day dresses, admiring the perfectly manicured lawn and the butterflies flitting about the blooming bushes, when a car pulled into their drive and drove up to the house.

A clean-cut, thirty-something man got out carrying a bouquet of flowers and came up her steps, smiling.

"Flowers for Tansy Sullivan," he said.

"That's me! I'm Tansy Sullivan," she said, and stood as he came toward her.

As she held out her hand to accept the flowers, he placed an envelope in one hand and the flowers in the other.

"Tansy Sullivan, you have been served," he said, and turned and jogged down the steps, then drove away, leaving Tansy in shock.

She was still standing, watching the petals of a white daisy falling onto the porch as the reality of what had happened began to sink in. She laid the flowers on a side table and sat back down to open the envelope. She saw the words, and then the world began to spin. *This can't be happening. How? Who? What the hell am I going to do?*

And then she heard the roar of another car engine and saw her husband skid to a halt and get out running.

She leaped to her feet, clutching the court summons against her breasts, and began backing up as he came up the steps. She could tell by the look on his face that he knew.

"What's that in your hand?" he shouted.

"Um, I just—"

He snatched the papers away, read, and then rolled his eyes. "Perfect! Just perfect! Not only will everyone know what a slut you are, but you're dragging my name through court for this bullshit lawsuit. Alienation of Affection! My God. Oh, my God!" he shouted.

"I don't even know what that means," she whined.

"Then you're not only a slut, but you're also a stupid slut. It means you've been named in a divorce based on adultery."

"Paul, I'm so sorry! It was just a fling, and—"

"Get out!" he said.

"No! Wait! What do you mean, get out? This is my house, too."

"Not for long," he said. "Pack your shit and get. I've already fired your lover boy. You go cry in your beer with the two other women also named. What a disaster. An adultery scandal. I can't stay in this town and have any level of decorum about myself or my business."

Tansy froze. "What other women?"

He paused and then threw back his head and laughed. "You thought you were special? You really thought it was just you? That's rich!"

"Shut up! Shut up! Stop laughing at me!" she screamed. "What other women?"

"Sue Ritter and JoJo Walker are also named. I wonder if they believed they were exclusive, too? The joke is on all of you, and it's no more than you deserve. Now pack your clothes and get out. Go ask your daddy for a lawyer, then tell him why you're going to need one. And your chances of getting any kind of alimony from me are slim to none," Paul said, then opened the front door and stood, waiting for her to go inside.

Tansy's oh-so-perfect world had just come down around her ears, while Randy Arthur had moved on to the Lone Bridge library and was entering the building. He walked up to the man at the front desk, carrying yet another bouquet of flowers.

"Delivery for Sue Ritter," he said.

"Wait here," the man said quietly, then got up and disappeared between the stacks. A few moments later, he returned, followed by a tall blonde in her mid-thirties.

"I'm Sue Ritter. How can I help you?" she said.

"These are for you," he said, smiling.

"How nice!" she said, and held out her hands. As she did, he laid the summons in one hand and the flowers in the other.

"Sue Ritter, you have been served," he said, and walked out.

Sue gasped, gave the clerk a wild look, and then dashed into her office. A few moments later, a scream came out of the office, and then the sound of crashing furniture.

Workers ran toward her office, found an overturned chair, and Sue passed out on the floor with the papers still clutched in her hand.

"Call an ambulance!" one of the workers cried, while the man from the desk took the papers and read them.

"She doesn't need a doctor. She needs a lawyer," he said.

Randy was three deliveries down and one to go, as he headed home. He had JoJo Walker's address in his GPS, and as he came upon the house, realized he had passed it on his way into town. He took the turn up into the driveway, then got out with the last envelope and the last wilting bouquet, ran up the steps, and knocked on the door.

Moments later, the door opened. He smiled. "Delivery for JoJo Walker?"

"I'm JoJo Walker," she said, and held out her hands.

Like before, he put the envelope in one of her outstretched hands and the flowers in the other.

"JoJo Walker, you have been served," he said, and then went back down the steps and drove away before JoJo could blink. She stared down at the wilted flowers and the envelope, then backed up and closed the door. She knew it wasn't good news. Summonses never were. She tossed the flowers in the trash and sat down on the sofa to open the envelope. The moment she took out the summons and saw the words on the paper, her face went numb.

"Oh my God," she muttered. What a mess this was going to be. And then it dawned on her that this might be her lucky day.

If Cal was getting divorced, then that would mean he would finally be free. They could be together without having to sneak around. She didn't mind the gossip if she got Cal for the consolation prize. She was about to congratulate herself when her cell phone rang. She glanced at Caller ID and frowned, then answered.

"Hello?"

"JoJo, it's me, Tansy Sullivan. Have you heard yet?"

"Heard what?" she asked.

"That Cal and Bitsy are getting divorced. She filed adultery charges as her grounds and named all of us."

JoJo's stomach rolled. "What do you mean . . . all of us?"

"You, me, and Sue Ritter. He was seeing all three of us behind Bitsy's back, and she found out. We're all being sued for Alienation of Affection and named as part of the adultery he's accused of. We're her proof that he was cheating, and she's dragging us into court at the divorce proceedings."

"I don't believe it," JoJo said.

"What? That she's naming us, or that we were all so stupid we didn't see his game?" Tansy said.

"I have to go now," JoJo said, then hung up and ran.

The last time JoJo had been sick enough to puke had been one New Year's Eve when she was still married to her second husband. That time, she'd over-indulged in champagne. This time, it had been because of an overabundance of sex with someone else's man.

She needed a lawyer.

———————————

At Paul Sullivan's orders, Brenda closed the agency early.

Paul was gone, and she was on her way out the back door, talking on the phone to her mother as she went.

"Momma, you will not believe what just happened!" And then she unloaded, spreading the news even further.

Sue Ritter regained consciousness to the news that she was being fired, and to add insult to injury, that she wasn't the only woman Cal had been seeing behind his wife's back. She hadn't felt this stupid since she'd given an old man a lap dance and a heart attack when she'd still been working in Vegas and had had to go home in disgrace. She was already on the phone with a lawyer, trying to find out if the city of Lone Bridge had to pay off the remainder of her contract to fire her, or if she was going to go over the falls of shit's creek, homeless and broke.

It was almost noon when Bitsy got Charlie Cowan's text.

They've all been served. Change the locks on your door.

She had already been warned to do this, so she pulled up the locksmith's number in her contact list and made the call. Three rings later, a man answered.

"Elmer's Lock Shop."

"My name is Bitsy Yarbrough. I need to change the locks on my house. It's kind of an emergency. Front door and back, and as soon as possible."

"I have time this afternoon if that's good for you. All I need is directions to your house," Elmer said.

Bitsy gave him the address.

He read it back to her, and she confirmed. "Yes, that's right, and thank you." Now all she had to do was wait.

About an hour later, her phone rang again. Her heart thumped when she saw the caller's name pop up on the screen.

She'd been expecting it, but she put the call on Speaker, for the simple fact she didn't want the sound of his voice so close to her ear, and then answered.

"What!?"

Calvin winced. "Bitsy, I . . . I just . . ."

"The day of our anniversary, I was doing laundry and found lipstick on the collar of your work shirt. Even as I was using up the last of my stain remover to get it out, I knew it wasn't any color I'd ever used. When I went to write down 'stain remover' on my grocery list, I noticed the pen you'd left on the notepad was from Rogers' Motel, and I told myself it was a gimme pen. You could have gotten it anywhere. But when I went back to sort more laundry, I found a blue pop-off nail caught on the elastic waistband of your underwear, and that was impossible to ignore, so I went looking for more evidence and found a half-dozen ballpoint pens from other motels. I saved them all with the fake blue nail."

Cal groaned. "So that's—"

"Shut up, Calvin, I'm still talking. After that revelation, my yet-to-be-repaired-car began to make sense. When we were on the way to town to shop for my new car, and you stopped to help Art put up his bull, I was picking up the receipts that had fallen from behind the visor. That's when I saw a pair of black lace panties and yet a different color of lipstick under the seat where I was sitting. And then a pink hairbrush and another tube of lipstick in the glove box. *None of which were mine!!!* I put them in my purse for safekeeping. More evidence to hang you. The giant hickey on the back of your neck the next morning after you came home from the bar was the last straw. That was when I hired a private detective. There are lots of them in Jackson, and he's been following you around ever since. I have pictures of you with all three women, going in and coming out of motels, and passionate kisses in the back parking lot of the library, and in the front yard of their homes, and on their porches, and you are dead meat as far as guilt goes. Do you understand me?"

"Yes," Cal said. He hurt in a thousand places, but the worst one right now was his heart.

"You completely disgust me. I thought about killing you, as in completely ending your life just like you had just ended mine, but I opted to divorce you instead. I have two lawyers. One for my personal self, and a divorce attorney with a shark-bite reputation for destroying cheating spouses and abused spouses. You have no grounds to fight this. Try it, and I will bankrupt you. Are you still listening?"

Now his voice was down to a whisper. "Yes."

"I don't want alimony, because after our divorce is final, I don't want contact with you in any way, ever again. But you will give me fifteen thousand dollars in cash on the day we sign the divorce decree. That's one thousand dollars for every year we were married, and for the birthday gift, and the Christmas gift, and the anniversary gift that you always ignored, and for all the flowers you never gave me. There is no bargaining over this, and whatever your lawyer tells you, mine will destroy you and him. Understand?"

Bitsy could hear him crying, and she didn't care.

"Bawl your head off, buddy, and know that I have yet to shed a tear. You are lucky you're still breathing. When Southern women get mad, they get even and cry later. This is all on you. Don't call me again. I've changed the locks on the house. You set foot on this property, and I will shoot you. The next time and last time I see your face, it will be in court."

At that point, she ended the call, and as she looked up, she saw a white van, with an Elmer's Lock Shop logo, coming toward the house.

One more thing to do before this day was over.

Cal was still crying and waiting for another blast of recrimina-tions when he realized she'd hung up on him. He had a cracked rib from the choking incident, a bruise on his jaw the size of an orange from being punched in the face, and he was still not completely healed from the barbed wire.

He was homeless, jobless, and laying low in a motel in Jackson. He had enough money in the bank to tide him over, and the savings for his retirement, which was about to be fif-teen thousand dollars less than it was right now, and as soon as he healed and this divorce thing was over, he was heading to Colorado where his family lived now. He'd look for work there.

Insurance adjusters didn't have to be sinless in their private lives. They just had to be reliable and good at their jobs. He'd made a mistake. A huge mistake. But everybody made mistakes. Surely, he could be forgiven for being human. At least that's the story he was running with.

CHAPTER NINE

Fisher had put off shopping until he'd completely run out of necessities and was downtown running errands. He'd gone to the pharmacy first and was on his way up front to check out, when he overheard two women talking about Calvin Yarbrough getting beat up by his boss and fired from his job. *Ah . . . the word is out, and Sullivan's retribution got painful. Well hell, dude. What did you expect?* he thought, and walked past the women to get in line.

His next stop was the supermarket, and it was the topic in every aisle he went down, and then the same thing again at the gas station when he stopped to refuel. He went home with a smile on his face and put up his purchases. It was always a good day when things came together.

Later in the evening, he checked the tracker he'd left on Cal's truck, saw it was at a motel in Jackson, where he'd obviously holed up to stay out of the line of fire. He'd go to Jackson and remove it on the day they all went to court.

As he was locking up and going to bed, he thought of Bitsy, alone in that big house. He didn't know if she was crying yet, but he would have put money on "No," being the answer. Then he pulled back the covers, got in bed, and turned out the lights. Even after he'd closed his eyes, he could see her face, looking up at him that first day in the Clothes Closet, her eyes shimmering with unshed tears. Her voice had been shaking, but there'd been a set to her jaw as she'd set up getting her revenge, and by God, she had done that in spades.

When he finally fell asleep, he dreamed of her in his arms, leaning back within his grasp, and looking up at him, her long hair hanging over his arms. She was laughing.

The For Sale sign in front of Bitsy's house had turned her life into a holding pattern. Until the place was sold, she couldn't move forward. Until the divorce was final, she couldn't make plans for her future. The words, "Until," and "If," and "When," and "Maybe," had become her restraints.

When she went to town to get groceries, she was stared at. Nobody blamed her for being angry, but she'd set herself apart by her decisions and being different in a small town was a death sentence to acceptance.

For the first time in her life, she saw the shallowness of their thoughts and prayers and was beginning to understand what Fisher had meant when he'd said he would always been invisible here.

She didn't realize until they no longer had contact, that he had earned a place of respect in her life. She didn't go to the Clothes Closet anymore, so a random meeting was unlikely to happen.

The first Sunday after the big reveal, her pastor had begun preaching a sermon about wifely duties and honoring wedding vows. The second time he had looked directly at her, she'd stood up from her seat in the pew, lifted her chin, and had given Pastor Samuels a look he wasn't likely to misunderstand, then she'd walked out. Straight up the aisle with purpose in every step, and she had never gone back.

He'd called her twice at home, but she hadn't answered. Then he'd come to her house. When she'd opened the door to his knock, she'd just stood there in silence, forcing him to speak from the doorstep.

"Bitsy, may I come in? I'd like to talk to you."

"You said what you needed to from your pulpit, so you can say what you have to say on my doorstep," she replied.

He sighed. "I'm afraid you misunderstood my—"

She interrupted. "I misunderstood nothing. You said nothing about denouncing unfaithful spouses or cheating women in your sermon. Only wifely duties and honoring wedding vows. I wasn't the one who broke them. I wasn't the one who dishonored a spouse. And after what my husband has put me through, do you actually think I am going to stand here and listen to another man begin mansplaining anything to me? I heard what you said aloud to the entire congregation, and you were looking straight at me. You judged me without being in my shoes. You aren't supposed to judge people. You had the audacity to think you could say what you said just because of that white collar around your neck. When this house sells, I'll be gone. But until then, do not expect to see my face in your church again. I am the victim. How dare you point a finger at me?"

And then she closed the door in his face and turned the lock.

It was the click of that lock that ended Samuels' expectations of making peace. He dropped his head and went back to his car, a chastened man.

He had underestimated her. He'd seen her silence as a measure of guilt, when in fact, she'd been restraining herself from coming undone.

The next Sunday, he admitted to the congregation that he'd misjudged her and made an elaborate apology. But they were the only ones who heard it. Bitsy Yarbrough was done with the house of public opinion.

Then two months before they were due in court, Bitsy's house sold. The realtor brought a family of five to view the house, and they fell in love with it. The wife wanted to keep the chickens as part of the sale, and the three children were enamored of all the places to play outside. They even used the wrap-around porch for a racetrack, just like she and her daddy had done.

It felt right.

Bitsy had no other feeling but relief when the contract was signed, and the earnest money received. After the closing, she would be five hundred and eighty-five thousand dollars to the good. Now she had to settle on what she was going to do to make a living, where she was going to live, and had less than two months to figure it out and move.

So much to do in not a lot of time.

Late October

Bitsy's alarm went off just after seven a.m. She shut it off, then lingered a few moments more beneath the warm covers, staring up at the pale pink and gray coffered ceiling and the elegant little crystal candelabra hanging over her bed. It, and the big porch across the entire front of the house, were the reasons she'd bought this two-bedroom, one bath cottage in Jackson.

She'd been in residence almost three weeks now and was mostly unpacked. She'd brought the furniture from home that had meant the most to her and sold the rest at a one-day auction in the front yard of the farm and had pretended her heart wasn't breaking.

She'd stayed inside the entire day, collected the profit from the auctioneer, less his fee, and kept telling herself not to cry, because it still didn't compare to the day she'd lost her parents.

What she'd had to give up was just stuff. It was people who could not be replaced.

Two weeks ago, she finally got a job with a company that staged homes for sale, and she'd also made a career decision and was studying for a realtor's license. Now, she had a home and a plan for her future.

But today, she was off work and studying was on the back burner, because this was the day of the divorce hearing. She was to meet Charlie Cowan in front of the Hinds County Courthouse on Pascagoula Street East at ten a.m. They would go to a specific courtroom, and according to Charlie, her revenge would then be completed. The guilty parties would have suffered a sufficient amount of humiliation and disgrace, and she'd finally be free. It was everything she'd asked for. All she had to do now was figure out what to wear and be on time.

Retha Dubois, her book club buddy, was the only person from home who had sincerely empathized with what had happened and had stayed in touch. She had already warned Bitsy that the courtroom was likely to be full of people from home.

Bitsy didn't know what they expected to see. But she had a few surprises of her own. She'd had her hair cut and restyled in what the stylist called an Italian bob that curved around her face and fell just below her chin. She had a few new outfits in the latest fashion, new makeup, and was going in like she was going to war.

Now it was time to get out of bed and face the enemies one last time, so she threw back the covers and headed for the shower.

———

Fisher had been parked in the parking lot for almost an hour before he saw Calvin Yarbrough drive up, park, and get out. He watched as Cal started walking toward the courthouse, met up with another man, probably his lawyer, and then watched as they went in together.

A couple of minutes later, the three women began arriving. It was amusing to watch them puff up their feathers as they glared at each other, then walk in single file, a good ten feet apart, as they, too, headed for the courthouse.

Fisher knew Charlie Cowan on sight and recognized him when he parked and got out, but instead of going inside, he stood on the sidewalk, obviously waiting for his client.

Less than five minutes later, a little red Camaro came speeding off the street and into the parking lot.

Fisher caught himself leaning forward, as if the need to get close to her was innate. When she parked and got out, he couldn't believe what he was seeing—like watching a butterfly emerging from a cocoon.

She'd done something glorious to her hair and makeup and wore three-inch heels. The orange and turquoise pattern of her long-sleeved, knee-length dress made her bare legs look longer. The pang of regret that washed through him dissipated as quickly as it had pierced. She was beautiful and elegant and even farther out of his class than she'd been before.

He waited until they had gone into the courthouse, and then he went straight to Cal's truck, removed the tracker, tossed it in the seat of his car, then went inside. He'd been part of documenting the downfall, but he needed to see this to the end. He slipped into the courtroom just before the doors closed and took an aisle seat at the back of the room.

He immediately spotted her and her lawyer sitting halfway down and could tell by the straight set of her shoulders that she was braced for discord.

Stay strong, darlin'. Don't let them see you cry.

Charlie leaned over and whispered in Bitsy's ear. "This isn't going to take long. Stay focused on the questions the judge asks and feel free to elaborate on your answers at will. Remember, this isn't a trial. You're not being judged by a jury. You are just stating your truth as to why you want out of this marriage."

"What about the women's lawyers?" she whispered.

He winked. "They're about as worthless to this hearing as tits on a boar hog. You have not asked for damages. You have simply named these women as proof of adultery. They're going to have to sit there as guilty as sin without any excuse for their illicit behavior, and if any of their fool lawyers try to argue any level of innocence, thanks to the photos and physical evidence, we've got that covered."

Bitsy eyes welled, but she furiously blinked back the tears. *Worthless as tits on a boar hog. I haven't heard that since Daddy died.* And then a couple of minutes later, the court clerk called out the next case on the docket.

"Elizabeth Yarbrough versus Calvin Yarbrough. Petition for divorce. Accompanying lawsuits for Alienation of Affection, Elizabeth Yarbrough versus Tansy Sullivan, Sue Ritter, and JoJo Walker. Come to the front."

The judge frowned, glanced down at the docket, then remembered the files he'd read earlier, and sighed. This was out of the ordinary, but since it was pertinent to the charge of adultery, and that dang law was still on the books, he was going to have to deal with it.

Calvin got up with his lawyer and followed him to the front of the courtroom as they took a seat at one of the tables, followed by three red-faced women who were being seated beside him with their lawyers lined up in chairs behind their clients.

Cal gave his lawyer a nervous look, then heard a slight rumbling of voices, a few gasps of surprise, and turned to see what all the fuss was about.

His first thought was, *who's the woman,* and then he recognized his wife coming down the aisle with a man he assumed was her lawyer.

His first emotion was shock. She gone from one of the chickens in the hen house to a peacock. And even as he sat there telling himself that analogy didn't work, because the glamorous peacocks were male, she sailed past where them and took a seat at the table on the other side of the aisle, leaving her lawyer to take the chair between them.

Charlie stood. "Your honor, this divorce is not being contested, but there are extenuating circumstances that have brought this divorce to court, and it is important to my client to make those known. And to do so, I would ask for Elizabeth Yarbrough to take the stand."

Bitsy stood, calmly walked toward the judge, and took her seat in the witness stand. As she scanned the faces in the courtroom, she saw Fisher. She hadn't expected him to be here, but seeing his calm, steady gaze gave her courage. Then she shifted her focus as the judge spoke.

"Mrs. Yarbrough, you have filed a petition to divorce your husband and have brought it before this court. Is it still your desire to dissolve this marriage, and if so, on what grounds?"

"On the grounds of adultery, and yes, I want it over. My husband has broken every vow he made to me on the day of our wedding. He has deceived me and lied to me, and he has had illicit assignations with three different women, who I have known and considered to be friends."

"And how did you come by this knowledge?" the judge asked.

"It was a series of events, beginning on the day of our fifteenth wedding anniversary. There was lipstick on the collar of one of his good shirts. It was not my color. Then there was a blue pop-off nail caught in the elastic of his underwear. After the shock came anger as more clues began to appear. I had to decide if I was willing to go to jail for murder or just file for divorce. You are witnessing my choice."

"At that point, did you confront him?" the judge asked.

"No, sir. What I did was hire a private investigator to get all the proof I needed on him and his 'other woman.' What I didn't expect was to find out there were three of them . . . all being played by my husband, the Lone Bridge lothario. Once I found out, I did see the irony of cheaters being cheated on."

There was a twitter of laughter in the courtroom that the judge instantly hushed with a bang of his gavel.

"And what, exactly, did you learn from his investigations?" the judge asked.

"That he'd been at it for years. My lawyer, Charlie Cowan, has all the information I gathered. Affidavits from motel clerks with copies of room registrations going back five years. The clerks knew all his women by their first names. They are who he partied with. I was his leftovers. The hardest part after that was knowing there are people from our hometown who knew it was happening and chose to protect him and his reputation, while he was blighting mine. He has destroyed my life, broken my trust and my heart, and those women who sit there beside him today are equally to blame. They are as selfish and heartless as he is, and they share in his guilt."

"Are you requesting monetary compensation from any of these people?" the judge asked.

"No! I do not want their money. I want the world to see their truth. Look at them. There they sit with their fancy lawyers, frowning at me with all their indignation and guilt. I don't know how they expect to be exonerated. My private investigator got both photographic and physical evidence on all of them.

Coming out of motels with my husband. Passionate kisses and embraces with him on their porches, in the doorways of their homes, and in parking lots behind their places of business. My daddy would have called them tramps. I know they have no self-respect. As for my husband, I have nothing to say about him that's fit for polite company. I don't want alimony. I don't want anything from him, except out of my life. He will, however, be repaying a debt he owes to me. Fifteen thousand dollars upon the finalization of this divorce. One thousand dollars for each year we were married, in repayment for every birthday, anniversary, and Christmas gift he never gave me, and then I never want to see his face again."

Tansy Sullivan's lawyer stood abruptly. "Your honor, are we not allowed to speak on behalf of our clients? How can we be certain those photographs weren't manipulated? AI and photoshop are common practices now and . . ."

Charlie stood up and pointed toward the lawyer. "You want to challenge her veracity? Then I will demand DNA samples from all three women and compare them with the black lace panties found under the seat of Calvin Yarbrough's truck, and the blonde hairs from the pink hairbrush found in the console of his truck, and the DNA from three different colors of lipstick found in his truck, and a blue pop-off nail found on Mr. Yarbrough's underwear. If your clients are so certain they are innocent, then you can pay for the costs of those tests to clear their names."

Three women glared at their lawyers, whispering in hisses and gasps, then the lawyer who'd spoken shook his head.

"I withdraw the challenge," he said, and sat down.

From the back of the room, another man stood. "Your honor, my name is Fisher Means. I am the bonded and licensed private investigator Mrs. Yarbrough hired to get the evidence she needed to take her husband and his women to task, and I will submit my original photos for testing to prove none of them are doctored."

At that point, the room went silent.

Bitsy's heart was pounding. Calvin wouldn't even look at her or the three women sitting beside him. The lawyer who'd spoken was already sorry he'd ever opened his mouth. Charlie hadn't moved a muscle, and Fisher was still standing. Waiting.

The judge pounded his gavel. "Mrs. Yarbrough, is there anything else you wish to say?"

She shook her head. "No, sir."

"Mr. Cowan, do you have anything further to add?"

"No, sir," Charlie said.

The judge glanced at Calvin. "Mr. Yarbrough, do you have anything you wish to say to the court before the divorce is granted?"

"No," Calvin said.

The judge frowned. "I will say, Mr. Yarbrough, that you are sadly lacking in empathy and honesty. You need to do better." He pounded the gavel again. "This divorce has been granted. Lawyers, bring your clients into my chambers to sign the final papers. JoJo Walker, Sue Ritter, and Tansy Sullivan, please stand."

At that point, Fisher turned and walked out of the courtroom. There was a scraping of chairs against the wooden floors as the three women stood.

Sue Ritter was crying.

Tansy Sullivan was frowning and flushed.

JoJo Walker was just flat out embarrassed.

By now, the judge was disgusted with the lot of them and raised his voice for effect.

"All of you are charged with Alienation of Affection that led to the breakup of a marriage. You have been found guilty of those charges, and while you are not being sued for monetary gain, this will go on your permanent record. Your own special little rap sheet, so to speak. And I will give you the same verdict I gave Mr. Yarbrough. You are all lacking in shame, empathy, restraint, and honesty. You are dismissed."

They filed out of the courtroom with their lawyers, parted company in the lobby, and made a run for their cars as Fisher watched from a nearby bench.

Charlie escorted Bitsy into the judge's chambers, with Calvin and his lawyer right behind them.

She signed her name where they told her without looking at Cal or acknowledging he was there. When he laid the cash on the judge's desk, to his humiliation, she stood there and counted it in front of everybody.

"Bitsy, damn it. Don't you trust me to—"

"No, I don't," she snapped, and kept counting, then nodded at the judge. "It's all here."

"Then we're out of here," Cal's lawyer said.

Cal stood a few moments longer, staring at her.

When she saw what he was doing, she took a step forward. "Git away from me."

"You look crazy," he said.

"Oh, that's from being backstabbed. Fuck off, Calvin. Nobody here cares what you think."

He flushed a bright, angry red, but before he could say more, his lawyer, Frank Shannon, grabbed him by the arm and led him out of the judge's chambers, talking nonstop beneath his breath.

"Mr. Yarbrough, I honestly don't know why you hired me. Clearly, the story you told me was as fabricated as your life. You didn't have an innocent leg to stand on. You have just gotten off big-time, and the best thing you can do for yourself now is get as far away from that woman as you can. You mess with her again, and she'll see you put in prison. The lifers would have a fine time with a pretty boy like you. Do you understand?"

Cal's anger turned to horror. "Yes, yes, I understand. When I leave here, I'm heading to Colorado. I just . . ."

"You don't have permission to be angry. You don't even have the right to challenge anything she says or how she feels. You broke everything. Accept that and start over," Frank said, and pointed to the exit.

Cal pivoted and walked out.

Frank Shannon just shook his head and went out of a side door to his car.

By the time Bitsy and Charlie were back in the lobby, the people who'd been in the courtroom were gone.

Bitsy shook inside and tried not to let it show when she put her copy of the decree in her purse.

"Mr. Cowan, thank you for helping me. Thank you for doing this *pro bono*. Thank you for everything," she said, and held out her hand.

Charlie wanted to give her a hug, but he could tell by the look on her face that one ounce of empathy would send her over the edge, so he just smiled and took her hand, instead.

"Believe me, it has been an honor to meet you. I know this is a hard day for you, but the ugliness is over. Tomorrow, and all the days thereafter, are the rest of your life. Your choices. Your decisions. Good luck to you, Bitsy Yarbrough."

"Thank you, and my next step is no more Bitsy. Just Liz, and I'm changing my name back to the name I was born with . . . Collins."

He laughed, and the sound echoed around her.

"That's called, 'Wiping the slate clean.' You go, girl. I have another client to see here in about an hour, so I'm off to another courtroom. Go treat yourself to lunch."

Bitsy went out the front entrance, then began walking down the steps. She was heading for her car when she saw Fisher coming toward her. His long, lanky stride was now as familiar as his face. Her entire focus shifted as she stopped to wait for him, and then he was standing before her.

"You did good, lady. You were magnificent. You look like a million bucks, and you burned them good," he said.

She took a breath, but no words came out. There was a tightening in her throat, and her eyes were beginning to burn.

Fisher sighed. She was pale and trembling, and the dam within her was breaking.

"Aw hell, honey. It's over now. It's okay to cry," and when he opened his arms, Bitsy knew she was coming undone.

She walked into his arms, and when they curled around her, she began to sob, then couldn't stop, and still he held her without motion, without words, standing fast.

When she could finally talk without choking, she took the handkerchief he offered and wiped her eyes.

"Oh my God. I could not have done this without you. Thank you."

"You're welcome," he said.

Then her face twisted into an expression of such despair. "Ah God, Fisher . . . I am so freaking alone, now."

"You still have me," he said. "I've always been here. I'll always be there for you. Are you okay now? Come on. I'll walk you to your car."

She nodded and unlocked the car with the remote as they drew near. He opened the door for her then stepped aside to help her in, and as he did, she paused and put her hand on his arm.

"I don't know where you go next or how far you travel, but will you make me a promise?" she asked.

He smiled. "Probably. What do you want?"

"Don't lose me."

His smile slipped. "I promise."

She got in the car.

He closed the door and watched her drive away with his heart.

CHAPTER TEN

Late December

Liz Collins had emerged from the ashes of Bitsy Yarbrough's life. She didn't look like Bitsy, but there were plenty of days when she still felt like her—like the nights when she went to bed alone and the meals she ate alone. She was getting to know people through her job and got more male attention than she cared to deal with, but she was healing.

The upcoming Christmas would be the first time in her life she would spend it alone, and she was so despondent she couldn't bring herself to put up a tree or decorate the cottage in any way.

It was a chilly, rainy day as she drove home from work. When she pulled up in her driveway, she saw a box near her front door, slightly hidden from the street view for safekeeping. She unlocked the door, scooted it inside, and then turned on the lights before locking herself in for the night. Curious as to what was inside the box and who it was from, she carried it into the kitchen and set it on the island.

The postmark was New York City, which intrigued her. She got a knife to cut through the packing tape and opened it to find a red envelope on top of the Styrofoam packing peanuts. The name, "LIZ," was written on the front. In her mind, that eliminated anyone she'd previously known, and she took out the Christmas card inside.

Merry Christmas, honey. Keeping my promise not to lose you. Eat some peanut brittle for me.

But instead of signing his name, Fisher had drawn a fish wearing a Santa hat.

Her eyes welled. This card alone had just made her whole Christmas, but now she was curious as to what he'd sent. She thrust her hands into the bits of Styrofoam until she felt an oblong box. She pulled it out, cut through more packing tape, removed the lid, and gasped. There was another note lying on top of the most beautiful blue and white porcelain vase she'd ever seen.

I found this in an antique store. They said it was Wedgewood, whatever that means. I thought it was beautiful, and it made me think of you.

Liz lifted it out of the tissue around it, carried it to her granny's marble-top sideboard, and set it in front of the mirrored back.

"You didn't forget me," she whispered, then put the Christmas card and note beside it.

She got her phone, took a photo of the vase on her sideboard, then pulled up the last contact info she'd had on him, and sent the photo along with a text.

I hope this is still your number. I wish you were here so I could hug your neck. Your gift arrived today. It's stunning. I love it so much. Thank you for not losing me.

Merry Christmas to you.

--Liz

Fisher was on a plane to Wyoming and didn't get the text until he landed. His heart skipped when he saw the photo and then read her message. He told himself not to read anything into it that wasn't there and waited until he got to his motel to reply.

Hey, honey, I'm working a case in snowy Wyoming. Not a lot of snow happening in Mississippi. Have you ever built a snowman? I'll build one for you. Sleep tight and keep rocking your fine self.

Liz was asleep when his text came through, and she didn't see it until the morning, but it put a smile on her face.

No snowmen in my past. I can't wait to see the picture. Make sure you're in it.

Fisher was on his way back from a meeting with his new client and had stopped to get some food to take back to the motel. It was snowing again, and he was frustrated. There wasn't much chance of beginning what he'd come to do until the weather cleared. As he drove, his phone dinged a text.

As soon as he got inside his room, he sat down to read it, then smiled. Now he had a snowman to build for his Mississippi girl. Only she wasn't really his girl. He just wanted her to be.

Hours later, there was a snowman in the motel parking lot wearing an old cowboy hat. Fisher got the desk clerk to take pictures of him posing with it, and then sent them to Liz.

My latest client. He's a cold-hearted cowboy without much to say. I promise to stay in touch when I can.

--Fisher

It was the beginning of their long-distance friendship.

Whenever something new happened for Liz, she told him, and when he was off to another location, he told her where he was.

When crazy stuff happened on the job, like opening a box of dishes to stage a dining room in a house that was for sale, and finding a tiny mouse looking up at her, shaking with fright. And how she'd snuck it out of the house and let it loose in the garden, because she knew what it felt like to be afraid.

When she passed the test for her realtor's license, he was the person she told. And when she got her first job at a realtor's office, then when she sold her first house, Fisher was who she told.

They communicated often, off and on, over the next two years, never going longer than a week without at least saying hello. She never knew for sure where he was on any given day, but as long as she didn't lose him, she didn't care.

She just didn't realize how important Fisher Means had become to her until he sent a message that worried her.

I'm going to be out of pocket for a while. Don't worry. It's just this case I'm working. I won't have this phone with me while I'm gone. I'll have a SAT phone for emergency use only. I just want you to know how much you and your messages mean to me.

--Fisher

After that, her world went silent. One month passed, then six weeks, and she was in what might have been considered a full-blown panic when she finally got a text.

She was in an empty house, waiting for the prospective buyer to arrive, when her phone dinged. She read the text with huge relief that he was still alive, and horror at what he wasn't telling her.

It's me. Stuff happened. I didn't mean to go AWOL. Just got out of the hospital. Still in one piece, but with a new scar and a limp that's supposed to go away. Are you okay?

Liz was crying and didn't even know it. Her hands were shaking as she replied.

Other than being out of my mind worried about you, I am fine. OMG! Fisher! Don't ever do this to me again. I thought I'd lost you. I didn't know what happened, but I knew something had.

Fisher read the text with his heart pounding. This two-year, long-distance, one-sided love affair was killing him.

You can't lose me unless you want to. If I die, you're listed as my next of kin, because you are the only person alive who sees me. Only I don't know how you see me, or what you think about me as a man, or if you even see me that way, at all. I have no idea what's happening in your personal life, but you are all that's going on in mine. I miss your face. I miss your voice. As soon as I can drive again, if it's okay, I'm coming to see you.

Liz read the text, then read it again to make sure she wasn't trying to read between the lines, but it was there. A declaration of what he felt for her. She felt the flush rising up her neck and then her face. All of a sudden, she was dizzy, then broke out in a cold sweat. She'd never fainted in her life, but it might be about to happen now. She had to sit down on the stairs to keep from falling.

Had he just said that? Did he mean what she thought he meant? Had Fisher Means just gone from pen pal to someone to love? She was staring down at her phone, rereading the texts, and the longer she sat there, the more certain she became that he was already that guy in her heart.

She texted him back, then hit Send.

When she didn't immediately respond, Fisher sighed. He'd probably just messed up his last chance to at least be her friend. He was sore as hell and hurting, and he'd been putting off taking his pain meds because they made him sleepy. He'd also been putting off contacting her until he could at least make complete sentences again without falling asleep. He was reaching for the pill bottle when his phone dinged. He pulled up the text and began to read.

There's this guy I know. He sends me gifts. He makes me laugh, and I didn't know how much I loved him until I thought I'd lost him. I was crying the last time I saw your face, but I remember that hug. You held the pieces of me together. You kept me from falling apart. I promise not to cry when I see you again. Get well. Come see me. I owe you a hug . . . and so much more.

"Thank you, lord," Fisher said, and sent one last message.

Give me three weeks. I'll take the hug and all that comes with it. Love,
Me.

Then he reached for the bottle of pain pills, shook two out in his hand, swallowed them without water, and then eased himself back down on his pillow and closed his eyes, as he waited for the drugs to kick in and the pain to ease.

There was still an entire week of his life he didn't remember. When he had been in and out of consciousness, wondering if he was dying and regretting all the things he'd never said to her. He'd made a promise to himself that if he survived this, he would say what was in his heart and take the consequences. This was way more than he'd imagined, even in his wildest dreams.

The last thing he was thinking as the drugs pulled him under was the irony of all the years he'd been in a foreign land, fighting a war not of his making, only to come home and nearly get killed on an interstate in a ten-car pile-up that had started with a farmer on a John Deere tractor.

Fisher fell asleep thinking of his Mississippi girl. He'd seen the fury in her. And he'd seen her cry. She wasn't ashamed of emotion. Her passion would be off the chart.

Liz had learned the easiest way to get past what Cal had done to her was to laugh about it, and today, she and Andie, her nail tech, were talking about her life before moving to Jackson.

"So, you've only been here three years or so, but have you always been a realtor?" Andie asked.

"Oh Lord, no. I was the typical Mississippi country girl who married her high school sweetheart," she said, and then she began relating the downfall of the marriage and telling the story about finding lipsticks and black lace underwear, and the blue pop-off nail stuck to his underwear, and how she'd thrown their anniversary cake out to the chickens.

The sixty-something woman in the chair beside them had been listening to Liz's story, but when she heard Liz say, "I gave the cake to the chickens," she laughed out loud.

"Pardon me. My name is Della Worthington. I don't mean to be nosy, but I couldn't help but overhear. You are an absolute delight. Did you know who the other woman was?"

Liz shook her head. "Not at first, but I kept finding more clues and hired a private investigator. He discovered my ex was seeing three different women, and they didn't know about each other."

Della gasped. "I would have been devastated. What did you do?"

"Oh, I *was* devastated, but my mama always told me never to let my enemies see me cry. I didn't just want justice. I wanted revenge. So, I filed for divorce on the grounds of adultery and named all three of the women as abetting the dissolution of my marriage, then I filed Alienation of Affection charges against each of them. I dragged their sorry asses into court with him. They were mad at him and horrified at what I'd done to their reputations. It's hell being outed in a small town."

Della laughed. "You are a remarkable young woman who traded a chicken house for selling other people's houses. The irony is perfect. What's your name?"

"I took back my maiden name. It's Liz Collins."

"I have a property I am planning to sell here in Jackson. Do you have a card?" Della asked.

Liz nodded. "I do. Just a sec. Don't want to mess up my manicure." She eyed a nearby nail tech who was stocking a shelf of nail polish. "Hey, Carl, would you help me here, please?"

Carl heard his name called, stopped what he was doing, and hurried over to where Liz was sitting. "What do you need?"

"Would you unzip that pocket on the outside of my purse and get out one of my business cards," Liz said.

"Oh, sure thing, hon . . ." Moments later, he pulled one out. "Here you go."

"Could you give it to Mrs. Worthington for me?"

Della took the card and dropped it in her purse as she stood up. "Expect my call. I'll be in touch," she said, and left the salon.

After she was gone, Andie leaned over, whispering. "That woman is one of the socialites of Jackson. Old family. Old money."

Liz's eyes widened. "Good to know," she said.

And that's how Liz wound up sitting beside Della Worthington today, as she was signing final papers for the sale of her house.

The two million, five-hundred-thousand-dollar house was Liz's biggest sale ever, and it had all come about because of that appointment at her nail salon.

When all of this was over, Liz was going to bank seventy-five thousand dollars as her fee from the fifty-fifty split with her agency.

She was so excited; she couldn't wait to get home tonight and call Fisher to tell him what she'd done. She hadn't heard from him since last week, but she knew he'd been going regularly to physical therapy and was waiting for a doctor's release before he could get behind the wheel of a car again.

And she knew that when they were finally face to face once more, their lives were going to change forever, and in the very best way.

She and Della parted company with a handshake.

"Thank you again for the opportunity to represent you," Liz said. "It has been a pleasure to work with you."

Della smiled. "Oh, honey, the pleasure has all been mine. I've probably told your story of taking your husband and his 'other women' to court a dozen times these past few months. You are remarkable, and I would expect your reputation for fierceness, both in life and business, to serve you well in the years to come."

They parted company, and then Liz went back to the office to file all the paperwork. She walked into a small round of applause from the other realtors and a high-five from her boss for a job well done. It felt good to be recognized for her diligence, and by the time she'd finished, it was time to go home.

Traffic was, as usual, a mess between five and six p.m., but she'd long ago learned what shortcuts it took to get home quicker.

As she turned the corner and headed down her block, she was thinking about a long soak in a hot bubble bath, when she noticed the SUV parked at the curb in front of her house.

She pulled up into the driveway and got out, glanced back once at the darkened windows of the SUV, and then got as far as the steps when she heard someone call her name.

She turned, and then froze. Fisher was walking toward her with that long, lanky stride, that wonderful, almost handsome face, and a barely perceptible limp. She dropped her briefcase and her purse on the porch and started toward him, and moments later, threw her arms around him.

He grinned. "My Mississippi girl. Long time—no see," he said.

She was laughing when she leaned back in his arms and looked up, and he remembered. *Just like in my dream.*

And then he lowered his head and kissed her.

EPILOGUE

Liz and Fisher's wedding was a real-life version of a line from an old Johnny Cash song called, *"Jackson."*

"They got married in a fever, hotter than a pepper sprout."

The fire in Fisher's woman had not surprised him. He'd always known she would ignite his life.

As for Elizabeth May Collins becoming Elizabeth Means, she took it as a sign from God that there were such things as second chances.

Things getting better the second time around.

Everything getting better with age, just like her mama and daddy's marriage.

Like the look she saw in Fisher's eyes when she caught him watching her. That quiet, enduring, forever promise he'd made to her at the altar.

There was no more mad left in his Mississippi girl.

It had been loved right out of her.

RAIN DOWN ON ME

SHARON SALA

RosettaBooks®

DEDICATION

Love never really dies.
It just goes into a holding pattern until you're ready to take another chance.
I dedicate this story to people like me, who found love the second time around.

CHAPTER ONE

Russellville, Arkansas:

Max Bridger was leaving the house that had sheltered him, with what was left of the woman who'd raised him, on a quest to fulfill her dying wish.

He had been dreading this day for weeks, and now that it had arrived, he was torn between wanting to get it over with and the grief that came with it.

The weather report was iffy. Rain was predicted around noon or later, but leaving this early meant he'd be home well before any of that occurred.

Since his muster out of the military was so recent, his choice of civilian clothing was still sparse, and old Levis, a sweatshirt, and hiking boots for the trip were all he had. But he had packed a change of clothes in his backpack, in case he was soaked by the time he completed his quest.

At the last minute, he went back and put a hooded rainproof jacket into the backpack, pocketed his wallet, grabbed his keys, and left the house. When he got into the Jeep, he buckled the backpack into the passenger seat, gave it a quick pat, then backed out of the driveway.

Today was a bitter end to life as he'd known it.

Retiring from the military after twenty-five years of service then coming home to find Deidre Lewis, the woman who'd raised him, in the last stages of pancreatic cancer had been an unexpected end he had not seen coming. She'd given him roots, purpose, and more love than he'd ever known, but had passed before her sixty-sixth birthday.

As he drove away from the house, he was remembering his homecoming three months earlier.

Max had been on the road since mustering out of Fort Liberty, and all he wanted was to get home to Dee. It had been eighteen months since his last visit, but this time there would be nothing to rush away for. He was home for good.

He breathed a quiet sigh of relief as he passed the city limits sign of Russellville, Arkansas. He'd lived there since the age of nine. Gone to school there. Played football and baseball for the high school teams, and knew the streets like the back of his hand. When he finally pulled into the driveway and parked, he half-expected her to come running out to meet him. She knew he was coming home for good, but she didn't show.

He didn't think much of it as he palmed his keys, grabbed his bags, and hurried up the steps to let himself in. The moment he closed the door behind him, he called out.

"Mom! I'm home!"

Then he heard a weak voice coming from down the hall.

"I'm in here, honey!"

He dropped his bags and headed to her bedroom, then stopped in the doorway, shocked by the sight of her. She was at least twenty pounds thinner than the last time he'd seen her and wearing a sock cap, which he supposed was to keep her head warm, since all her hair looked gone.

"What the hell?" he said, then rushed to her bedside. "Why didn't you tell me you were sick?"

She patted the bed beside her. "Sit here, love."

"What's wrong?" he asked, as he eased down beside her.

"Final stages of pancreatic cancer. Incurable. I didn't want to worry you, because there was nothing you could do. I'm dying, but not this minute. I've been waiting for you to come home. You were in too many war zones the past twenty-five years for my peace of mind, and I'm worn out from praying to God to keep you alive. I wasn't going to be cheated out of seeing my boy again, after all that praying." His eyes welled as he kissed the palms of her hands, then held them against his cheeks.

Dee grimaced. "Don't cry, Maxie . . . don't cry. I've made peace with all this, and your presence in my life has been a God-given gift. Even though MaryJo gave birth to you, you're the child I took to raise. I am so proud of the man you became."

He shook his head. "I don't remember anything good about her. You're my mom."

Dee gripped his hand tighter. "She loved you, darling."

"She was an addict. She was chasing the next fix, not chasing after me," he said. "You, and every bouncer and dancer in the club took better care of me than she did."

"I know, but she was just as sick in her addiction as I am now with cancer. A disease is a disease. The tragedy was you being the one to find her body. That was a hell of a thing for a nine-year-old child to see."

Max shook his head. "I've seen far worse since in war-torn countries," he muttered, then stood and kissed the side of her cheek. "At any rate, I'm home, you're here, and I'm going to unpack. You and I are doing this together, understand?"

Dee finally gave way to tears. "I don't know how to die, but I'm guessing all I have to do is let go, and having you here now takes all the scary away from the thought."

He kissed her cheek again. "I've got this. You just rest. Love you."

———— ◆ ————

Two months later, she was gone. And here he was, three weeks afterward, on his way to scatter her ashes at Falling Water Falls up in the mountains above Russellville. The day was clear, but his heart was heavy. The finality of it all was weighing on him as he drove. Once again, life had thrown him a curve ball he hadn't seen coming, but he'd made her a promise he intended to keep.

Normally, there would be plenty of cars on this road. The Ozarks were beautiful this time of year, and the hiking trails and waterfalls were favorites of both locals and tourists. But today, the traffic was sparse, and he was guessing the morning weather reports of an impending storm front were likely responsible. He wasn't worried, and it made the trip easier not having to deal with traffic. He had plenty of time to get to the falls, scatter the ashes, and still make it home before the storm hit.

All of his years in the military had taught him to be prepared for anything, but this morning he hadn't given any thought or consideration to the local wildlife, and he should have.

One minute he was driving along, admiring the fleeting glimpses of sunlight coming through the forest around him, when a flash of sun bounced off the hood of his Jeep and into his eyes. He blinked, and when he looked again, there was a full-grown deer standing in the middle of the road.

He swerved to miss it, and hit a small tree on the side of the road, instead. The collision was bone-jarring. His head hit the driver's side window as his safety belt tightened against his chest. Then to his horror, the small tree gave way, and he and the car began sliding down the side of the mountain, gathering speed at an alarming rate.

Everything was a blur of green, coupled with the slap and cracks of limbs and bushes against and beneath the body of the vehicle, until it slammed to a halt, caught in the heavier tree growth below.

He woke up with blood running into his eye. His head was throbbing, and he was in enough pain that for a few moments, he couldn't think what to do.

He glanced up where the rearview mirror used to be, but it was lying on the dash beside the tree limb that had come through the windshield, barely missing his head. He was on his own, and so far out of sight of the road above that he knew he'd never be found unless he got himself out.

He turned off the engine, used the key fob to unlock the doors, then found his cellphone and tried to call for help, but there was no cell service. The backpack with Dee's ashes inside was still buckled in the seat, and he wasn't leaving her behind. He released his seatbelt, reclined his seat, then ducked under the limb to release the backpack, too. He grabbed hold of it, and began crawling into the back of the Jeep, but the doors were jammed.

His head was pounding as he began kicking until one of the doors popped open, and he eased himself out. But once he was on solid ground, the slope was so steep that standing upright was almost impossible.

He leaned slightly forward to get better footing so he wouldn't slide backwards, took a swipe at the blood running down the side of his face, then shook off a moment of nausea before strapping on the backpack and began to climb.

For every yard of distance he covered, he slid a back a foot, catching himself by digging the toes of his boots into the earth, and grabbing at bushes, clawing at trees, crawling over the stubble of what the Jeep had destroyed.

Slowly he began making headway. What had seemed impossible was happening. He couldn't see the road yet, but he knew it was up there, and traffic was passing. He didn't bother shouting for help. They wouldn't hear him, and he needed to save his breath for the climb.

Skye Raley woke with the sunrise, and went through her usual morning routine while listening to the weather. Her home—a big sturdy log cabin—built years ago on the mountain above Russellville, had once been her parents' holiday destination. Her move to this place had been both escape and self-imposed exile, but the solitude had healed what life had broken.

When she heard there were thunderstorms predicted to hit the area by noon, she began to hurry. If it rained too much, the low-water bridge between home and the main road would flood, and she wouldn't be able to get out until the water went down. She'd been putting off making a grocery run, but now it was a necessity, so she uploaded a piece to her daily blog that she'd previously written, and went to get ready for the trip down the mountain.

At the age of thirty-five, she'd been a widow longer than she'd been a wife. She had a brother, Sean, in Oregon, a sister Marie, who lived in Los Angeles, and her mother, Donna, who had moved to Florida after Skye's dad passed away.

Skye had been twenty-three years old, and working as a physical therapist when she'd married Paul Raley, a fireman who worked for the City of Hot Springs, Arkansas. They'd settled into their happy little home, and were there for four years before Paul died on the job, and her fairy-tale life came to a horrendous halt.

By the time all of the details of his death had been dealt with, she was numb. Learning she would receive monthly widow's benefits answered one question, but everything about the city reminded her of him. She couldn't sleep. She wasn't eating. She began dreading going to work each morning to the looks of sympathy on everyone's faces. Emotionally, she was gone.

It was the call from her mother that had saved her sanity.

"Skye, darling . . . the last time we spoke, you mentioned how difficult it was to stay in Hot Springs alone. It occurred to me that, if you don't mind the isolation, the family cabin outside of Russellville is still there."

Skye was surprised. "I thought you sold that after Dad passed."

"I thought about it, but I didn't. It's in good condition, but it's been empty a while. I've talked to your brother and sister, and we all agree that, if you want it as your home, then I'm going to deed it to you."

Skye started crying. "Mom . . . I don't know what to say other than thank you. Yes, a thousand times, yes. I can't bear to be here, and that cabin was everything special when we were kids. All the Christmases and summers we spent there . . . It has nothing but wonderful memories for me."

"Then it's yours. I'll FedEx you the keys and the little book your dad kept about the upkeep of stuff. You move at your leisure, and I'll have my lawyer deal with the deed. The utilities are on. If you need me, I'll fly back to help you."

"You've already saved me. You don't need to help me move. Tell everyone thank you for me. You all mean the world to me."

After that, Skye's despair shifted to purpose. She still grieved the loss of Paul, but she'd been left behind to figure this out on her own. Between her widow's benefits and a rent-free home, it eased the financial pressure.

She was still working as a therapist once a week in a physical therapy clinic in Russellville, and at random times when they needed extra help. But she had refused to work there full-time. The long drive up and down the mountain each day wasn't something she was interested in doing.

At first, beginning *Skye on the Mountain* as an online blog had been for her. But that had been eight years ago.

Since then, she'd written about weathering blizzards, flooded roads, and power outages. About the wildlife, and the old bear named Grumpy that meandered through the woods around her cabin now and then, and an owl named Greg, who lived somewhere in the trees outside her cabin and hooted at her every night.

As time passed, she gained a following and advertisers that added to her income, and she'd thrived. The isolation was a small price to pay for the security, solitude, and comfort of the big log cabin, and it had healed all the raw, sad pieces within her.

Today was just another day. The predicted weather was just another storm. She had her grocery list in her purse. The empty gas cans were in the truck bed to be refilled and on hand for the generator in case of power outages. Just to be safe, she grabbed a raincoat as she went out the kitchen door and into the garage. As she was backing out, she made sure the garage door was down before driving away. In the mountains, anything left out or uncovered was fair game for bears and raccoons.

The boards across the wide, low-water bridge rattled as she crossed it, and then a couple of minutes later she was at the main road and heading down the mountain.

Max was still climbing, but flat on his belly now and trying to catch his breath. At best guess, he was still a hundred yards from the top. It had taken him more than thirty minutes of getting one yard up and sliding one foot back just to get this far, and he didn't dare look back for fear he'd slip again. He just needed a minute to reorient himself and give his strained muscles a rest.

But he laid there too long, and one minute turned to two, and he was close to passing out when he heard a large vehicle on the road above. The sound roused him enough that he shifted his backpack, dug his fingers into the dirt, and then reached for the closest bush. As soon as he had a good grip, he started climbing again, but this time without stopping. If he was going to pass out, he needed to be on flat ground when it happened.

When he finally reached the top and crawled out onto the main road, he was so exhausted every muscle in his body shook. He went from his hands and knees to sitting upright, trying to decide whether to go back down the mountain for help or finish what he'd come to do and go up.

It was the soldier in him that decided the issue. He was mobile, and to hell with hurting. He had a mission to complete. He never thought to check for cell coverage again. He just pushed himself upright, swiped at the seeping blood, readjusted the backpack, and started walking toward the falls. One step, then another, and then another—uphill all the way.

He thought the sun had just gone behind the clouds until he heard a clap of thunder and felt the air turning cooler with every step. The first raindrops hit him in the face, and then began falling harder. He paused to get the hooded jacket out of the backpack and put it on, then pulled the hood up over his head before shouldering the pack and moving on.

Rain was now a curtain between him and the world. It blurred his vision to the point that everything before him looked like a mirage. There was no place to take shelter, and the traffic he'd heard on the road earlier was absent. The air was as cold as the rain, and the higher up he walked, the colder it felt. He didn't know he had a rising fever. All he knew was that the cold felt good on his face.

He didn't know where he was now, or how far he had left to go, but the decision to go up instead of down might become the end of him. He was staggering and sweating beneath his sodden clothing, wondering why he'd stayed alive all those years in the military just to come home and die on a mountain, in the rain.

————————

Skye shopped with an eye to the clouds and wasted no time heading home. She had a month's worth of groceries in the back seat of her pickup truck, three gas cans full of fuel in the truck bed, and an order she'd picked up at the deli to take home for lunch.

She was more than halfway there when it began to rain, which prompted her to speed up. She had to get back across the bridge before it flooded, or she'd be spending the next few days back in town.

Within five minutes of the first drops hitting her windshield, it had turned into a deluge. Her windshield wipers worked overtime, and her fingers gripped the steering wheel so tightly her knuckles had turned white.

Then, between the wiper swipes, she saw something moving on the road ahead. At first, she thought it might be a deer or a bear, but in this rain, most animals took shelter. As she came closer, she realized it was a man. A big man, stumbling and staggering.

Her heart skipped as she watched him stumble far too close to the edge of the road. Either he was going to fall in front of her or down the slope. She didn't know if he was drunk or high, or if he'd been injured. But she couldn't bring herself to drive past him and leave him out in this storm.

And just like that, the decision had been made. She'd been bringing home strays all her life. What was one more? If he was a bad guy, he would have to get well before he could kill her. So, she slammed on the brakes and stopped in the middle of the road, pulled the hood up on her raincoat and got out on the run.

———

Max didn't hear the vehicle behind him. He was just struggling not to pass out when all of a sudden there was someone beside him. He got the vague impression of a woman's face. Thinking he was dreaming, he swiped his hand across his face to wipe away the rain, but she was still there talking, and then he felt her arm around his waist and her voice shouting to be heard above the rain and rolling thunder.

"You need to get out of the storm. Come with me," she said.

One moment the rain was in his face, and then he was in the front seat of her truck with his backpack in his lap. She was a blur as she circled the front of the truck to get in, and then she was in the seat beside him.

He still wasn't sure this was happening, or if he was hallucinating, and reached toward her, touched the side of her face, then dropped his hand in his lap. "You're real. I thought you were an angel," he mumbled, and then leaned back, still mumbling beneath his breath.

Skye thought she heard him saying something about "going to heaven in a red Chevie truck," and then he closed his eyes.

"Hang tough, mister. I have to get us home before the road floods," she said, and took off again, driving as fast as she dared.

He closed his eyes, and knew whatever happened next was up to her. Wherever she was taking him, it wasn't home. Home didn't exist anymore.

Skye glanced at him once just to make sure he was still breathing, and then noticed there was blood on the side of his face. She hadn't seen it before because of the rain. He'd either had some kind of accident or been in a fight, but right now, he wasn't a danger to anyone but himself.

She kept her eyes on the road, driving into the wind-driven rain until she finally came to her turn-off, made a quick left, and headed into the forest on the gravel road, anxious for the sight of the bridge.

A few inches of water were already moving over it when she arrived, but she'd made it in time. She drove through the flow, and as she sped the last thirty yards toward the house, pressed the remote to raise the garage door.

By the time she got there, the door was up. She drove inside and hit the remote again, finally breathing easy as it closed behind her. Rain was hammering the roof and blowing against the windows, but they were safely inside. Now all she had to do was get him into the house, which turned out to be easier said than done.

She jumped out and ran to open the door that led into the kitchen, then circled the truck to get to him, but he was already fumbling at the latch on his seatbelt. She reached inside and released it, then patted his arm.

"Okay buddy, we need to get inside. Let me have your back-pack, and I'll—"

He pushed her hand away. "No. I promised," he muttered.

She sighed. "Okay, that's fine. Can you stand up?"

He slid out of the seat and stood.

Moments later, her arm was around his waist. "Lean on me," she said, and so he did.

They made their way into the cabin with him stumbling and mumbling, then down the hall to one of the spare bedrooms, dripping water all the way.

"Sorry about this buddy, but you need to get dry and warm. Put your backpack down, and hold out your arms. I'm going to help you out of your clothes, and don't freak. I've seen naked men before."

He blinked, slowly lowered the backpack, then steadied himself by putting his hands on her shoulders.

She started with removing his jacket, then his belt and shirt. She worked his sodden clothing down around his ankles and pulled back the covers on the bed. She couldn't help but notice how physically fit he was, but it was the bruising that was beginning to appear that worried her most. "Sit please. I need to get your boots and pants off."

Max sat, but the moment he felt the soft mattress beneath him, he laid back.

"Alrighty then," Skye said, and untied and removed his hiking boots, then the rest of his wet clothes. She started to help him get his legs up on the bed, when he waved a hand in the air.

"I can do it," he said, and scooted himself into the bed.

She pulled the covers over him and checked his pulse. It was strong and steady, but when she felt his forehead, it was too warm, and the cut was still oozing. "Your head is bleeding. I'm going to go get my first aid kit. Can you tell me your name?"

"Max . . . I'm Max."

"My name is Skye. Rest easy, Max. I'll be right back," she said, and ran to the bathroom to retrieve the first aid kit then hurried back into the bedroom.

She moved with purpose, cleaning the open wound, applying antiseptic to the cut before pulling it together with little butterfly strips and a gauze pad over the cut to absorb the seeping blood. The whole time she was working, she was also studying his face.

She didn't know if he had passed out, or if his eyes were closed against the pain. She guessed he was probably mid-forties. His nose had once been broken, and he had some fairly horrific scars on his back. His eyebrows were as black as his hair and lashes, and she already knew his eyes were brown. He had a broad fore-head and what she would have called a stubborn jaw. He was a good-looking man, and she couldn't help but think of the people who must be worried out of their minds at where he was.

"Max, can you hear me?" she asked.

He didn't answer. She was worried about concussion, or a more serious brain injury, and dared to open an eyelid enough to check to see if his pupils were dilated. They looked normal, but bruising was already forming on his chest. There was dirt beneath his fingernails, and his hands and legs were severely scratched. Best guess was he'd been in a wreck.

She tried to call emergency services, but her cell phone had no signal. So, here they were, and she still had a truck full of groceries and fuel to unload. The fuel would be fine in the truck bed until the rain had passed, but she needed to get her food in the house. She emptied his pockets of their contents, left it all on the table beside his bed, then gathered up his wet clothes and took off on the run.

As soon as she had the clothes in the washer, she brought the groceries inside, ran to check on him again, and found him still sleeping, then she ran back to the kitchen and began put-ting things up.

She hadn't eaten breakfast, so she started a pot of coffee. As soon as it was done, she poured herself a cup, grabbed her food from the deli, and took it back to the bedroom to keep an eye on him while she ate.

The backpack he'd refused to relinquish was on the floor beside his bed. She couldn't help wondering what was in it that was so important, but wasn't going to snoop. Whatever it was, it couldn't fix what had happened to him.

The battery on his cell phone was down, and she still had no signal, but she'd found a charger cord when she'd emptied his jacket pockets, so she plugged it in. After checking him one more time, she sat down, took her first bite of the cold shrimp and pasta salad, and made herself relax. For now, she'd done everything she knew to do for him until he woke up enough to tell her where all he hurt.

She ate in silence, listening to the rain and to him muttering in his sleep. When she noticed his hands kept clenching and unclenching, and the dark lashes on his eyelids were fluttering, she guessed he was dreaming.

School was out, and Max was in line with the other fourth graders waiting to be picked up. Today was Thursday, which meant Ray, who was a bouncer at the club where his mama, MaryJo, danced, would be taking him home. Ray did Tuesdays and Thursdays. Corky, the other bouncer, did Monday and Friday. DeeDee, who danced at the same club, did Wednesdays. This was nine-year-old Max Bridger's normal. And when Max saw Ray's old Corvette pulling into the line of waiting parents, he called out to his teacher.

"Miss Ellie, Ray is here. Can I go?" Max asked.

"Yes, but walk, don't run," she said.

Max obeyed, and was grinning at Ray when he got out of the car and opened the door for him.

"Get in kid," Ray said. "Look at those clouds. It's gonna pour before I get you home."

Max jumped into the passenger seat, dumped his school bag in the floorboard, and buckled up as Ray got in.

"Is that my snack? Max asked, pointing to a bag of chips and a can of Mountain Dew.

"You know it," Ray said, smiling as he watched the brown-eyed boy tear into the bag of chips. When Ray got the all-clear from another teacher doing bus duty, he pulled away from the curb and drove off, talking as they went. "Did you have a good day, buddy? Today was spelling test, right? How did you do?"

Max stuffed a chip in his mouth as he popped the tab on the can of pop, chewing as he answered. "I got an A," he said, and grinned.

Ray stopped for a red light and winked at him. "Way to go! You keep studying and get yourself really smart. Don't wind up like me. Do something important with your life, you hear?"

Max nodded. Ray and Corky and DeeDee all said the same thing. He liked it when they bragged about him. Mama didn't know today was spelling test day, so she wouldn't be bragging. She didn't know anything about Max's life. They just lived under the same roof.

When it started raining, Ray turned on the windshield wipers while Max ate the rest of his chips, absently counting how many times the wipers swiped in a minute, then downed the whole can of Mountain Dew before Ray pulled up into the driveway.

"Okay kiddo, here you go. Go tell your mama I'm waiting to take her to work, and she needs a raincoat."

"Okay Ray. Thank you for the snack," Max said, then grabbed his book bag, jumped out of the car, and took off running. He wore the key to the house on a chain around his neck and pulled it out to unlock the door. "Mama, Mama, I'm home!" Max shouted, then slammed the door shut to keep out the rain, and dumped his bookbag on the sofa. MaryJo didn't answer, but he headed for the kitchen, following the sound of the radio.

She was sitting on the floor, leaning against the cabinet beneath the sink. There was a hypodermic needle stuck in her arm, and a dirty strip of elastic still tied around her arm. Her eyes were open, but she wasn't moving.

"Mama? Mama? Are you okay?"

When she didn't answer, he squatted down beside her and patted her face. It was cold. She needed a blanket. He shook her shoulder to wake her up, but when he did, she fell sideways onto the floor without a word.

Max's heart skipped. He patted her face again. "Mama. Mama. Wake up! Wake up!"

He was waiting for a response when he saw a cockroach crawl out of her hair and across her face. When she didn't blink or scream, that's when he knew she was dead. He scrambled backwards in horror, jumped up and ran for the door and out into the rain, wild-eyed and screaming.

Ray's heart dropped when he saw Max's face, and he got out on the run, picking the boy up. "Maxie, Maxie, what's wrong, buddy?"

But Max didn't stop screaming, and that's when Ray went back into the house with him, saw MaryJo on the floor, called 9-1-1, and then the police.

And then he called Dee.

Deidre Lewis was getting ready to go to work when her phone rang. She saw it was Ray, but when she answered and heard Max screaming, her heart stopped.

"Ray! What's wrong?"

"Max just found MaryJo. She's on the kitchen floor with a needle in her arm. Looks like she's been dead for hours. I've called 9-1-1 and the cops. I need help."

Max woke abruptly as the dream began to fade, but he was disoriented by the unfamiliar surroundings. He remembered seeing an angel, but couldn't remember how he'd gotten here.

Then he saw a young woman sitting in a chair near the window by his bed. She had a cup of coffee cradled in her hands and seemed lost in thought as she stared through the rain-drenched panes.

There she is. There's my angel. Is she real, or am I dreaming?

He thought about trying to get up, then realized he was naked beneath the covers. He had a vague memory of someone helping him get undressed. His head throbbed, but when he touched the place where it hurt the worst, he felt the bandage.

Clearly, the angel he thought he'd seen was a real one, with hair the color of cinnamon, a profile of solemn beauty, and a gentle touch. He'd never felt her tending to his injuries.

As if sensing she was being watched, Skye abruptly turned to look, then leaped up with a smile and came hurrying to his bedside.

"Oh, thank God. You're awake!" She laid her hand on his forehead to test the temperature of his skin. "You're still feverish, and you must be confused. I know you're Max, because you told me your name earlier. My name is Skye Raley. I have a hundred questions, and you probably do, too. But let me get you some water. Are you allergic to anything?"

"No allergies, and yes, I'm Max. Max Bridger."

She patted his hand. "Good. I'll be right back. Are over-the-counter pain meds okay?"

He squinted against a stabbing pain. "Yes, and thank you," he said, then watched her dart out of the room. He could hear her footsteps as she hurried away, and then found himself listening for the sound of them coming back. He had a moment of *déja vu*, and being in a MASH unit somewhere in Iraq, waiting for a doctor to come stitch up a shrapnel wound on his back.

Only this time, he hadn't been carried off a battlefield. He'd been picked up off a road in a storm and taken to shelter under the care of a woman named Skye. The name fit the angel she was to him. She came hurrying back with water and Advil, and sat down on the side of the bed beside him.

"Can you sit up a little?" she asked, then when he did, the covers slipped down around his waist. The bruises across his upper body were telling. One ran across his chest, where a seatbelt would have been, and the other was along the left side of his rib cage, on the same side of his body as the cut on his head. She'd seen him naked, and she'd already seen the two scars on his back, one of which was a good eight inches, and long since healed. Without commenting, she shook two pills out into his palm, then handed him the bottle of water. He swallowed the pills and handed her the bottle back.

She set it on the table within his reach. "Max, there's a bathroom behind that door if you need it. But I'm kind of afraid to let you get up on your own. You were staggering all over the road when I found you."

"I'm naked," he said.

She shrugged. "I'm the reason you're naked. Don't worry. I didn't faint. I had a husband once . . . for four years. He was a fireman in Hot Springs. He was killed on the job, but that was in another lifetime," she said, then grabbed the lightweight blanket from the foot of the bed. "Your sarong awaits."

Max liked her. She was matter of fact and kind. But when he threw back the covers and sat up on the side of the bed, he grabbed the mattress with both hands.

"The room's spinning. Give me a sec."

"Take your time," Skye said. "Neither of us is going anywhere until it quits raining and the water goes down. The low-water bridge into this property always floods, but it runs off just as quickly."

Finally, Max stood, and when he did, Skye wrapped the blanket around him like a sarong. "Okay, lean on me as we go," she said, and felt him slide a hand across the length of her shoulders and hold on.

He made it back to the bed on shaky legs, then eased himself down onto the mattress with relief, dropped the blanket, and slid back between the covers.

As soon as he settled, she sat down beside him.

"Is there someone you need to call? A wife. Children. Any kind of family?"

"My mom, Dee, was my only family, and she's gone. Never married, and no children. Came close to getting married once, but military life and constant moving did not appeal to her. That was years and years ago."

"Understood," she said. "So, what happened? How did you get hurt?"

"Had a wreck. A deer jumped out in front of me. I swerved to miss it, hit a tree. Then went over the edge."

Skye's eyes widened. "Wait. What? You went off the side of the mountain?"

He nodded.

"Oh my God, Max. Oh, my God. How far?"

"Far enough that I had no cell signal. Took me a really long time to crawl back up to the road. I think I slid backwards more than I moved forward, but it put all my army survival skills to work."

"You served in the military?"

"Twenty-five years. Colonel Bridger, recently retired. Over and out. Then I came home to find my mom, Dee, in the last stages of pancreatic cancer."

Skye's eyes welled. "I'm so sorry—for such a horrible accident, and for . . ." Her voice broke. "Just everything."

Max reached for her hand. "I've always associated rain with the worst day of my life until you. You have forever erased every negative aspect of it, and I am grateful."

The last time she'd purposefully held a man's hand in this way, he had been lying in a casket, and she had been trying to find the words to say goodbye. But now she needed to know the story behind the rain.

"If you don't want to tell me, then forgive me for asking. But what's the story with the rain?"

"It's not a pretty story," he said.

She shrugged. "I've had my share of bad, sad days."

He saw patience and compassion on her face and then let himself go there. Back to that time.

"I was nine. Came home from school one day in a downpour, and found MaryJo, my birth mother, sitting on the kitchen floor with a needle in her arm. She was an addict. I thought she was asleep, but she fell over when I touched her. I still didn't get it until a cockroach crawled out of her hair and across her face. Her eyes were still open, but she didn't blink, and that's when I realized she was dead. I ran out into the rain, screaming. Don't remember much after that except Dee taking me home with her. She was a dancer at the same club where MaryJo danced. Everybody at that club was responsible for raising me, getting me back and forth to school, helping me study . . . the whole nine yards. They were the people who kept me out of foster care. They took care of me for the first nine years of my life, and Dee was already my legal guardian. When MaryJo died, Dee quit dancing, moved us to Russellville, and became Mom. She got a job as a teller in a bank, and that's where I finished growing up. I joined ROTC in high school, and after I graduated, I went straight into the army with her blessing."

Skye was in shock. "Is she part of the promise you have to keep?"

"She's all of it. She wanted her ashes scattered at Falling Water Falls. That's where I was going when I nearly got side-swiped by a deer."

Skye looked down at the backpack beside his bed. "Her ashes are in that bag, aren't they?" she said.

He nodded, and now that I think of it, I have a change of clothes in there, as well. I don't know if they got wet, too."

"Oh, no," Skye said. "Would you like me to check?"

He nodded.

She pulled the bag between her feet and unzipped it, pulled out a pair of jeans, a long-sleeved pullover, socks, and underwear.

"Good backpack," she said. "They're dry. I'll leave them out for you." She saw the black box tucked into the bottom of the pack as she zipped it back up. "Everything else is safe and secure."

CHAPTER TWO

By nightfall, Max had eaten soup and crackers, been up twice, and was back in his own clothes. He also checked the backpack for himself to make sure the container with the ashes was still intact.

Once Skye had cell service again, she contacted the Russellville police to let them know about his wreck, then called her local doctor. He checked Max out via a zoom consultation, with a request for him to come in for a thorough checkup once the weather cleared, and then afterward, the doctor gave Skye added instructions.

"Skye, if you have any concerns about Mr. Bridger's health, don't hesitate to call," he said.

"I will, and thank you so much," she said. As soon as the consultation ended, she turned to Max. "Do you feel okay with all that?"

His mouth turned up at one corner just enough to pass for a smile. "You might be the kindest, most considerate woman I've ever had the pleasure to meet. Yes, ma'am. I am very okay with that."

Skye sighed. "I know, I know. My whole family calls me Miss Fixit. I'm probably a lot to deal with, but it's who I am. As a kid, I was always bringing home some stray cat or dog, or finding an injured animal and bringing it home to fix."

Max shook his head. "You misunderstand me. I am most grateful you rescued me. Most women wouldn't have."

Skye shrugged. "I didn't know if you were sick, hurt, or drunk, but I told myself you'd have to get better to kill me and kept driving."

He was watching her expressions with a growing sense of respect. He chuckled, and then shook his head. "Not laughing at you. Just the way you said it. I know that's a valid concern for every woman. You're something else, and I assure you, I hold strong self-sufficient women in high regard. The woman who raised me was like that."

Skye saw sadness in his eyes, but she wasn't going to ask him one more thing about his past. Everyone had a story. Whether they told it to the world or not was for them to decide, so she changed the subject.

"I saw the weather report earlier. The storm front is stalled over the area, which means this rain is likely to continue. I'm sorry you've been stranded here, but I'm glad for the company."

"I'm glad for the company, too," he said, and realized he meant it.

Skye picked up the remote and turned up the volume on the TV. "Since we know it's still raining, no need wondering what the weatherman has to say. I get Netflix. Want to watch a movie?" she asked.

"We could watch *Noah*, that movie with Russell Crowe about the biblical flood. Maybe we could get some pointers on building an ark," Max said.

Skye laughed. "Good suggestion, but I think we've both had enough rain in our lives for a bit. What's your favorite genre?"

"Anything that doesn't involve a war," he said. "I'll watch King Kong movies all day long."

"Oooh, yes! *Kong: Skull Island* is one of the best. I know that's on Netflix at the moment. Are we good with that?" she asked.

"We are so good with that," he said.

"You only had soup and crackers. Do you want a sandwich or some popcorn with your movie?"

And just like that, she'd included him in the event as if they were old friends.

"You don't need to bother with . . ."

"I'm not bothering. I'm using you as an excuse. I never watch a movie without a snack and a drink in hand. Holdover from the days when we all went to the theatre to see movies."

He smiled. "Then I'm having what you're having."

"Deal," she said, and leaped up from the sofa and flew out of the room.

Max heard doors banging, dishes rattling, and in less than five minutes, she came back with a charcuterie tray of meats, cheeses, snack crackers, and corn chips with a bowl of salsa on the side, plus two, twelve-ounce bottles of Mountain Dew.

When Max saw the bottles of pop, he flashed back on the snacks Ray used to bring him after school. The drink was always Mountain Dew.

"That looks fabulous," he said.

"That's just the savory tray. I'm going back for the sweet one," she said, and disappeared.

He laughed, and the sound startled him. He hadn't laughed in months, but it felt good—like someone had opened a door in his memory that had long since been shut. When she came back, she had two forks, two plates, and a smaller tray with cookies and a bowl of peanut M&Ms.

"I like the way you think," he said.

She handed him a plate and a fork. "Help yourself. I'm going to find the movie."

Within a few minutes, they were sitting on the sofa, their drinks in the cupholders in the console between the cushions, and the trays of snacks on the coffee table in front of them, watching Kong standing on a mountaintop roaring out across the prehistoric valley below.

A low rumble of thunder sounded off in the distance, but there was no wind and no lightning. Just a steady downpour running off the roof and onto the already rain-soaked ground below. The low-water bridge was completely submerged, but tonight it didn't matter.

If they hadn't been strangers to each other, and if Max wasn't still holding on to the burden of Dee's ashes, and if Skye hadn't been so leery of letting her guard down, they could have almost called this a blind date. One of those first meeting times when you have to decide if it's a hit or a miss. If they'd had to vote, it would have been a 'so far-so good.'

The movie was over, and the remnants of their feast were little more than crumbs, as Skye turned off the TV.

"That was fun," she said. "What made you such a fan of King Kong movies?"

"Ray loved them, and I loved Ray," he said.

"Who's Ray?"

"One of the bouncers at the club where Dee and MaryJo danced. He and Corky, the other bouncer, took turns taking me to school, and then picking me up to take me home. Ray taught me how to tie my shoes, how to open doors for girls, and how to spit."

Skye smiled. "So, spitting is an important thing for little boys to know?"

His eyes almost twinkled. "I guess. Ray thought so, anyway."

"Do they know what an amazing man you turned out to be?" she said.

Max stilled. "I wouldn't say I'm all that."

"Then I'll say it for you," Skye said, then glanced at the clock. "It's late and you have had a miserable day. You need to rest," she said, and then began gathering up their plates.

"Skye . . ."

She paused and looked up. "Yes?"

"Thank you for rescuing me," he said.

She shook her head. "You rescued yourself. I just gave you a ride."

"You took me home. To your home. You let me into your world, and I do not take that lightly," he said.

"I know. I tend to act first and think later, but in this instance, my first instinct was the right one." Then she continued to gather up the trays and plates.

"Let me help," Max said.

Skye eyed the darkening bruise on his cheek. "That bruise on your cheek is really purple now."

"Yeah, but my hands and legs are fine. I'm still going to carry one of these trays," he said.

She grinned. "Point taken and thank you."

As soon as the dirty dishes were put in the dishwasher, she wiped down the trays and put them back in a cabinet.

Max could tell she was nervous. They were about to spend a night under the same roof, and all he could think to do was lighten the moment.

"Does the door to my room lock?" he asked.

Skye turned and looked at him. "Yes. Why?"

"Not trying to insult you, or hurt your feelings, but I'll just feel more comfortable if I know you can't come storming into my room later, all full of lust and passion, and take advantage of me."

She blinked, and then burst out laughing, and threw the wet dishrag at him.

"In your dreams. Go to bed, Max Bridger."

He caught the dishrag in mid-air, laid it on the island, and walked out laughing.

She took that sound to her bedroom, paused as she closed the door, and then wondered as she turned the lock, if it was to keep him out or keep herself in her own bed where she belonged.

Max fell asleep quickly, but woke abruptly the first time he turned over. It was painfully apparent that all of the muscle injuries he had suffered were making themselves known. He got up to get some water and took another couple of pain meds before getting back in bed.

It took longer to fall asleep, but he made himself focus on the sound of rain on the roof and finally drifted off again . . . and went straight back to the chaos of war. It was his subconscious response to the pain from the wreck, translating it to pain from the shrapnel wound on his back.

It faded when he rolled over onto his side, and for a while, he slept peacefully until he heard the central heat kick on. It was just before four a.m., and he'd had enough of the bed.

He showered, dressed in his other set of clean clothes, and then headed to the front of the house. He didn't want to start coffee because that might wake Skye up, so he opted for caffeine in bottle form and got a Mountain Dew and a couple of cookies, then sat down in the dark in the living room, using sugar and caffeine to distract himself from body aches.

Every time Skye was sick or exhausted, she relived the last day of Paul's life. It always began with her in the shower and the scent of coffee wafting into the room, which told her Paul was making his to-go coffee before heading out to work. And tonight, that dream intruded.

It was the first week of the new year.

Snow was still on the ground and Paul was going back on his twenty-four shift this morning. Skye had known before she and Paul had gotten married that this would be their life, and when the alarm went off at six a.m. that morning, he bailed out of bed and headed for the shower.

Skye got up, grabbed her robe, and adjusted the thermostat to start warming the house as she headed for the kitchen to make coffee and put some bagels in the toaster. She was reaching for the eggs when she heard the water go off, which meant he'd be in the kitchen within the next ten minutes, so she began scrambling eggs.

She poured a cup of coffee to let it start cooling, buttered the bagel slices when they popped up, and dished up the eggs just as he walked into the kitchen.

"Wow, honey. Assembly line speed. Thank you!" he said, then noticed she hadn't made anything for herself.

"You're not eating?"

"I'm having coffee with you. I'll make mine after I shower."

He kissed her on the cheek and sat down. He ate as fast as he showered, and with an eye on the clock. His shift began at seven a.m., and he wouldn't be home until this time tomorrow morning. Then he'd be off for two days, then back on the twenty-four shift again.

He was chewing his last bite when he got an alert on his cell phone. He glanced at it and stood abruptly.

"Three alarm warehouse fire! Gotta go," he said, grabbed his coat and keys, and was out the door.

Startled by the abrupt departure, Skye didn't realize until he was already out the door that she didn't get to tell him goodbye. She didn't get to say the magic words . . . come home to me.

The dream shifted here, as it always did, to that knock on her door and the captain from her husband's station with that look on his face.

And then the dream ended there every time.

Except tonight.

When the door opened in the dream, it wasn't the captain on the doorstep. It was Paul. But his face was a blur. She could hear him talking, but his mouth wasn't moving.

"Skye. My Skye. We loved. So much. But I'm gone. Let me go. It was not your fault. Your magic words could not have saved me. You didn't die, so don't bury yourself alive. Be happy. Live every day with joy."

She woke abruptly, with her heart pounding. There were tears on her cheeks, but there was a peace within her she hadn't felt in years. It was a little before seven a.m., but after what had just happened, she didn't want to go back to sleep. So, she got up, showered, and dressed.

Afterward, she slipped into her office and uploaded a new post for *Skye on the Mountain*, then thought of the breakfast yet to be made and took care to be quiet as she headed for the kitchen.

She glanced into the living room as she went through the cabin turning on lights, and saw Max sprawled out on the sofa. Startled and fearing he'd gotten worse instead of better, she ran to him and immediately felt his forehead for a fever. But the moment she touched his head, he opened his eyes.

"I'm okay. Just too damn sore to get comfortable for long."

Skye breathed a sigh of relief. "Oh my God, you scared me. Is it sore muscles?"

He nodded. "Mostly."

"I have something that will help. Come with me."

Max was too tired and sore to deny the possibility of relief. So he got up, but instead of going back to his bedroom, she led him into her bedroom, turned on the lights, and pulled a wooden stool before the biggest window.

"Take off your shirt and have a seat. That way I can do front and back without you having to lie down or roll over on already sore spots."

He pulled the shirt over his head and sat. He eyed the blue and white colors throughout the room and the king-size bed up against one wall, then saw Skye coming out of the adjoining bathroom carrying a small handbasket full of jars and bottles.

She was all business as she set the basket on her dresser and sorted through the contents before choosing a round crock-like container about four-inches tall with the circumference of an oatmeal box. The moment she removed the lid, the scent of mint was in the air.

"Are you allergic to anything topical?" she asked.

"No, but that smells good. What is it?" he asked.

"Just some stuff I use on my patients."

He frowned. "Are you a doctor?"

"No, a part-time physical therapist for a clinic down in Russellville. One more question . . . I can see the bruises, so I know those places are bound to be sore, but are any of the scars on your back sensitive to touch?"

"No. They're old and long-since healed," he said.

"Okay then. Try to relax. I'm still going the gentle route," she said, then dipped her fingers into the fragrant ointment and started rubbing it in at the back of his neck and then his shoulders, going back now and then for more.

As soon as she had the surface of his back lightly coated, she went back to his neck and started massaging the tense muscle structure until she felt the knots releasing then began working along the length of his spine.

Max hadn't said a word since she began, but when his head dropped forward and his eyes closed, she knew he was getting relief.

"Moving to your chest and ribs," she said softly, and switched her position from behind him to in front of him.

The moment Skye stepped between Max's legs, his head came up and his eyes opened. They were face to face, so close he could feel her breath on his face. Then he saw his reflection in her eyes, and for a moment, he let himself believe it was his own salvation he saw.

"You have the prettiest green eyes I've ever seen," he said.

Skye's heart skipped, and then she began lightly applying the ointment in the darkest bruises with the palm of her hand.

"Thank you," she said, and then smiled. "My brother, Sean, called me 'Froggy' when I was little, because my eyes were as green as the little tree frogs in the woods. So, of course, I wanted my eyes to change to another color so he would stop."

"Did he stop?" Max asked.

"Only after Mom made him. I'm the youngest of three. Sean is the oldest, Marie is the middle child, and I'm the baby. This cabin was the Wray family gathering spot when we were growing up."

"Your maiden name was Ray?"

"The Irish spelling of Ray . . . with a W."

"Ah . . . Wray. I guess you come by those green eyes honestly," he said.

She glanced up briefly. "I suppose I do," she said, and then applied the last bit of ointment onto the bruise on his left shoulder. "When you hit the tree, did it throw you into the driver's side door?"

"Yes. That's where the cut came from. The rest of all this came from crawling up through all the brush and trees I mowed over before landing in a thicket. The blessing was that the car never rolled. It was just a wild ride on the way down."

She shook her head, frowning. "It's a miracle you lived, let alone were able to get yourself back up to the road. It's also why your shoulder is bruised and why the muscles are knotted up on this side of your neck. You used your upper body strength for the climb." She stepped back, eyeing the upper part of his chest and then nodded. "I think that should do it."

She turned around, retrieved his shirt from the back of a chair and handed it to him.

He pulled the shirt back over his head and was easing his arms into the sleeves when she took the basket back to the bathroom and then began washing the ointment from her hands. Even after they were clean, her skin still bore the lingering scent.

She walked back into the room to find him still sitting on the stool but looking out the window to the woods beyond. She walked up behind him and put a hand on his shoulder.

"It's beautiful here, isn't it?" she said.

He nodded, then glanced at her. "Everything here is beautiful."

It was the look in his eyes that made her heart thump. It was time to get out of the bedroom.

"I'm going to make coffee and buckwheat pancakes. Are you interested?"

He grinned. "You ask a man my size if he wants to eat?"

She laughed. "Dumb question?"

"Well, unnecessary at best, and yes, ma'am, I am more than interested," he said, and followed her down the hall and into the kitchen.

"You sit," Skye said, as she began making coffee. "I don't want you undoing the good I just did. And today you spend the day on the sofa in front of the TV or in your bed. It's still raining, and the front hasn't moved. Hopefully it will come to an end, at least by tomorrow, and then we'll have to wait until the flooded creek crests. Guess you're stuck with me."

"No worries. I will treasure every minute I get to spend here. I'm in no hurry to exit the premises," he said.

She flashed him a quick smile and then began breaking eggs in the bowl for the pancake batter, added buttermilk, baking soda, a little vegetable oil, then the buckwheat flour. Minutes later, she was flipping pancakes like a pro and piling them up on a plate. Butter, syrup, and molasses were on the table as she brought the pancakes with her, then sat down.

"Help yourself, Max. Did you take anything for pain this morning?"

"A couple of what you've been giving me, but that was at about four a.m."

She frowned. "You're due another dose," she said, and bolted out of the room, then came back a few moments later and put the pills on the table beside his plate.

He looked up. "Sit yourself down, darlin' and quit fussing over me. These pancakes are so good. You need to eat while they're still hot."

She blinked at the word, darlin', wondering if he even knew he'd said it, then sat and did what he'd said because it saved her from having to talk. All of a sudden, she didn't know what to say.

Water dripped from the eaves. The sky was clearing. And in the quiet of the cabin, they could both hear the rush of water running over the low-water bridge.

Max was thinking to himself about the randomness of life. How starting a day to complete one task had turned into a near-death experience, but then a rescue from an angel with green eyes had changed everything. He thought of the ashes he had yet to scatter, but there was no rush. A day. A week. A year. None of that meant anything to his mom now. He was the one left behind again.

He glanced at Skye when she wasn't looking—then at the curve of her cheek, the shape of her mouth, the quiet strength within her—and thought about her self-imposed exile. She'd lost the man she loved. Would she ever love another? *I could easily fall for the woman she is, but is she even an option? A relationship might be the last thing she wants.*

Unaware she'd become the focus of Max's silence, Skye finished eating, got up to top off his coffee, and then began cleaning up, because that's what she'd been doing every day for the last eight years. Going through the motions.

Alone.

Her mother and siblings still came to the cabin for Easter and Christmas. They stayed in constant contact. One or more of her family would call her or video chat with her every week, but she knew they all worried about her living up here on her own. What she didn't do was dwell on their fears. That was on them. She felt safe here, and the occasional glimpse of wildlife coming and going in the woods had become commonplace, not something she feared.

She'd found injured birds and fed them until they healed. She'd made a winter shelter once out behind the shed for a crippled raccoon and had fed him until he'd left on his own. One day he'd been there, and then he'd gone.

She'd been rescuing strays and hurt animals all her life, but Max was the first human she'd taken in to heal, and it was working. He was getting better, but the weather was not.

She had no idea when she would be able to cross the bridge, but when that happened, he'd be gone, and his absence would be missed. He'd filled up the empty space in the cabin, and if she was of a mind to let him in, he might become the one to fill up the empty space within her heart. But he was a stranger, and it was scary to be vulnerable. So, she'd stay in her caretaker shoes instead of risking her heart.

"Max, it's a little cool this morning, but if you want some air, the view from the front porch is beautiful and peaceful, even when it rains. The water rushing over the bridge sounds like its own little waterfall. Your jacket is clean and hanging on the hall tree as you go out."

"Will you come with me?" he asked.

She hesitated, but the longing in his voice was her undoing. "Yes, sure. Just let me get my jacket."

As she'd promised, the continuing downpour and the elevation of the cabin made the morning almost chilly. She thought of the gas cans still in the back of her truck, but there was no hurry. Moving them to the shed could have wait.

They sat side by side on the bench, glanced at each other, smiled, then looked away.

Max sighed. "Awkward as hell, trying to make conversation with a stranger, isn't it? All I can say is, I wish you weren't . . . a stranger, I mean. I'm really sorry you lost the man you loved."

Skye looked at him again, but he wasn't looking at her. He was looking down the drive toward the road.

"Thank you. The strange part now is that I've been widowed far longer than I was married. Some days I don't even think about it. Other days I feel like life is passing me by. I came up here to heal, and I did. What surprised me was that I didn't miss city living, and the longer I stayed here, the more settled into solitude I became. I don't feel like I'm a hermit, but I think I learned early about what mattered most. Not the new clothes or getting my hair and nails done. No more lunching with friends or going to parties. All of those things were erased from my to-do lists a long time ago."

Max shifted so he was facing her. "What if one day, someone came along who really wanted to get to know you . . . with the option of a relationship becoming a possibility? How would you feel?"

Her heart skipped. "It would depend on the someone. I wouldn't want to pretend just for the sake of never being alone.

I would want love. Deep and abiding . . . and passion. I miss that. I miss that heartbeat skip. I miss laughing with someone. I miss love. But for me, either there's an instant attraction, or there's not."

She watched him nod, then look away, and knew then he would never ask without a sign. He wouldn't insert himself into her life without an invitation. And she also knew that if she said nothing now, she was going to regret it for the rest of her life.

"So? Did all that scare you off?" she said.

Max looked up at her again. "I don't scare easy. But I also know how to read the signs, and the last thing I would ever do was make you afraid of me."

Skye leaned forward, then put her hand on his arm. "There are no 'Keep Off the Grass' signs on me. There are no 'Trespassers Will Be Shot' signs on this property. This is just me, thinking you might be the best stray I ever brought home."

A slow smile slid across Max's face as he reached for her hand and threaded his fingers through hers. But before either of them could take the conversation further, Skye caught a glimpse of movement from the corner of her eye and turned to look toward the creek, trying to focus through the rain when she suddenly gasped. "That's old Grumpy."

Max followed her gaze. "That's a really big black bear."

"And something is wrong with him," she said, as she got up and walked to the edge of the porch.

Max followed, watching the bear staggering and weaving back and forth.

"So, that bear has a name?"

She nodded. "It's one of the park rangers' tagged bears. See the tags in his ears! I've got to call Avery Nelson. He's the head ranger in the area," she said, and reached for her phone.

Max stood aside, watching the bear and listening to the conversation she'd put on Speaker.

"Avery, this is Skye Raley. Yes, the weather is a mess, for sure, but that's part of why I'm calling. One of your tagged bears is on the north side of the creek running through my place. You need to get some men here fast. He's either sick or hurt. He's staggering and stumbling all over the place, and I think it's Grumpy."

"Well damn it," Avery said. "I'll get some men headed there ASAP. I don't have to tell you to stay away from him."

"No, of course not, but the rain is really heavy, and my low-water bridge is flooded at the moment. Hurry. He might wander off," she said.

"Just keep an eye on him for me. I'm dispatching my men. Even if it leaves the area, you'll be able to tell them which way it went."

"Yes, I will," Skye said, then took Max's hand. "We need to sit back down and stay still," she said.

They sat with Skye holding her phone, and Max put his arm around her shoulder. She knew it was a gesture of protection and was glad of his presence. They sat motionless and silent, watching the bear swaying back and forth on all fours until it suddenly fell over and didn't move.

"Oh no. Poor Grumpy. I can't imagine what has happened to him," she whispered.

"You did the right thing when you called for help. Now we just wait with him, right?"

"Yes," she said, then moments later, Avery called her again.

"Is he still there?"

"Yes, but he fell over and isn't moving anymore," she said.

"I'll radio the rangers enroute to tell them the incident is critical," he said. "Call me if anything changes," he said.

Skye's heart was pounding. When she finally saw a dark green Ranger truck come around the curve in her drive, and another one right behind it, she breathed a sigh of relief.

"They're here, thank God."

"You did good, Skye. They'll take it from here," Max said, and gave her hand a quick squeeze.

The bear was being pelted by the rain, but when it heard the vehicles, it raised its head and instead of slipping into the woods as it would normally have done, fell back without trying to run.

Both rangers were already out, and both of them were carrying guns. One was a dart gun. The other was a hunting rifle, if worse came to worse.

"If they shoot the rifle, we're in the line of fire," Max said. "We need to get inside now," and without asking, he grabbed her hand and took her into the cabin. Once inside, they moved to a window on the far side of the living room to watch. Skye was shivering. Max grabbed a blanket from the sofa and draped it across her shoulders.

"Thank you, but I'm shaking as much from the fear of what happens next than I am from the cold. Lord, I hope they don't have to put the old bear down. Grumpy is the oldest bear on the mountain."

Max was standing behind her, looking over her head as the rangers began moving closer. Again, it was the instinct to comfort her that prompted him to put his arms around her shoulders and pull her closer.

Slowly, her shivering stopped as they watched one ranger with the dart gun fire. The bear reacted when it hit, but it didn't try to run. And when another ranger arrived with a big cage on the back of a trailer, the local vet was right behind him. They all rushed to where the bear was lying.

Max and Skye watched from the window as the vet began his examination. Afterward, they rolled the bear onto a heavy canvas and began pulling it toward the catch cage, then they dragged it inside. Once the bear was inside the cage, they used a winch to pull it back onto the trailer, tied it down, then backed out and drove away.

Skye got a call from Avery as the last ranger was driving away.

"Skye, thank you again for calling," Avery said. "It was Grumpy. The vet says the bear is sick, not injured, and doesn't know for sure what's wrong until he can run some tests. At any rate, if he can be saved, it will be thanks to you."

Skye felt sad. "Thanks for letting me know. I hate the thought of not seeing him rambling through the woods anymore, so I'm going to hope for the best," she said, and then disconnected and glanced at Max. "The bear wasn't injured, but he's sick. They're running tests."

"I'm sorry," Max said. "It's hard when we lose someone or something that matters to us, isn't it?"

She frowned and then looked away. "Fate is so out of our hands."

"Which is why we shouldn't waste the time we're given," Max said.

Skye nodded. "Truth, for sure, but I think you need to rest for a while and let the analgesic ointment do its thing."

He saluted her. "Yes, ma'am."

"Don't give me that look. I'm not bossy. I'm just right," Skye said, and pointed down the hall.

"This is me, going to bed now," he said, and was smiling as he walked away.

CHAPTER THREE

Max sat down on the side of the bed to take off his boots, but the moment his head hit the pillow, he breathed a sigh of relief. Skye was right.

He pulled a blanket over himself, closed his eyes, and went to war. Back to the battles, and the deaths, and the roadside bombs, and the men under his command who hadn't make it back to camp.

Unaware that Max's dreams had taken him to a place of unrest, Skye when into the garage to get meat from the freezer and took it inside to thaw for later, then made herself a cold drink and headed to her office to catch up on the blog. There were always questions waiting for her, and comments to read, so she settled in, logged onto the site, and started reading questions and answering as she went.

About an hour later, her phone rang. She glanced at the Caller ID and answered.

"Hello, this is Skye."

"Skye, it's me, Reggie. We need you to cover for one of the therapists tomorrow. He has clients beginning at nine a.m. to just after three p.m."

"Sorry, Reggie, but I can't. My road is flooded. It's still raining, and I'm going nowhere until the water subsides. I also sort of rescued an accident victim on the way home yesterday, and now he's flooded in with me at the moment and recuperating in my home."

"Good grief," Reggie said. "Does he need a hospital?"

"Oh, we've already been that route. We did a Zoom exam with my personal doctor right after I got him home. As far as I'm concerned, he's a walking miracle. He swerved to miss a deer and went off the side of the mountain. The trees' downslope finally stopped the slide, but he had to rescue himself and climb back up to the main road. I almost didn't see him for the downpour, but by that time he was staggering. I loaded him up and took him home. Nothing is broken. He's past the stage of any kind of serious concussion, but he's bruised and scratched up. That happened yesterday. He woke up this morning extremely stiff and sore, so I used some of that mint analgesic on him like we use at the facility."

"Well, good call," Reggie said. "You know what to do, so I'm confident he's in good hands. Hope he gets well without issues. Catch you next time, okay?"

"Absolutely," Skye said, and disconnected, then went back to her blog and did a live "Chat With" session for about an hour with some of her followers.

She was just about to sign off for the day when she heard footsteps in the hall and looked up just as Max walked in.

She smiled. "Hey you. Were you able to get some rest?"

He didn't mention dreams because he didn't want to talk about them. So, he focused on her instead.

"I did, and I am minty-fresh, to boot," he said.

She grinned. "I was just finishing up here. Give me a sec, and we'll go scrounge up some lunch."

"I heard the click-clack of the keyboard as I was coming up the hall," he said.

"I was behind on answering questions from my daily blog. It's called *Skye on the Mountain*."

His eyes widened in surprise. "You have a public blog?"

She shrugged. "I started it not long after I moved here, because I was beginning to realize how thoroughly I'd isolated myself. So, I just wrote my story, and then kept writing. I gained some advertising, which adds to my income, and now I have online followers from all over the world."

"What do you write about?" he asked.

"Just stuff I do, and the animals I see. And the weather, and the hassles of life . . . good and bad," she said.

He sat down in the chair next to her desk. "Are you going to write about rescuing me?"

"Never without asking you first," she said.

"Then write away. People should know what an amazing person you are."

"I won't use your last name, but I would love to tell them about this really brave man named Max, who went off the side of a mountain and then turned around and rescued himself," she said.

He nodded. "Fine with me, just promise you won't leave out the part about you saving me."

"Deal. But right now, I'm thinking about tomato soup and grilled cheese sandwiches. Feel free to stretch out on the sofa to watch TV, or follow me to the kitchen and be my taste tester."

The thought went through Max's head that she didn't have to ask. Two days. Two days was all it had taken for her to break the wall around his heart, and she wasn't even trying. He was at the point now that he would follow her anywhere.

"I think I should introduce you to yet another shining facet of myself. I am the world's best taste tester," he said.

Skye was watching the way the light caught in his hair, turning the thick black thatch to almost blue, and the way his eyes twinkled when he was teasing. Then she realized he was waiting for her response. "Your modesty becomes you. You're hired."

"I'm just being honest. I'm not the best cook, but I am a formidable nibbler."

She laughed, then pointed to the door. "So, go on with you, Max Bridger. I'll get out the goods to make lunch, and you show me what you've got." Minutes later, he was sitting at the table with his own little plate, testing out three different kinds of cheese and a few apple slices to go with them.

"And how does the royal taster rate the cheeses? Does he want cheddar, Havarti, or Provolone in his grilled cheese sandwich?" Skye asked.

"Could he have Cheddar and Havarti?" Max asked.

"Two sandwiches, or both kinds of cheese on one sandwich?" Skye asked.

"Yes," he said.

She blinked, and then burst out laughing. "Clearly, I have forgotten what it means to feed a big man. Two sandwiches with two kinds of cheese, coming up."

Max swallowed past a sudden lump in his throat as her laughter rolled through him. It had been so long since he'd felt any kind of joy that it took him by surprise. Watching his mom wasting away before his eyes had numbed him. When she'd finally taken her last breath, he'd been so relieved she was no longer suffering that he hadn't cried, and even now, he had yet to shed a tear.

Part of his problem, and he knew it, was that he'd lost his roots. He didn't know where he belonged anymore. The army had been his life for twenty-five years, and always with Dee in the background, keeping home in his heart. But retiring from the military, then going home to a dying woman, had changed the whole dynamic of his life.

He took a drink of the iced tea Skye had given him and then leaned back to watch her at work. She was so much more than pretty. And the more he learned about her, the more amazed he became. She'd found her own way through a traumatic life event and made peace with it. He understood that process. He knew how it felt.

Their backgrounds couldn't have been more different, but life had dealt them similar blows. Her husband and father. His two mothers. He and Skye's paths had crossed because of fate. What happened next was up to them.

When she came toward the table carrying their plates, he sat up.

"Soup's coming up," she said, and went back for the bowls. As soon as she sat down, she looked up and smiled at him from across the table.

"Max Bridger, I'm so sorry for what happened to you, but I'm really glad you're here."

"I'd do it all over again for the pleasure of your company," he said. A long look passed between them, and then Max picked up his glass. "A toast to the angel who saved me in the storm. To Skye on the mountain."

Skye's eyes welled. "Then I must thank you, as well, for giving back something to me that I thought I'd lost."

"What's that?" Max asked.

"An emotional connection to another man. Not asking you for anything. I just wanted to say that out loud—to hear myself admit it was real."

Max's heart thumped and then kicked back into a normal rhythm. Hearing those words gave him hope there could be more. "Is the phrase, *I feel like I've been waiting for you all my life*, too corny?"

Skye sighed. "No," she said, then picked up her spoon to taste the soup. "It's still a bit hot. Don't burn your tongue."

"Got it," he said, then dunked the corner of one of the sandwiches in the soup and took a bite, rolling his eyes as he chewed and swallowed. "It's all about the cheese and the crunch, right?"

She nodded. "The buttery crunch sells it every time."

They kept the rest of their conversation on the light side as they ate. He shared stories of his life being rocked to sleep in the back room of a club of exotic dancers and burped by the bouncers. And how they'd protected him from becoming lost in the foster care system by being the family MaryJo couldn't give him.

"They had a closet in the dressing room that became my personal nursery. They removed the door and emptied all of their costumes out of it, shoved a baby bed inside it, cobbled up some shelves, and got away with it for almost three years before Social Services found out. After that, my babysitters were whoever was off work at the club until I started school. I guess I became accustomed early on to the music in the front of the club and the noise. The back became a no-smoking area because of me. Of course, I don't remember this happening, but as I got older, they never let me forget that one of my favorite teether toys was the cup of one of the exotic dancer's padded bras. And they taught me to count with the dollar bills that got stuffed into their costumes."

Skye laughed, and clapped her hands in delight. "Max! That's amazing. The absolute best daycare in the world. A dozen helpers for one special baby."

"I never thought about it like that, but I guess you're right," he said. "It was just my world."

"And there I was, the youngest of three children. I grew up with all of the perks, and it still didn't make my life impervious to failure or despair. I met an old man in the park in Hot Springs not long after Paul's death. I was sitting alone, absently tossing peanuts to the squirrels, when he just appeared in front of me. I couldn't have guessed his age if I tried, but he had the clearest blue eyes I'd ever seen, a long graying beard, and long dark hair well past his shoulders. He was dressed in a suit. His shoes were shining, and the walking cane in his hand had a hammered silver handle. The first words out of his mouth were, 'You are at a crossroad.'"

"What did you think when he asked that?" Max asked.

"That he was about to try and pass himself off as some physic for a fee."

"I probably would have thought the same thing," Max said. "So, what happened?"

"It was like he'd read my mind. He said, 'I didn't come for your money. I came with a message. You will find new purpose, but not here. Look to the mountains. Life waits for you there.' Then I blinked, and he was gone. I swear to God, one second, he was in front of me, blocking out the sun in my eyes, and then he just disappeared." She sighed. "I never told anyone this before, so if you repeat it, I will say that you lied. And this all happened after Paul died, and before my mother deeded me this place as my home. I have come to believe that there is but a small curtain between this world and the next, and sometimes, the people we meet are really angels in disguise."

Max reached for her hand. "I don't doubt that for a second. That's why I first thought you were an angel—because you came when I needed one most."

She gave his hand a quick squeeze and then let go. "At least you don't think I'm crazy," she said.

The meal ended, and then they cleaned up the kitchen together. Max hung up the dishtowel as Skye put the last of the dishes in the dishwasher.

"If I wasn't here, what would you be doing now?" Max asked, as they moved into the living area and sat down.

"Walking to the mailbox to get the mail. It's full of two days' worth by now. I used to mow the grass around the cabin, but I figured out that deer keep it eaten for me. All the wildlife precludes the urge to plant flowers or grow a garden. I'd never get anything grown for them eating it to the ground. I like to read in bed, so I'm always uploading books on my Kindle. And when I want to hear voices, I watch TV. What are some things you like to do in your downtime?" Skye said.

"This may sound weird, but I honestly don't know. Everything is organized and programmed in the military and having leave isn't like planning a holiday to somewhere fun. I thought I'd discover all that when I came home, but you know how that turned out. Now I can't think beyond fulfilling Mom's last wish. It's weighing on me like a light I left on, and until I do that, I won't be able to turn it off," he said.

He sounded lost and Skye knew how that felt. But when the water did go down, he would leave, and then they'd both be lost again. Some days life sucked eggs, but she didn't want to be the one to deter his quest.

"Whenever we can get out, you can take my truck to the falls. It's not far from here," she said.

He leaned forward, his elbows on his knees as he stared at the floor, then looked up.

"Would you go with me?" he asked.

Skye answered without hesitation. "Absolutely."

He sighed. "Thank you."

Before she could respond, his cell phone rang. He glanced at the caller ID.

"My insurance agent," he said, and answered. "Hello, this is Max."

"Max, this is Clyde Burns. First of all, how are you?"

"I'm okay. Nothing broken. Just sore and bruised. Did you find the Jeep?" Max asked.

"That's why I'm calling. We had to use a drone to find it. Apparently, the wind and rain from the second wave of storms shifted it from where it first landed. It is now at the bottom of the canyon. It's been totaled out, and since it's a brand-new model, we'll be sending you a check for full replacement. I just need to confirm your current mailing address is the one in Russellville."

"Yes, that's correct," Max said.

"Duly noted," Clyde said. "Okay . . . take care and let me know when you replace your vehicle. We'll get you insured ASAP."

"Thanks, Clyde. I'll be in touch." Max disconnected, then looked back at Skye. "They had to use a drone to find the Jeep. He said the last storm likely shifted it enough that it slid the rest of the way into the canyon. Good thing I wasn't trapped in there waiting to be rescued," he said.

Skye paled. "Oh my God."

"Exactly," Max said. "If that wreck had to happen, I'm really thankful it wasn't raining when it did, and I didn't have to cope with trying to climb a mountain in the rain. I also didn't have anyone shooting at me or firing missiles at my location. In the grand scheme of things, the fact that I was still mobile when the slide ended was the first miracle. You finding me was my second."

Skye hesitated, measuring her words before she spoke. "Do you believe that when certain things happen, it's meant to be?"

He locked into the look she was giving him, wondering where she was going with this. "Are you talking about fate?"

She shrugged. "Maybe. I readily accept that a lot of things happen to people because of other people's actions. But there's a part of me that's always felt like I chose a road, and the rest came with it before I was born. And that whatever I encounter along that road is happening for a reason. Either I'm meant to learn something I didn't understand before, or I'm helping someone else learn it."

The hair stood up on the back of Max's neck. He moved toward her, and moments later, they were sitting face to face.

"I have lived with this same belief all my life. It's how I survived a drug-addicted parent. I was always telling myself that MaryJo kept me when she could have given me up to the state. That something within her had needed to keep her baby to make her life mean something. During all I witnessed and lived through in service to my country, then going off the side of a mountain and still being alive after the crash, I have accepted it as part of the road. The fact that I still believed and accepted the appearance of an angel in a storm was just another stop on the road I was traveling, until I woke up to you. It doesn't matter that I only met you two days ago. In my heart, it feels like you've been waiting for me to arrive."

Her eyes widened. She reached for him then, cupping his face, taking care not to touch all the places where he'd been hurt.

"I don't know what happens next, Max Bridger. I don't know where your road takes you after I take you home. I don't have a claim on any part of you. You owe me nothing. But I know that if I don't let you love me before you leave, I will regret it for the rest of my life."

Then she was in his arms, feeling his hands on her body, and his mouth on her lips, and it felt like home.

"My bed, so I will remember you there with me," she whispered.

He picked her up in his arms.

"Max, you'll hurt yourself," she said.

"I know how to hurt. But I don't think I'll know how to be without you," he said, and carried her down the hall.

The first time they'd been in a bedroom together, she'd undressed him, but not this time. Clothes came off with abandon, and then they were lying face to face. Without saying a word, he reached for her, slid his hand beneath her hair and moved forward.

Skye was wondering what it would feel like to kiss him when she felt his mouth on her lips. One staggering, endless kiss later, and she had the answer. It was soft, relentless, seduction that ended with a gentle nip to her earlobe, and then his hands were on her body, tracing every curve with his fingers and then his tongue.

Her fingers were in his hair, and the room was spinning. She could hear the hammer of her own heartbeat in her ears as he rose above her, and then he was in her.

The wet heat enveloped Max as he slid inside her body. Her soft, incoherent whispers rose between them as he began to move. Her breath was warm on his face. She was intoxicating, and he couldn't slow down. He'd been too long without a woman, and she'd been too long without a man. Within a few short minutes, the end result was inevitable.

Skye had already lost focus on everything but the climax she could feel coming, then between one breath and the next, it washed over her in a blinding flash of ecstasy. When it did, she took Max with her, leaving him spent and breathless.

Twice, he tried to speak but couldn't voice what he was feeling, then rolled over, taking her with him.

Once again, they were lying face to face, but her vision was blurred with tears, and unaware that he was drowning in them.

Max wanted to say 'I love you' but it was too soon. She wouldn't believe it, so he said nothing.

Skye didn't regret one single moment, but she already knew that losing him was going to hurt in ways she had never experienced.

Instead of pillow talk, they clung to each other without moving, without talking, while the sun began to set.

Finally, Max raised up on one elbow and looked down at her face. "That was the single most perfect moment of my life, and if you regret it, I don't want to know."

She shook her head. "Regret? For feeling treasured? For being loved in a way I didn't know I needed? Don't ever doubt you are forever in my heart."

Tears were running down her cheeks as she got up and disappeared into the bathroom. He heard her turn on the shower and thought about joining her, but she'd closed the door between them, and it felt like the finale of the greatest day of his life.

He got up, gathering his clothes as he went, and walked down the hall to his bedroom to shower. When he came out, he smelled food cooking and headed for the kitchen.

She turned at the sound of his steps. He could tell she'd been crying, but she smiled at him anyway, and the world settled back down on its axis.

"It got late on us," she said. "I'm making breakfast for dinner. Biscuits are almost done, and then we can eat. I hope you like them."

He thought of all the years in mess halls, MREs in the field, the food in the officers' mess, and smiled. "Remember those two grilled cheese sandwiches? So, I like biscuits even better."

"If you want to hear my little waterfall, take a peek at the bridge."

He went out the front door onto the porch, peering through the shadows to the creek beyond. The rain was still falling, and the water running over the bridge sounded like it had also captured the wind within it. It wasn't an actual roar—closer to rushing hiss. And she was right. The road was still impassable. He was past ready to honor his mom's last wishes, and at the same time, so sad to think about leaving Skye that it hurt to draw breath.

He glanced up at the darkening sky. "If anybody up there is listening, I want her. Please let her want me back." When he went inside, Skye was putting food on the table. "Smells good, looks amazing, and you were right. The water is crazy, and it has yet to crest. You're still stuck with me."

She shook her head. "I'm not complaining. I'm just sorry your reason for even being here has been delayed again."

"You can't seriously expect me to complain after what we just shared," he said, and sat down.

She paused, then walked over to him. "Look at me," she said.

He did and saw tears on the verge of spilling down her face.

"This is not my 'I want you gone' face. This is my afraid face—afraid what you're feeling is all wrapped up in gratitude."

He sighed. "I have had gratitude for many people for many things, but it never felt like this. You'll just have to trust and believe me. Give it time. Give yourself time. I'm a man who never had the luxury of debating decisions. I have acted on my instincts all my life, and I'm still here. I know what I want. I want you to want me the way I want you. Not casual sex. Forever love. Just stop trying to figure out the details and let whatever happens, happen, and the biscuits are getting cold."

She sat down hard and passed the biscuits but couldn't quit shaking inside.

An owl hooted somewhere close to the kitchen window. Max heard it and paused.

She glanced toward the window. "That's Greg. He always comes to say hello before he heads out on the hunt."

The corner of his mouth tilted slightly. "You named your owl?"

She shrugged. "He's not really my owl. But I pretend I matter to him."

"Well, you don't have to pretend that you matter to me, because you do. Pass the butter, please."

They managed to make small talk all the way through the meal. After, while Max was helping her clean up, his phone rang as they were cleaning up. He glanced at Caller ID and frowned.

"A realtor has called me every week since Mom passed, reminding me that if I decide to sell the house, he wants to list it. Damn buzzard," he muttered, and let it go to voicemail.

"How awful," Skye said. "There's so much paperwork involved in dying. Everybody wants a piece of what's left. I went through it with Paul. I saw Mom going through it after Dad passed, too. I'm sorry that's happening, Max. Truly sorry."

He shrugged. "Not your fault, honey, but I've been ignoring calls and haven't bothered to check email since you brought me here. I guess I need to do that, okay?"

"Of course, and have a good soak in a hot bath. When you get out, I'll put some more minty stuff on your shoulders."

"Deal," he said, as he leaned down and brushed a kiss across her lips.

CHAPTER FOUR

Skye was already in her nightgown, lying on the bed watching TV when he walked in, wearing nothing but a big bath towel wrapped around his waist. She turned off the TV, picked up the jar of ointment beside her, and rolled out of bed. She was about to open the jar when he stopped her with a look.

She froze. Even with the distance between them, she felt the intensity. Slowly, she put the jar aside, pulled her nightgown over her head and stretched out on the bed she'd already turned back.

He dropped the towel and slipped into bed beside her. He was hard and aching as she reached for him.

"Make love to me, Max."

He rose above her, then slid into the soft, wet warmth of her. She moaned as he began to move.

Greg the owl sounded off on his way past the window.

It was the last conscious thing they heard as the lovemaking began. Time stopped. The first time had been out of their control, but this time the tension built slower. The tease for a climax kept ebbing and flowing. Their hearts were beating faster, and their movements more urgent, and then the climax hit, shattering focus and breath. Satisfied and satiated, he pulled the covers up over both of them and just held her.

Skye was wrapped in his arms, her head on his shoulder, knowing how utterly perfect they were together. "Oh Max . . . what am I . . .?"

"Sleep, darlin'. Just sleep. You can start your worrying all over again tomorrow."

Making love to Skye might have been the best thing Max had ever experienced but losing her was going to be the worst. By the time the new day dawned, the rain had stopped. Yet even in the bedroom and behind a closed door, he could still hear the rushing water.

He'd been awake since before daylight watching her sleep. She lay on her side facing him, and he quietly waited for her to open those beautiful green eyes. Finally, he saw her stir and laid his hand over hers.

She woke up. "You're still here. I was dreaming you were gone."

"Sounds like a nightmare to me," he said, and kissed her the rest of the way awake.

They made love without haste, touching, stroking, until he slipped his arm beneath her and rolled her on top of him, then he was inside her. His hands were at her waist, holding her fast, rocking her into a whole other level of ecstasy, until she collapsed in his arms. He rested his chin against the top of her head waiting for his heart to slip back into a normal rhythm.

"Sweet Lord, Skye, you're under my skin. You're in my blood. How does this work? You tell me, because walking away from you and this isn't happening."

"I can't lie. I don't want to lose you, but you still have something important you need to do for your mom, and I have a favor to ask of you."

"Anything," he said.

"When I take you home, use that time away to re-assess how you really feel. Get your new car. Catch up on whatever still needed doing before you left home that day. You call me, and I'll answer every time. But I can't do all this with you without knowing it's forever. I survived loss once. But to have my heart broken when I've fallen this hard, this fast, would destroy me."

"I'll do whatever it takes to reassure you of that, okay? But I won't quit you. Now, no more sad face. No more worry. And I have a question."

"What is it?" she asked.

"Do you have any disposable razors?"

She ran her hand over his three-day growth of black whiskers. "Yes, I do, and there's shaving cream and aftershave to go with it. It's my brother's stash, but he won't mind sharing a bit."

She rolled out of his arms and walked into the guest bathroom to get the shaving kit and handed it to him with a kiss. "I'm going to shower and then make us some breakfast."

"Suits me, and thank you for the shaving stuff."

"We can thank Sean for that. He never gets home with everything he brings. Take your time. We're still stranded until the water goes down."

While he went to shave, Skye showered and dressed. She wasn't in the mood to cook, and decided on toast and cereal, which took no prep time.

So, she started the coffee then went to the office to upload a new post on her blog. As she was working, she got a text from Avery Nelson.

Thought you might like an update. Grumpy the bear is recovering nicely, and we'll be releasing him back into his territory in about a week. Just waiting to make sure the old guy has his legs back under him before we let him go. Thanks to you, Grumpy lives to grump another day.

Skye smiled. It was the best news of the day.

After that, the day seemed to slip away. She finally got to unload the fuel from the truck bed and cleaned it out for their trip tomorrow. One moment they were having lunch together, and then it was night.

They made love in the dark, hiding Skye's tears of regret for what was coming, and once again, they fell asleep in each other's arms. But the next morning, she woke up alone. When she heard the shower running in the bedroom down the hall, her heart skipped. Max was already up! Today was the day of scattering ashes and then taking him home.

She threw back the covers and went to wash up. She was getting dressed when she heard him come out of his bedroom. The cadence in his steps sounded like a soldier on the march. Today was going to be a hard day for him.

She left the room in haste and went straight to the kitchen. His backpack was beside the door leading into the garage, but he was nowhere in sight. She started coffee, put some bread in the toaster, got cereal from the pantry, then went to look for him and found him on the front porch with his hands in his pockets, looking out into the surrounding woods. There was a stillness within him she'd never seen, and then, as if sensing her presence, he turned, and she saw the look on his face. He was saying goodbye.

"Max . . ."

"You are a beautiful woman, and you live in a beautiful world. I was blessed to be one of your strays."

She reached for his hand. "You are far more than a stray. You're not going to lose me unless you make that choice. But you need to make sure what you feel is more than gratitude."

He shrugged. "I've had female doctors put my body back together. I've had Army nurses debriding dead skin from old wounds. I never once felt anything for them but gratitude. I didn't want to sleep with them. I didn't tell myself I'd fallen in love with them. I'm a grown-ass man who knows his own mind." He paused, looked away, and then back at her. "I think you're the one who's afraid of commitment. But that's how I roll. I would never judge your personal feelings as wrong. In my mind, you're worth waiting for." He touched her hair, then slid that hand back into his pocket. "I'm ready to go when you are."

Skye was taken aback. Her perception of him had just done a one-eighty. That wasn't a man trying to justify his feelings. He believed everything he said.

"Then I guess I'm going to have to have a 'Come to Jesus' moment with myself. I came outside to tell you breakfast is on the table. Just cereal and toast," she said, and went back inside.

Max followed.

Their conversation while they ate was brief and stilted.

Skye had issued her ultimatum, and Max had responded with a volley of reasoning she hadn't seen coming. The scary part was that he was right. She was afraid of her feelings. She'd been alone on the mountain too long. She'd forgotten what it was like to have a partner, but she wasn't going to start some big debate. It would be futile. Max Bridger already knew what he wanted. He wanted her.

Dishes went in the sink. The box of cereal went back in the pantry, and Skye kept reminding herself that Max's trip to the falls was a pilgrimage to see Dee off to her final resting place and nothing should interfere with it or him.

When they went into the garage, Max got in the truck, buckled up, but kept the backpack in his lap. Moments later, they drove away from the cabin, across the low-water bridge, down the gravel road to the blacktop, and then they headed up the mountain.

The day had yet to heat up, and the wind coming through the open windows put tangles in Skye's hair, but it didn't matter.

Her truck had become the hearse, and she the driver, taking Max and Dee on their last ride together.

Max was silent, and Skye couldn't begin to imagine the thoughts running through his head. A quarter of a mile later, she began slowing down, then pulled off into a lay-by. As soon as she killed the engine, she reached across the console and gave his hand a gentle squeeze.

"There are the falls. You can see them through the trees. Do you still want me to go with you?"

"I will always want you with me," he said, and opened the door.

She had a lump in her throat as she pocketed the keys and circled the truck bed to where he was waiting. After he shouldered the backpack, he reached for her hand. Today they were on the way to scatter the ashes of someone he loved. Tomorrow wasn't promised.

As they walked the short path through the trees, they could see the rain-swollen water in the creek, and the sudsy bubbles riding the crest as it rushed toward the rock fall, down into the pool below.

For Skye, being in the woods of the Ozarks always made her feel small. Some of the trees were almost as ancient as the ground in which they'd taken root. They always gave her a sense of timelessness, remembering the generations of people who'd come this way before.

And today, she felt even smaller, walking beside this man who had risen above the worst of life's tragedies over and over without breaking.

Max was ever conscious of the woman beside him, and the firm grip she had on his hand. This was his final goodbye to his mom, but he hadn't realized until now how grateful he was not to be doing this alone.

"The creek is really swollen from the rains," Skye said, as they approached its bank.

He glanced back at her, thinking her eyes were as green as this forest.

"Mom would love this day. She used to fashion boats for me to sail in the street gutters after it rained," he said.

"She was a good boy-mom, wasn't she?" Skye said.

Max had never thought of her in that way before, but it was true. As they reached the creek bank, he looked out across the water, wondering what it was about this place that had meant so much to his mom.

"Yes, she was. In every way. She didn't fuss about muddy shoes or a tear in my shirt. She was in her early twenties when she gave up everything for me. Even before MaryJo died, Mom . . . she was Dee to me then . . . was always there to pick up the slack. I didn't know until years later that MaryJo had designated her as my legal guardian."

"What a remarkable woman Dee was . . . and at such a young age! And that is a whole new way to look at MaryJo's life and how she thought. Even when she knew she was failing you, she was making plans to protect you." Skye paused a moment. "Remember what we said about being on chosen paths? If that follows, then you have to accept that MaryJo didn't fall off her path, and neither did Dee. They just chose the rocky ones." Skye said.

His eyes widened, and then he nodded. "I never looked at it that way before. But whatever it was MaryJo came to learn, I hope it was enough. I never knew who my father was because neither did she. Everyone who mattered in my life was a substitute for the ones who were missing. I don't trust easily . . . but I trusted you on sight. You took a chance when you brought me to your home. I will never forget that."

Max set the backpack on the ground and removed the little box of ashes. He paused a moment to assess the lay of the land, then stepped out into the shallows and began walking across the rocky ledge, stopping midway. The water was running swiftly, but his stance was steady as he hugged the box against his chest.

"Okay Mom, here we are . . . me and what's left of you . . . one last time. We already said our goodbyes. Death set you free of all the sickness and pain, and this is me honoring your last wish. Knowing you, you're going to love this last ride."

Then he took off the lid and turned the box upside down.

The ashes spilled out into the air, hovering for a second as if they couldn't decide which way to go, then caught a ride on the breeze at his back and were swept into the flow of air and water. As they fell, some defied gravity, while others chose oblivion as they washed their way downstream.

Max was still standing in the water, half-mesmerized by the fall and flow, when he began noticing green leaves floating past his feet, and then more and more, until there was a multitude of different leaves from different trees floating past him and spilling over the falls.

He turned abruptly, thinking there might be a limb or a branch coming up behind him, and instead, saw Skye kneeling on the creek bank, putting leaves into the water, one by one.

His breath caught. His vision blurred with a sudden rush of tears as he walked out of the water and up onto the bank. He dropped the empty box beside his things as she came toward him, and then she was in his arms.

Skye saw his tears. "I hope you didn't mind that—"

He shook his head and cupped her face. "That was the most precious, perfect thing you could have done to honor her place in my heart. I don't know what I have to do to prove what you mean to me, but you need to know you have fixed your place in my heart forever. You don't have to promise me anything. Your doubt will never change how I feel about you. All you have to do is figure out what you want, because I already know I want you." He kissed her one last time, slower, longer, and then turned her loose and went to pick up his things.

He started to walk away, then stopped, looked at the little wooden box in his hands and immediately walked off the path into the trees and knelt down beside a thicket of bushes. He turned the little box on its side, and pushed it against a tree, thinking it might become a shelter for any small creature in need, then got up and walked back to where Skye stood waiting.

Skye was so taken by what he'd just done that she couldn't speak. He'd taken a box that had held the remnants of a life and turned it into a shelter for another life, small and furry though it may be.

Chances with a man like Max were as rare as grabbing the gold ring on a merry-go-round. Sometimes you only got one chance. In that moment, she reached for him like a drowning woman reaching for a rock to cling to.

They walked back to the truck, hand in hand.

As Max got inside, she noticed the backpack was between his feet now instead of in his lap. With Dee's ashes gone, there was no longer anything in it that needed to be protected. But when she started the engine and headed back down the mountain, his hand was on her shoulder, still holding onto what mattered to him.

The ride down was silent until they got to Russellville.

"You have to give me directions from here," she said, as they drove into town, so he did. When they arrived at the address and pulled up in the driveway, she began to frown.

"Oh! Wait a minute! I've been to this house before!"

"What? When?" Max said.

"At least a year ago, maybe longer. The lady who lived here had suffered a fall, and her doctor has prescribed physical therapy for the strain and pain. Rather than have her try to drive herself to the therapy center, I offered to come to her house. Deidre. Deidre Lewis. I never connected her with your Dee."

Max shook his head in amazement. "I was overseas. I knew about the fall, but she blew it off as nothing and said she was fine."

"She told me she was sick and had fallen because she'd passed out," Skye said. "I recommended she get a Rollator . . . one of those four-wheeled walkers that has a seat, and she did. She was using it when I finished up her last treatment."

"I saw that in her bedroom the day I came home," he said. "That meeting with her is where you crossed my path. And the day you picked me up in the rain is where my path crossed yours. Meant to be." He didn't want to get out, but it was time. "Thank you for today, and for the ride home . . . and for taking care of Mom when I couldn't," he said, then he kissed the palm of her hand. "Meant to be," he said again, and got out of the pickup and went inside.

Skye sat watching as he walked away. Shoulders back. Chin up. The long, measured stride of a soldier. Before the door swung shut behind him, she already felt his absence.

He didn't look back, but he didn't have to. He already told me where he stood. I'm the one with decisions to make.

She backed out of the driveway and drove to the supermarket. She was back to cooking for one, but still needed to restock perishables, and maybe a twelve-pack of Mountain Dew for Max, just in case.

This morning while he was still asleep, she'd uploaded her blog about rescuing him. She called the piece, "Cloudy Skyes." She'd already written the blog to follow and titled it, "Soldier on the Mountain." She didn't know what would follow, but she knew how she was going to feel. Alone all over again.

Max walked into the house, closed the door behind him, and then stood within the uneasy silence. It was almost like he'd put the house on pause, and it had been waiting for him to return. When he'd driven away three days ago, he'd thought he'd be back before noon, but then life had happened, and Max had learned long ago how life had a way of changing plans.

He turned on lights as he went down the hall, dumped his backpack on the floor, and pulled off his boots and jeans that were still wet from walking out into the water. After putting on dry clothes, he went into the adjoining bathroom then paused in front of the mirror, eyeing the bruises on his head and cheek.

"You look like the tail-end of hard times," he muttered, then shrugged it off. The bruises would go away, but his feelings for her would not.

He left the bathroom and went back outside to gather the stack of mail from the mailbox on the porch, then started a pot of coffee and sat down to sort through it, tossing most of it as junk. After that, he moved from snail mail to his laptop and began checking email.

Tomorrow, he'd go car shopping. The insurance check would arrive in due time, but he wasn't going to wait for it. Now he was glad he hadn't already sold Mom's car. She'd left him everything, but her will was still in probate. In the meantime, he had access to her wheels.

He was already missing Skye, and she'd only let him out an hour ago. Dancing about with his real feelings was going to be a hard horse to ride.

Skye shopped quickly and left town with the same feeling she always had after Christmas was over and the family had gone home. Somewhere between a let-down and lonesome. She had zero regrets for making love with Max, but her self-imposed abstinence had been destroyed. It had been beautiful and perfect, but there was no way to deny she'd just made love to a stranger, and at her own invitation. The scary part was how badly she wanted him back, and how tenuously she viewed his vow to return.

It was well past noon by the time she got home and going inside with her groceries felt anti-climactic. The silence and solitude were familiar. She began putting up the groceries, then went to her bedroom to hang up her jacket and change her shoes. But the moment she sat down on the side of the bed to take off her walking boots, she caught the scent of him on her pillow. It was a kick in the gut.

She fell backward and rolled over, burying her face in the pillow, remembering the first sight of him, staggering in the rain.

The weight of him against her body as she helped him into the truck. Undressing him to get him warm and dry and seeing the bruises and old scars on wide shoulders and rock-hard abs, then the scrapes and cuts on his knees and legs.

Remembering how afraid she'd been for him as she'd kept watch while he'd slept.

The easy way they'd fallen into step.

How he'd made her laugh.

Being held in his arms as they'd made love.

She wanted him back, and she needed to get over herself. Max was right. She was the one dragging her feet, but for what? She hadn't realized how much she'd missed the company of a partner until she'd brought him into her home.

She had put herself away—like old clothes that no longer fit.

What the hell was she waiting for?

Later that evening, she went outside with a bowl of carrot tops and potato peelings to toss out into the trees, and thought of the little box Max had left under the bushes, picturing some tiny wood mouse making it his home.

Even as he was grieving, he'd thought to turn that little box into something good.

As she tossed the peelings into the grass, she thought about something her mother had told her after her father's passing.

Skye, honey...a good man always cares for those he loves most. He thinks of them before he thinks of himself. It's how the male psyche works. It's a part of the territorial DNA within the—to protect that which is his. Those he loves. The things he's responsible for. That inner sense of danger comes from the ancient DNA within us all. It's what saves us after the chaos is over—the drive to pick ourselves up and move on. You did that after Paul. I will do it now, and so will you, again. That's part of our ancient DNA, too.

Skye stood by the vegetable peelings, lost in thought as a rabbit came out of the bushes. It paused a few seconds, and then hopped a few steps closer and began nibbling on carrot tops. It was the perfect example of nothing going to waste and life moving on.

She smiled. "Enjoy your dinner, fuzzy butt," she whispered, and then she slowly backed away before turning around. But every step toward to the cabin, she kept hearing Max's voice.

I won't quit you.

"Ah, Max . . . I hope you mean it, because I'm about to bet the farm on you."

Max's afternoon had been productive enough getting settled back in, but when he had nothing left to distract him, he sat down with his laptop and found Skye's blog. He signed up to follow it, then started with the archived blogs first and opened Year One.

The posts were full of her thoughts and wishes—her funny days, and her sad days. And of the holidays with her family that had come and gone.

He ordered in and ate pizza as he read, going through two years of blog posts before the pizza was gone.

He glanced at the time, surprised it was already after nine p.m., and reached for his phone. Her number was in his contacts now. And his was in hers. But he wasn't waiting for her to call.

The phone rang twice, and then her voice was in his ear.

"Hi," she said.

He sighed. "Hi, yourself. Just wanted to hear your voice. Thought you might want to read me a bedtime story or something."

She smiled at his foolishness, and realized it was part of what endeared him most. "You are outrageous."

He grinned. "My teachers called me impulsive with a tendency for outbursts of unnecessary information."

She laughed again, and then a long silence followed.

"Skye, are you okay?"

"Yes. Sorry . . . I got lost in thought. I was thinking that I've laughed more in the few days we've spent together than I do in a month."

"Okay . . . I'll check class clown off the list. What else do I need to be for you? I miss your face. I called because I missed the sound of your voice. No comments required. I'm just letting you know what being without you feels like.

I'm going car shopping tomorrow. I may paint a bedroom or two. I am too young to be retired, and too old for all this romantic angst. I know what I know. When you close those pretty green eyes tonight, dream of me. I'll be dreaming of you."

"Well, for God's sake, you're not banned from the premises," Skye said. "When you get your new car, come see me. We can eat sandwiches, drink Mountain Dew, solve the world's problems, and feed the scraps to the squirrels."

This time, she was on the receiving end of his laughter, and it felt good.

"Then I'll see you soon. In the meantime, if you need help with anything, I'm your man."

"So, you keep telling me," she said.

"I'm a good teacher. I don't mind repeating myself."

"Goodnight, John Boy," she said.

He chuckled at the John Boy reference from *The Waltons*, an old TV series that had been a favorite of Dee's.

"Goodnight, Skye on the mountain. See you in my dreams."

CHAPTER FIVE

As soon as Skye disconnected, Max began gathering up the trash from his pizza order and carried it outside to the garbage, then locked up the house for the night. It was too early to sleep, so he went back to her blog, pulled up year three from the archives, and started reading.

It's my third winter on the mountain, and I am officially snowed in. I'm not gonna lie. It's a little intimidating. Can't see the road or the bridge. Surrounded by trees. It's like being in a foreign country. Can't speak the language. Don't know the rules. No travel guidebooks to explain how this works.

The upside is watching a herd of deer moving across my yard. They've already eaten the cornbread crumbs I tossed out for the birds. I'm going to have to figure out a hanging birdfeeder.

I found a little mouse in the garage. Instead of putting out a mousetrap, I made it a house out of an empty peach can, stuffed it with cotton balls and a handful of Cheerios.

No, I'm not that lonely. I'm just one of those people who's always bringing home the strays. Shelter in place, I always say.

Until next time,
Skye

"Shelter in place, indeed," Max said, thinking of a bombed-out building somewhere in Kabul where they'd taken cover while waiting for the air support of the incoming Apache Longbows.

Then he shook off the memory and went back to the blogs. He was officially a *Skye on the Mountain* fan, now. Her posts were so real, and so honest, and engaging, like her . . . like listening to her talk. No wonder she'd gained such a huge following.

The moment Skye had heard Max's voice on the phone, her world had settled into place, and the moment he'd disconnected, she'd felt the absence. Clearly, he had affected the gravity of her life. When she finally went to bed, as fate would have it, she did dream of him. And woke up aching—wishing he was lying beside her to make the hurt go away.

Her sleep was fitful, and by five a.m., she'd had enough. She showered, dressed, and then went to the kitchen long enough to make toast and coffee, then she went to her office to work.

An hour passed as she uploaded a new blog post, and then was going through the comments, answering reader questions, when her phone rang. She smiled when she saw caller ID.

"Hi, Mom. How goes the world in Miami?"

"Hello, darling," Donna Wray said. "Very same-old, same-old. You know I read *Skye on the Mountain* before I even read my papers, and I want to know about this Max fellow? Did he get well? Is he still at the cabin?"

"I'm fine, thanks for asking," Skye said, and then laughed when she heard her mother sputtering, trying to make excuses for asking about the man and not her own daughter. "Don't get all defensive. I was just teasing. The water receded enough yesterday that I was able to get out. I took him to the falls to spread his mom's ashes, and then I drove him home."

"Oh. Well. Then I guess you're safe and all," Donna said.

"I guess I am. But I'm not going to lie. He is definitely one of those 'once in a lifetime' kind of guys. Riveting life story. Recently retired Army Colonel Max Bridger. Forty-five years old. Really nice guy to know once I got his wounds cleaned up and his fever under control. The man was so lucky he didn't break any bones or have any internal injuries."

"I could tell by the way you were telling the story in your blog that he'd made an impression on you."

"Yes, he did, but the feeling is mutual. He's shopping for a new vehicle today. I'll see him again. Update me on Sean and Marie."

"Sean and his family are in Mount Ida, Arkansas, digging for crystals. His two boys are little rockhounds like their daddy, and Mama is along for the ride. I wouldn't want to be her," Donna said.

Skye laughed. "She married a geologist. I imagine she's prepared for all that. So, what's Marie doing?"

"Redecorating her house again. Gary the ever-patient husband took their little girl and went to stay at his parents' house while the painters and carpenters are on-site."

"Lord," Skye said. "One day I keep expecting you to tell me they're getting a divorce."

Donna gasped. "She's said nothing to me! Do you really think they're having trouble?"

"Mom, seriously? Something must be wrong. Whatever is going on with them, redecorating the house they live in over and over isn't going to fix a marriage."

Donna sighed. "You may be right. You're my baby, but you've always been the most level-headed child. You're strong and resilient."

"Because I had to be," Skye said.

"I've never asked about your personal life after Paul died, but do you date? Ever?"

"No. But Max asked if he could come back to see me on a personal level, and I said, 'Yes.'"

"Good. You're too young to bury yourself. Life is short and uncertain, and you and Max aren't children. If you have feelings for each other that fast, then don't let them wilt and die. You water your own garden. You don't wait for Mother Nature to make it rain."

Skye took heart in the wisdom of her mother's words. "Thanks, Mom. I'm really glad you called," she said. "Go stick your toes in the sand for me, okay? Love you."

"Love you, too, my darling," Donna said, and then disconnected.

Skye put down the phone, logged off her blog site, and left the office with her mother's words echoing in her head. *Don't wait for Mother Nature to make it rain.*

She was still thinking about her mother's advice when her phone rang. It was the physical therapy facility where she worked. It wasn't her day to work, so she knew before she answered there must be an emergency.

"Hello?"

"Skye, it's Robert. I'm so sorry to call with such late notice, but Shirley just took a header out in the parking lot. We're all swamped, and there's no time for us to work her clients into our schedules today. Is there any way you could come in? Her first appointment is at nine a.m. Her last one comes in at two p.m."

"Absolutely," Skye said. "I sure hope she's not seriously injured. I'll change clothes and head that way."

"You're a lifesaver. See you soon."

The anxiety he was feeling about Skye's indecision was making sleep difficult. It was three fifteen a.m. in Russellville, Arkansas, but it was 2003 in his dream, and he was on the ground in Iraq on his first tour of duty.

The night sky was on fire, lit up by the impact of rocket-fire and ensuing explosions. The rescue team moved from one burned-out building to another, following the sounds of the rapid-fire bursts of automatic weapons to find the location where four of their men were pinned down.

All of a sudden, Max heard someone yell.

"Incoming!"

He woke abruptly, his heart pounding, his body bathed in sweat.

"Damn it. A twenty-one-year-old nightmare! Are you kidding me?" he muttered, and swung his legs out of bed.

He yanked on a pair of sweatpants and went through the house turning on the lights, popped a coffee pod in the Keurig, slid a mug beneath the spout, then hit Start before going back to his room.

It was far too early to even think about car dealers, but here he was, awake and antsy. The bruising on his face was fading to green, but not nearly as attractive as her green eyes. He shaved away the black shadow of whiskers before he got in the shower. The hot water soothed his stiff muscles, and after he got out and dried off, he finger-combed his hair and called it quits.

His civilian wardrobe was sparse. He had to shop for a new car. Might as well check out the clothing situation while he was at it. After getting dressed, he went to retrieve his coffee and find something to eat, then added grocery shopping to his day.

He'd just begun to get used to his mom's absence, and now he was missing Skye. He'd actually gone to bed listening for Greg the owl to sound off, before he remembered the owl lived on the mountain with her, as did Grumpy the bear, and the birds, and the wildlife. Everything lived on the mountain with Skye, except him.

He sat down at the table with his honeybun and coffee and started reading more of Skye's blog. He was all the way to year five of her residence at the cabin. The post had been written on New Year's Eve. She was snowed in and alone, trying to decide whether to pop the top on pale ale, or a can of Mountain Dew, and watching them ringing in the New Year in Times Square on TV. She'd just commented about bringing in the New Year alone when he stopped reading in mid-sentence, stared at the phrase, then read it again, and again. He didn't know he was crying until he felt the tears on his face.

"No one left up here but me . . ." she'd written.

It was the same thing he'd thought his first night in back in the house after his mom's passing. There was no one left in his world. No one else was left in this house. No one left but him to call it home. He'd spent the next few weeks coming to terms with that until he'd gotten her ashes.

Until he'd turned around and fell off a mountain.

And met Skye.

He closed his laptop and carried his dirty dishes to the sink. That's when he realized the sun was up, so he opened the curtains on the kitchen window.

The sky was clear and cloudless.

A bird flew across his line of vision.

A squirrel was climbing down from the tree in the back yard.

A car horn honked out on the street. That would be the Uber for the lady who lived across the street. Wherever she worked, she took an Uber to and from the job every day.

He shifted his stance, swiped at the tears on his face, and went to get the keys to Dee's car. Grocery shopping first and then back home to put them up. By then, businesses would be open. Car dealers would be his next stop, and if he was still in the mood, clothes shopping afterward.

———————

Skye was glad for the opportunity to work. Staying busy today was a lifesaver. She'd been all set up to feel sorry for herself, and now she was doing what she did best—taking care of others.

The mint-scented ointment she used on her patients' sore muscles and healing joints was the same stuff she'd used on Max and Deirdre. As the hours flew by and the patients came and went, he was uppermost in her thoughts. When she was finished with the last patient, she went up front to the area where they had products for sale and bought a jar of the same ointment for Max.

The receptionist teased her as Skye was paying for it.

"Need a little healing for yourself, do you?"

Skye laughed. "Something like that. Any news on Shirley?"

"Just a nasty bump on the head. No concussion. And we've worked tomorrow's patients into the other therapists' schedules. Thank you so much for today!"

"Of course. See you when I see you," Skye said, and carried the little sack out to her car.

She was a little achy between her shoulders, and her hands and arms were tired, but as soon as she got in the car, she called Max. The call rang three times, and then his voice was in her ear.

"Hey, honey. Are you okay?"

She sighed. "Yes, I'm fine. Had any luck car shopping today?"

"As a matter of fact, I have. I'm at home, waiting for them to call so I can go down and pick it up. They're servicing it now. I drove Mom's car to run errands all day, but brought it back after I signed all the papers on the car. I'll catch an Uber and—"

"Oh, you don't need to do that. I've been at the therapy center all day. I was just getting ready to drop something off at your house before I went home. I'd be happy to take you back."

"That would be much appreciated. Did I leave something behind?"

"No, nothing like that. I'm leaving the parking lot now. It will take me about ten minutes or so to get to your house."

"I'll be watching for you," he said.

And just like that, all of the tired feeling and the achy stuff she'd been feeling were gone. That man was good for what ailed her, in more ways than one.

No sooner had she pulled up into the driveway of Max's house than he was out the door and headed for her truck. She smiled at the sight of him coming toward her, then unlocked the doors.

Moments later, he was in the seat beside her. Before she had time to say hello, he leaned across the console and kissed her square on the lips, then leaned back and buckled himself in.

"Hello to you, too." She was beaming from the unexpected greeting as she pointed to the little silver bag in the seat beside him. "That's for you."

"You got me something?" he asked, as he picked up the bag and looked inside.

"It's the stuff for sore muscles. I suspect you're still hurting and just ignoring it. Am I right?"

He grinned. "An angel and a mind reader. What's a man to do with someone like you?"

"Don't play all innocent, Bridger. You already proved yourself there, and you're doing okay. Where are we going?"

He laughed. "Crazy. We're going crazy, and also to the Orr dealership on Main."

Skye couldn't stop smiling as she backed out of the driveway, then headed uptown with Max talking all the way.

"Only one night away from you and the cabin, and I had a hell of a time going to sleep. There was too much city noise. I kept listening for Greg the owl to sound off, only to remember that Greg was up there with you."

"I thought you'd probably be glad to get home—back to civilization, so to speak," Skye said.

"Oh honey . . . I haven't had roots since the day I showed up at boot camp. And home was never a house. It was Mom who made the house a home."

Skye nodded. "I get that. Wherever makes you feel safe is home. And when you don't have people to supply that, you turn your surroundings into all the things that make you happy, and that becomes home. At least, that's what I did."

"Dragging my sorry ass into your safe place was a brave thing to do. I know I've said it before, but you are a remarkable woman, Skye."

"You're not so bad, yourself," she said, and stopped at a red light.

He turned to look at her. "I've been reading your blog. I thought it might be the best way to understand what you've been through. You shared yourself with the world when you began to post your daily stories, so I started at the beginning, and as I read, a lot of what you wrote resonated. I'm just beginning year six of *Skye on the Mountain*. You are wise beyond your years."

She shook her head. "I have never imagined myself as wise, but thank you for the compliment."

The light turned green as she drove through the intersection, but what Max had just said made her feel seen in a way she hadn't expected. He'd read the words she'd written in her loneliest, saddest days, and read the journey she'd taken to get where she was today. Another checkmark in the plus column.

"Oh," Max added. "Just so you know . . . we are no longer strangers. I have lived the last six years of your life with you through the words you wrote. So, you can forget about me being a stranger."

She chuckled. "Do you view it as a biography crash-course, or the cheat-sheet version?"

"Definitely the crash course. Soldiers don't take shortcuts. They plow straight through opposition to get to the target," he said.

"I never wanted to be in the line of fire . . . until now," she said, as she pulled up to the curb at the dealership.

"You're definitely my target, but there's no incoming flak. Just a whole lot of love waiting to be received. Thank you for the ride."

This time, she leaned over the seat and kissed him. "You're welcome. Use the ointment on your back, shoulders, and legs. You'll sleep better."

"I sleep just fine with you in my arms. Do you work tomorrow?" he asked.

"No, I'm home."

"If I invite myself to lunch and bring the food, will I be welcome?" he asked.

She nodded. "Always."

"Favorite food?" he asked.

"You bring what you like to eat. I might need to know all that," she said.

A shiver of longing rolled through him. "We're getting there, honey. Meant to be," and then he was out of her car and walking across the parking lot and into the building.

The moment he walked out of sight, she felt the tug of wanting him back. "Lord, I'm so done for, aren't I?" she muttered, then backed up and headed home, already thinking about seeing him tomorrow.

The drive home was inconsequential, but as she slowed down to turn onto the gravel road leading to the cabin, a small fox darted across the road in front of her and slipped into the bushes. Their presence was why she didn't have chickens.

And when she crossed the bridge and saw three deer eating grass in her yard, she rolled her eyes. They were why she didn't grow flowers or plant a garden.

The black bear she saw lumbering into the forest wasn't Grumpy, but the bear belonged here. She was the interloper, and they'd all made peace with her presence.

The one thing people and animals had in common was birth and death. All that happened within that timeline was just stuff. In her case, it had been Paul's death and her choice to quit people for the comfort of the family cabin and the isolation it offered.

For eight years, very little about that choice had changed until Max Bridger fell off a mountain, and she'd brought him home. Within two days, she'd gone to bed with him. It was the most outrageous thing she'd ever done, and the best decision she'd ever made.

Seeing him again today wasn't a coincidence. She'd bought that mint-scented ointment on purpose just to use it as an excuse to go to his house. From the moment she'd picked him up to taken him downtown, he'd kissed her hello, and then she'd kissed him goodbye as if they'd known each other for years.

He was reading her blog, but she didn't have anyone to talk to about him, and she was beginning to realize it didn't matter. She just wanted to hear him laugh and see him coming in the door, bringing life and energy, and maybe a blowing leaf at his feet, and know she was alive again.

She went to bed that night thinking about tomorrow and seeing him again. Her mind was made up. She was going to grab that golden ring. She was going to take the chance. She rolled over and closed her eyes. *He wants me. He said he won't quit me. And God knows, I want him.*

Max's new Jeep Wrangler was silver and black with all the bells and whistles—exactly like the one he'd wrecked. Same year, same make, same model, and this time when he headed up the mountain, he had flowers in the seat, their take-away lunch in a basket and buckled up in the back seat.

The black pants, gray and white long-sleeved shirt with the sleeves rolled up, and gray roper-style boots he wore were all new purchases.

He was as anxious about doing this right as a teenage boy in a rented limo and rented tux going to pick up his best girl for the prom.

The drive up was easy. Traffic was light. He passed a few backpackers on the road, and thought of the irony of already having left two pieces of his past on this mountain. His Jeep, which would rust forever at the bottom of the canyon, and Dee, whose presence would always be marked by the last place he'd left her.

He turned off the blacktop and onto the driveway heading to the cabin. The boards on the low-water bridge rattled as he drove over them, and as he pulled up to the cabin, she came out to meet him. Her feet were bare, her hair was down, and the blue dress she wore was the color of the sky above her. She was smiling.

He got out, caught her up in his arms, and swung her off her feet as he kissed her senseless before putting her down. Then he grinned.

"I just got that backwards, didn't I? Should have said hello first. Are do-overs allowed?"

"You don't have rules, Bridger. I'm seriously happy to see you."

He grinned, then got the flowers from the front seat and handed them to her.

Her eyes widened. "I haven't had flowers in forever. Thank you. They're beautiful."

"Just like you," he said, and then unbuckled the picnic basket from the back seat. "I bring tidings of great joy . . . and Chinese takeout."

She laughed and was still laughing as they started up the steps and into the house.

"I'm going to put these in water. The table is set. You're in charge of setting out the food, okay?"

He began pulling out carton after carton of different dishes until the table between them was full.

She carried the vase of flowers over, then set them toward the end.

"Clearly you enjoy Chinese. Duly noted, but I'm starving, and I don't have the patience for chopsticks. The last time I tried to use them to eat, I flipped rice up my nose. I thought Sean was going to fall out of his chair, laughing."

Max grinned. "I gotta meet that brother of yours one day."

"Oh, you will, I promise. But today is for us, and everything looks and smells so good."

At that point, they sat down, served themselves some of all the different dishes he'd ordered, with two fortune cookies on the table between them.

"You choose the fortune cookie you want. I'll take the other one."

She paused, then picked the one on the left. He slid the other one beside his plate, and they began to eat.

"So Chinese is one of your favorite kinds of food?" she asked.

"I like it a lot, but I've been to a lot of foreign places and learned to appreciate a multitude of ethnic foods. I got really good at using naan for a spoon to eat East Indian curries and stews. I love the taste of Greek and Italian foods. And the spices they put in Thai and Indian foods are amazing. But in the end, it's really hard to beat a good old American burger and fries. What about you?" he asked.

"I like just about anything someone else cooks. Cooking just for me, I get in a rut with my choices and wind up going with the path of least resistance. But I am a big fan of anything with shrimp."

"Then I did good," he said, eyeing two different shrimp dishes on her plate.

When they finished eating, they went for the fortune cookies. "You first," Skye said.

"Are we reading these aloud?"

"Sure. You don't really believe them, do you?"

"I believe in a lot of things unseen," he said, then cracked his cookie and pulled out the fortune. His eyes widened, and then he slid it across the table.

Skye took one look at it and gasped.

"*It's meant to be.*"

"Oh, my Lord," she said, then cracked her fortune cookie, read it, and burst out laughing.

"What?" Max asked.

She shoved it across the table. He read it and grinned.

"*Your credit is maxed out. Pay up.*"

"No worries. Your credit is still good with me," he said.

She picked up the cookie pieces and ate them. "You have to eat the cookie, or the fortune doesn't work."

"Who told you that? Sean?"

She blinked. "You mean that's not true?"

"Not one word of it," he said.

She rolled her eyes. "Oh, for pity's sake. I wonder how many years he's been laughing at me about that?"

"Don't worry, honey. I run interference for you now, remember?"

"Clearly, the opportunity for that job is necessary. I am so naïve."

"Nope. You trusted him to tell you the truth because you love him, but I hear siblings are allowed to break that rule," he said.

She rolled her eyes. "I wonder what other bullshit he's been feeding me through the years. Oh well, if it was bullshit, I didn't know it was happening. So, no harm, no foul."

"Let's get the leftovers put up. Would you like to take a quick ride in the new Jeep to the falls and back. Are you up for that?"

"I would love to."

He pointed at her bare feet. "You need shoes."

She took off to her room while he boxed up the leftovers and put them in her refrigerator, and then they were out the door.

Max reached for her hand as they went down the steps.

Skye thought of all the times she'd been up and down those steps on her own, and how many times she'd accidentally slid down them after it snowed. This being cared about and cared for felt good. But when she got into the Jeep, she stared at the dashboard in disbelief.

"Good lord. Is this a car or a rocket launcher?"

He grinned. "I'm done with rocket launchers, and it's not as complicated as it looks. Buckle up. Precious cargo aboard," and then they were gone.

The ride up went too fast for Skye's satisfaction, but when they reached the layby, he parked.

"You don't have to go, but I want to see if there's a new resident in the box I left behind. I won't linger, but I've been imagining it being inhabited."

"I do want to," Skye said. They got out and headed down the path toward the falls. A squirrel scolded them as they passed beneath its tree, and a little turtle on the path went into panic mode and ducked inside its shell.

When they reached the tree, Max squatted down to peer beneath the brush and saw grass and leaves inside the box.

"Something *has* taken up residence there," he said, as Skye knelt beside him.

"I see. Oh, look, Max. They've made a nest. I love this so much!"

"We better leave the bitty critter alone," Max said.

"Right," Skye said, and they walked away in silence until they were far enough away, and this time, she reached for his hand. "You're a really special man, Max Bridger."

He kissed the back of her hand, then put his arm around her shoulders as they walked. "You're pretty special, too, Skye on the mountain."

It was just after four o'clock when they got back to the cabin. Max pulled up to the house, then walked her to the door.

"Do you want to come inside?" Skye asked.

"Yes, but I'm not going to. I'm not turning you into my booty call. I love you, lady, and that's my cold hard truth. Today has been the best day. I'll be back if you'll have me. And if you're in town, you had better at least come by. I may be in desperate need to be resuscitated with a kiss or three. Okay?"

She smiled, hoping she was hiding her shock, because this wasn't even close to what she'd expected. "Definitely, okay. Thank you for lunch, and the flowers, and for bringing me back to life. Drive safe going home."

His eyes darkened as the smile slid off his face. "Home is where the heart is, darlin'. Call me if you need me." He brushed a kiss across her lips, then took the steps down two at a time and got back in the Jeep. He backed up, then waved at her before driving away.

Skye was still standing at the door long after he'd driven out of sight.

"Home is where the heart is." He meant me. I am his home. Why didn't I say it? Why didn't I say it back?

Two weeks later, they were still talking and spending time together, but it felt like they were in a holding pattern. She had yet to utter the words, "I love you," and he'd said it and showed it, over and over. He didn't know what to do or how to get through to her, but he wasn't even close to giving up.

He'd had the whole house painted inside and out, and replaced the back storm door, had the tile in Dee's ensuite bathroom replaced, and fixed a half-dozen drips and leaks.

Today, he was in the kitchen, moving tables and chairs back into place, and wondering what the hell he was going to do next to pass the time when he heard a thump behind him. He turned around and saw a cardinal perched on the window ledge. His heart skipped.

Mom loved cardinals.

"Mom, there's your favorite bird! I wish you were here to see it," Max said. "I could sure use some advice. There's a woman I love. She was widowed young and has lived the last eight years alone in a cabin on the mountain. We connect on every level, but I don't know how to get past her emotional wall. Sometimes I think I need to quit waiting for her to decide and do it for the both of us. She might say 'No,' but at least this waiting will be over."

At that very moment, the cardinal began pecking on the window.

Max blinked. "Is that a yes?"

The cardinal pecked again then turned around and flew away.

"Then here goes nothing," Max said, shoved the last chair into place, and went to change clothes. As he was putting on his boots, he heard a clap of thunder. "Damn it. That low-water bridge is probably going to flood again, and there she'll be. Her on one side; me on the other."

He jumped up, grabbed a duffel bag and began stuffing clothes inside. If she said yes, he was set. If she didn't, she'd never know he'd prepared to stay. Then it occurred to him that she might be at work and made a quick call. It rang twice, and then she answered.

"Hey, you! What's going on? Are the plumbers still there?"

"No. The painters and plumbers are all gone. I was just checking to see if you were home or at work."

"I'm home, why?"

"I think I left something behind the last time I was there. If it's okay, I'm heading your way."

"Always, but it looks like it's going to rain. Drive carefully, okay?"

"I will. See you in a few," he said, and headed out the door.

Skye was elated that Max was coming. She'd awakened this morning, ready to end her own personal stalemate. He needed to hear her say the words. He needed to know how much he meant to her. It was the most important "get-a-grip" moment of her life, and she wondered what he was coming to look for.

By the time Max left Russellville, the sky was getting darker. He took off up the mountain, determined to get to Skye before anything flooded, but the farther he went, the darker the sky became.

The first sprinkles hit his windshield as he turned off the blacktop. Gravel crunched beneath the tires as he sped through the trees, then across the bridge. He came to a sliding halt in front of the cabin as Skye appeared on the porch.

"You made it!" she said, and after he'd launched himself up the steps, she wrapped her arms around his neck. "I've missed you so much."

"I missed you, too, darlin'. More than you know."

"What was it you left behind?" she asked.

"You! The last time I drove away I felt like I'd lost a piece of myself. I love you, Skye. I don't want to spend another night alone. I want to wake up beside you every morning for the rest of my life."

She was laughing and crying as he cupped her face, holding his breath, and then she said the words. The big words. The hard words. The words he'd been waiting to hear.

"Consider it done! I love you, Max Bridger. You rocked my world from day one, and I don't want to do this life without you." The drizzle was turning into big fat rain drops falling on their hair and on their faces. "Come inside, love. We're going to get wet."

But Max wouldn't budge. "I don't care if I get wet. Rain brought you to me, and love brought me back. I would let it rain down on me forever if that was what it cost."

"Love costs nothing when you give it away. Come inside, crazy man. You're probably going to be flooded in with me again."

"I came prepared for a miracle," he said.

"Maybe God brought you and the rain because I was too big a coward to say the words, and I consider that my miracle. Get your stuff and come inside. I have already stripped you once of sopping wet clothes. I can do it again."

He bounded back down the steps, grabbed his duffel bag from the back seat, then ran back to her and reached for her hand.

"Meant to be," he said.

Thunder rolled.

The sky unloaded as they began to run.

www.ingramcontent.com/pod-product-compliance
Lightning Source LLC
Chambersburg PA
CBHW031941010726
47493CB00007B/2030